DEAD
VOICES

ESSENTIAL PROSE SERIES 156

Canada Council   Conseil des Arts
for the Arts   du Canada

ONTARIO ARTS COUNCIL
CONSEIL DES ARTS DE L'ONTARIO

an Ontario government agency
un organisme du gouvernement de l'Ontario

Canadä

Guernica Editions Inc. acknowledges the support of the Canada Council
for the Arts and the Ontario Arts Council. The Ontario Arts Council
is an agency of the Government of Ontario.

We acknowledge the financial support of the Government of Canada.

DEAD VOICES

F.G. Paci

GUERNICA EDITIONS
TORONTO • BUFFALO • LANCASTER (U.K.)
2019

Michael Mirolla, editor
David Moratto, cover and interior design
Guernica Editions Inc.
1569 Heritage Way, Oakville, (ON), Canada L6M 2Z7
2250 Military Road, Tonawanda, N.Y. 14150-6000 U.S.A.
www.guernicaeditions.com

Distributors:
University of Toronto Press Distribution,
5201 Dufferin Street, Toronto (ON), Canada M3H 5T8
Gazelle Book Services, White Cross Mills
High Town, Lancaster LA1 4XS U.K.

First edition.
Printed in Canada.

Legal Deposit – First Quarter
Library of Congress Catalog Card Number: 2018963268
Library and Archives Canada Cataloguing in Publication
Paci, F. G. (Frank G.), author
Dead voices & other stories / F.G. Paci.

(Essential prose series ; 156)
Issued in print and electronic formats.
ISBN 978-1-77183-318-9 (softcover).--ISBN 978-1-77183-319-6
(EPUB).
--ISBN 978-1-77183-320-2 (Kindle)

I. Title. II. Title: Dead voices and other stories.

PS8581.A24D43 2019   C813'.54   C2018-906388-2   C2018-906389-0

Contents

Hot Stove 1
Bookman Goes Batty 29
Dead Voices 55
Prime Time Challenge 83
Nick and Francesco Visit Canada 115
Johnny Reno Does Manhattan 145
Recon Radio 171
The Switch 195
The Hearing 223
Z Goes Shopping 257

About the Author 287

Hot Stove

Mark wolfed down his lunch in the staff room and walked down the hallway to Mike Corelli's office. He was in his teaching fatigues of grey khakis, a blue tie-less shirt, and a black leather vest, with his pepper and salt hair buzzed down to the minimum.

These days the school was a battle zone. In order to keep a vigilant eye for land mines and enemy fire at all times, one had to be calm and collected. What the boys called *solid*. At the present moment, however, he wasn't. He was on edge, somewhere between angry and disgusted. *Angry* would be too noble for the setting and situation and *disgusted* would too ignoble for his character and image. On edge would be closer. About halfway between the joke they called a school and his inextricable involvement in the joke.

He was on edge for having to live a lie every day, for not being appreciated by a son who loathed him for all the compromises he had made, to use his son's word—though one had to hear him say it with his ever present sneer, mouthing it as if it reeked of fertilizer. On edge for having to play his wise-cracking clown self with the staff. On edge for having to listen to Mike's pious announcements each morning over the PA and having to attend Mass with his classes every so often and sit through sermons rendered by smug idiots in vestments who thought they were conveying pearls of wisdom. On edge for sitting through ridiculous Department meetings headed by a woman so officious in her duties her smarmy English accent drove him up a wall.

The one thing he had to look forward to was Hot Stove League where the guys crapped on appearances and compromises, where they were who they were—with no bullshit.

Every so often one of the five from the staff hockey team would call a Hot Stove meeting and they'd shuffle into Mike's office during the long common lunch and make as if they were still in the dressing room in their skivvies, putting on the pads and armour of battle, lacing on the skates, getting ready for the big game.

In Hot Stove they'd forget they were teachers, fathers, husbands, compromisers, bullshit artists, or whatever else they normally functioned as, and became soldiers, predators, hunters, warriors—a bunch of old-timers who had seen their glory years long ago and still laced up the skates for the love of the game. Hot Stove was their way of keeping the embers warm after the season, keeping the dressing room spirit alive, shooting the shit—as real shit instead of pious shit—and swapping hockey lore, and cutting their ties to the world of fakery and compromise.

The first time Mark had played for the team he had forgotten how the guys were in the dressing room. It had been a long time since his university years when he had last laced on the skates, and even then he was but a shadow of his prowess as a kid. It was as if he had entered another world. Like the years he had played shinny on the outdoor rink in his industrial neighbourhood, freeze his ass off, and then come into the wooden shack with the pot-bellied stove and thaw out and hear the guys being guys.

Though he had been a quiet kid and never swore, he'd always feel at home in the shack with the guys who respected his talents on the ice. He could still smell the wood and see the glow of the black stove, on which they'd throw snow from their sticks and skates and watch it sizzle.

Through the years, with the changes in staffing, he had seen players come and go. At one time he was part of the Lit Line, three guys in the English Department who could actually play hockey. It was an anomaly they never tired of bragging about. Since then the other two guys, Tony Chan and John Perlini, had transferred out of the school and he had been left alone to defend the gates of civilization and culture against the barbarian hordes.

Every so often anyone could be walking by Mike's office and join them. They could be students or staff members, the custodial staff, the Educational Resource Workers, or the Spec Ed kids—anyone who didn't take himself or herself too seriously.

They also called themselves the Original Six, in loyalty to the guys who had stuck it out through thick and thin, even though one of them had left.

Though he wasn't as dedicated to hockey as the other guys, he could feel the chains of his slavery melting away when he stepped into Hot Stove. The guys were merciless in their jibes, their criticisms, their honesty. And he liked nothing better than to engage in battle with them and give them the gears. His self-appointed mission was to steer their passion for hockey, wittingly or otherwise, into more noble channels. He was out to lift them from being mere jester-jocks, he told them, to scholar-athletes who could cite Plato and Rocky Balboa while digging their skates into the ice and snapping a hard one top shelf. In this gargantuan endeavour he was aided by Mike, who himself had intellectual pretensions along with his jock pedigree.

"We may have started as jocks," Mike had told the guys once, "but the Professor and I have risen out of our lowly hockey upbringing to blaze a trail through the literary world."

Mike never missed an opportunity to remind them of his mental virtuosity in order to offset his lack of talent in goal. Along with being the chaplain, he was the acknowledged school jester, a guy who could go from church-mouse-serious to dressing-room-jokester in a heartbeat. Long gone were the days when the chaplain of the school was a priest, a guy with a black suit and a collar and on a different plane of existence. Though Mike was pious enough when the occasion warranted, he was solid as well, just one of the guys in and out of the dressing room.

Mark was unmistakably the least talented on the team. The boys didn't mind, however. As long as you could lace up the skates and give it a go and laugh at yourself, you were a member of the club. And he gave the team its intangible weapon, they said. While Mike was their Catholic prophylactic, their holey goalie in a mask, he was their literary mascot, their grey-beard, their Billy Shakes on skates. It was all about having some fun on the ice and then having a few beers afterwards, as Jamie said. But

Jamie had been good enough, in his early years, to have played in the O and was only in his late thirties and was still damn good on his skates.

As a team they played against the cops and the firefighters for charity events at Christmas and Easter in the hockey arena a stone throw from the school. They had the most fun, however, at tournaments in Brampton against other school teams.

After him in age came Marty, who taught biology and chemistry and was chock-full of hockey lore. He had been an usher as a kid in the old Maple Leaf Gardens and had seen plenty of NHL games, not to mention OHL and other pro leagues. He could give them little stories of Harold Ballard and the Leafs teams when it was like soap opera in the old arena. Though his skills on the ice had long deteriorated, Marty could still play a decent game. He was in good shape, lean and bony, with dark hair and a five-o'clock shadow at noon. He was also no slouch in his academic creds, having acquired a doctorate in biology.

Mike, who was in his mid-forties, was of average height and a little soft at the waist, with a shock of straight black hair going to grey, and a mischievous grin. He was married and had two kids. A movie nut and a great fan of the Stooges, he often sported a Three Stooges tie as a badge of his calling. When he stood at the lectern addressing the student body in the gym before a Mass he'd crack a few jokes, keeping the kids in good cheer, and then get them serious by reminding them in a solemn voice that they were now in a church. Mike could make even the most dour student smile with his humour and playful disposition. In goal he wore these ancient brown pads that he got from Johnny Bower, he claimed, and flopped around like a fish out of water, every so often making a fantastic save as if by divine providence. He wasn't just a goalie and jester-chaplain, however. Just recently he had been granted a doctorate, after many years of study, on the noted Canadian Jesuit theologian, Bernard Lonergan. Mark had read his dissertation on pastoral care, and every so often he and Mike would meet to discuss the finer points of theology. To keep in the know, Mark himself had done some study on Lonergan.

Next in age was Wally Thorburn, who taught Math and was in his early forties and happily married with three young kids. Wally played hockey in the old-timers industrial league, coached the boys' and then the girls' team, was a dedicated Leafs fan, and was raising his kids, two of whom were girls, to be hockey fanatics. Like Mike, he was well-liked, had a fun-loving disposition, and was able to let the politics of the school slide off his back. He reminded Mark of a cross between the young John Wayne —with his lean good looks and his short brown hair—and Fred Astaire, with his jaunty walk. Mark told him he was the only guy who could feel at home riding the range and get off his horse and take Ginger over the dance floor in a two-step.

The walk was everything. Mike walked on the balls of his feet, slanting forward, like the irrepressible French film comic, Jacques Tati. Marty walked upright on solid feet, slow and ponderous, as if nothing could faze him. And, Jamie, the youngest in their group, walked like a cross between a ballet dancer and jungle cat.

Jamie was the most physically imposing in their group

and, indeed, in the whole school. He stood six-four, with a hard-muscled body, a chiselled face and square jaw that was topped with a lick of black hair, and the widest grin imaginable. He had a lot to smile about. Besides having the body that he kept buffed with constant work-outs, he had a glow about him, that great athlete's sense of confidence that could make any physical challenge look easy, not to mention a mind that wasn't too shabby either. Hockey hadn't even been his first sport. After playing a little in Junior A, he had been a star in varsity football, a quarterback who could've gone pro if not for a serious knee injury.

The students called him Superman. He had come dressed as the superhero on Halloween one year, with the whole shebang—the cape, the blue tights, the big logo, and the red shoes—and looked so not-out-of-place in the costume that the name had stuck. Of the five of them, Jamie was the only one not married. Jamie didn't have to get married, he said. He was getting laid so easily he didn't have to bother. He taught Phys Ed and a little Religion.

Mike's little office was adjacent to the chapel and down the hallway from the Phys Ed Office and gym. If the group got too large, however, they'd adjourn to the chapel next door, which was bright and airy and looked over the back lot of the football field.

In late September they were all anticipating the start of the NHL season and the upcoming hockey pool, an annual event that was set up by the Commissioner, Wally, and his Co-commissioner of Hockey Operations, Marty. In matters of hockey, Marty sometimes deferred to Wally. In everything else, Marty deferred to no one.

Mike's office door was always kept open. He was in

dress pants with his Three Stooges tie and a blue sweater and sneakers, sitting at his desk, looking at some paper work.

"How-do, Professor," he said. "I'm just getting some forms ready for the retreat."

Mark chose one of the two padded seats. The other two were wooden chairs from the chapel. Mike had a small book shelf for his theology and pastoral care books and bibles. An unadorned wooden cross hung over his desk, which was littered with paper and books.

"Anything to report?" Mark asked him.

"You mean before the plebs arrive?"

He thought of taking some of the edge off by lifting his mind out of the petty and into the noble. Just the past week they had discussed something taboo in the school, the nature of the Deity. Mark had tried to convince Mike that when Homer spoke about the Greek gods on the battlefield of Ilium, he didn't mean actual people who lived on Mount Olympus or in the clouds, as depicted in the movies. In his joker's tone, he said that when the Bible writers said that the Lord Yahweh or Adonai or HaShem spoke to the Israelites, they didn't actually mean they heard a voice from out of nowhere. It wasn't meant literally, Mark said, because the Lord was the poetic embodiment of their identity as a people. If the Israelites needed to be war-like, the Lord spoke to them and told them to slaughter their enemies, including all the children. If they needed to be solid and strong as a people, the Lord told them to be loyal and follow the Torah. If they needed to be loving and peaceful, the Lord spoke to them as a loving and peaceful Father. If they sinned and became disloyal and worshipped other gods, the Lord told them by voice or by prophet, to shape up.

No way, Mike said. It wasn't poetry at all. It was dead serious. He used some of the terms from his mentor, by way of Aristotle and Aquinas and Whitehead, to speak of a transcendent reality, whatever that was. Mark tried to convince him that the Catholic theologians, in trying to get away from the Biblical God, had drained the Deity of poetic-blood, and that the power of language could only be lived through its poetry.

When they went over the issue again, however, before the others arrived, the pressure got the better of them. As soon as Wally sauntered in with his wry grin, they stopped on cue.

"You guys talking shit again?" Wally said. "Borrring."

"If it isn't the Commish himself," Mike said. "The self-appointed leader of the Hockey World. The Commissioner of Pools and Recreation. The Pooh-Bah of plebeian reality."

"You can't block my shots with those big words, buddy. You're like a Shooter Tutor, man, a board with so many holes in it I can put anything by you with a simple wrist shot."

"You see how he sees the world through hockey eyes, Professor? I'll bet he conceived his kids on ice."

"How the fuck do you do that?" Jamie said, barging in as he usually did. He was in his track pants and a tight school maroon polo shirt, showing off his physique and biceps.

"With frozen sperm," Mark said. "Delivered low and hard on the stick side."

"Oh, OK, I see. He bulged the twine. He put it in be-tween the pubes. And he got a hat trick, eh, Wally?" Jamie said, giving out a boisterous chuckle.

Marty was always the last to arrive. He was casually attired in loose khakis and a short-sleeve shirt, his dark visage already showing a shadow of a beard. With his aplomb, he sat down on the remaining chair like a duke in his castle.

"How-do, Marty," Mike said.

"*Gravitas* has arrived," Marty announced with his wry grin.

"If you're *gravitas*, I'm *hilaritas*," Jamie said.

The first order of business was the upcoming NHL pool draft. Wally negotiated the time and the venue. He wanted a larger turnout this year, however. He was expecting them to recruit more females into the action. The ladies appreciated his humour much more than the guys.

"Jamie," he said, "can't you get some of your women friends on staff to come in?"

"Take off, eh, Commish. No way. They're all pissed off at me."

"Why's that?"

"I bang them and leave'm, that's why."

"Oh, fuck, here we go," Marty said, shaking his head. "Let's not go there, fellas, OK."

"How many has it been, Superman?" Wally asked him.

"I don't wanna brag."

"You've already bragged," Marty said, his eyes narrowed. "We're only establishing the numbers now. And this is supposed to be a Catholic school."

"Hey, Catholic girls are bunnies like anyone else. And I've been ordained as a love-priest to take care of the bunnies for Easter. Are we solid on that?"

"We're solid, Superman," Mike Corelli said with a big grin. "But we other mere mortals have been ordained to remain loyal to our woman of choice and we need to derive vicarious enjoyment from your amazing exploits. Tell us what it's like to bang'em and leave'em. Help us to re-live our former glory between the sheets."

"What glory between the sheets?" Wally said, raising his eyebrows at Mike.

"I may be chaplain now, but I wasn't chaplain in my younger years."

"Shit," Jamie said. "You couldn't stop the puck then and you can't stop it now."

Mike curled an imaginary cigar, doing his Groucho. "Hey, I may not stop the puck now, but I had a hell of a time with vulcanized rubber."

Jamie shook his head. "You're so full of holes, Mike, you don't know which end to put the rubber on."

"Does that make any sense?"

"Who the fuck cares?"

Wally gave Jamie a big smile. "Doesn't it get boring after a while, though?"

"It's the other way around, Commish. The same woman over and over. C'mon, what's that like? After eating the same three burgers, I'm ready to hurl, dude."

"If that's how you look at them," Marty said. "You obviously haven't eaten a gourmet meal with all the courses and the wine and the violins."

Jamie gave him a big grin. "Oh, I've tasted a few."

"Oh, yeah?" Marty said. "With the right feelings?"

"You fucking kidding me?" Jamie said, turning to Marty. He paced the small office. A couple of his big steps and he had to turn around. "Is he going into touchy-feely territory? Not in Hot Stove, please."

"Why not?" Mark said. "Why do we have to restrict

ourselves? Are we hockey players and mere boys—or are we more? Are we not men as well?"

"Some of us excel in all categories," Jamie said. "And some peter out."

Mark put on his serious face. "A man, after all, is more than just a hockey player, is he not? He's a son and a father and a husband. He works for his family and lays down his life for his family. He's a warrior, sure, but does he not have feelings as well? If you prick a man, does he not bleed? If you tickle a man, does he not laugh? If you hurt a man, does he not cry?"

"Yeah, if he gets it up the ass," Jamie said, giving them his fist-pump.

"We're talking feelings, Superman. We're talking about taking the Enterprise where no man has gone before."

"Yeah, into the Big Bang."

"No, Superman. Into the deep recesses of the heart."

"Let me remind you, Professor, that Superman can have feelings to show his sensitive side, sure, and he may have been married in the past, but he can't stay married. If he ever stayed married, he'd lose all his power as a super-hero. He'd never be ready to save the world at any second. He'd be washing the dishes with Lois Lane instead."

"That's the thing, see," Mike said. "Superman's sup-posed to be the ultimate good guy, isn't he? Superman and Lois ... they have the bond that shall remain nameless in Hot Stove League."

"Absolutely right. But that's just the show for the kid-dies, Mike. In reality Superman has to satisfy the needs of all women, bar none, or else he's not truly Superman."

"I think you're mixing apples and oranges, Superman,"

Mark said. "The *übermensch* is not the comic-book and movie Superman. They're two totally different fruits."

"Are you trying to insult me?" Jamie said. "I can mix anything I want with my superpowers."

"Right," Marty said. "But can you turn time around and bring us back to the Pleistocene period when the earth was one big skating rink?"

Jamie grinned. "I can clean your ass, off and on the ice, that's a solid."

Marty raised his narrow eyes to Jamie. "Oh, can you?"

"Boys, boys," Mark said. "We're in the chaplain's office."

"All right, all right," Mike Corelli said. "As chaplain, I have to steer this ship into uncharted territory, even though I may be jeopardizing my dubious status as a hockey player."

Jamie and Wally frowned. Mark was shaking his head.

Mike twirled his cigar. "Navigator, take us to the far reaches of space, where no hockey player has ever been. Take us to *amore, amour, amor, eros, cupid, agapé*."

"Fuck, give me some oxygen," Jamie said.

"Borrring," Wally said.

"I've been to the planets *amore* and *amour* and *cupid*," Jamie said. "But I've never been to *eros* and *agapé*. Are you going to home-school us, Mr. Chaplain?"

"Are we in a fucking retreat?" Wally said. "Borrring."

"No, let him speak."

"I'll tell you who they are," Wally said. "Jack Eros played for the Leafs way back. He'd drop the gloves every chance and give someone a knuckle sandwich. And Jacques Agapé was a Montreal Canadien, if I'm not mistaken, who'd go into the corners with a pocket-full of eggs and not break one."

Marty smiled at Wally. "I know where you got that."

Mike went ahead, indifferent to their comments. He tried to explain the difference between the two words in his best doctoral voice. He became so stiff and serious, however, that he made everyone uncomfortable, which threatened the loosey-goosey spell in the room. Sensing it himself, he stopped and suddenly twirled his imaginary cigar.

"Well, I gave it a shot. Those are my principles, but if you don't like them, I have others."

"All right, all right," Jamie said, taking over. "Let's put a few things into perspective, shall we? Let's get solid here, boys. In Hot Stove we may act like boys, but we're all men. At least the last time I looked. And a man likes sex, pure and simple. A man is supposed to love all women, or as many women as possible. A man wasn't made to stay with one mate for long. Look at the animal kingdom where many of the males mate'm and leave'm. Where they fight to have their own pride of females. It's just nature weeding out the weak and keeping the strong."

"Yeah, in the animal kingdom, sure," Wally said. "But animals don't play hockey, dude. And we play hockey. That means we have responsibilities to the team. As a husband and a father we have to take care of our team. The team comes first—and there's no 'I' in team."

"The same old clichés," Mark said.

"Why do you think it is a cliché, you chooch?"

"I don't know. Why don't you tell us."

"That I will," Wally said, nodding, getting off his horse and ready to do the two-step. "I'm going to edify you guys, all right, because it's quite apparent you need some edifuckation." He raised his finger as if to address the troops. "In the first place, the husband has to have strong feelings for his wife, OK. Call it love if you want. It starts with passion and hot sex, sure, but eventually it settles down and changes and becomes other things as well. They fight and bicker and settle into their roles on the team. They come to depend on each other for different things. They build a home as a team, work as a team, raise their children as a team. They may individually go through slumps, bad years, catastrophes, but if they've created a strong bond the union will save them. That's what love's all about, boys. Not the romantic stuff of the movies, but living it out day in and day out as a team."

"You mean," Mike said, "the husband stays a Leafs fan his whole life?"

Wally grinned. "Yeah, you stay solid, dude."

They all stared at Jamie.

"Well, I'm not a true fan, I guess. I play the game, boys. There are those who play and those who watch. You guys can be the spectators. I'm the player, man, the super-player."

"Maybe you're just afraid of taking the plunge," Marty said. "Don't you ever want to have kids? Then you'd have someone your own age to play with."

"He probably has a few out there he's not even aware of," Mike said.

"No way, dude," Jamie said. "Unless I used a holy condom."

"The same old story, a tale of love and glory," Mark said, shaking his head. "As time turtles onward into the dull horizon."

Mike's face beamed. "Remember this line, Professor? Peter Lorre says to Bogey in Rick's Cafe: You despise me, don't you, Rick? And Rick says: If I ever gave you any thought, I probably would, yeah."

Mark couldn't recall Rick actually saying he loved Ilsa in *Casablanca*. She definitely said it. But he was old-school. He didn't have to say it. It was written all over his face. And in the end he had gotten the letters of transit for her and her husband.

He tried to explain to the boys that old-school guys would find it embarrassing to express their feelings in words, that if you had the feeling you didn't say it, and if you said it, nine times out of ten, you didn't authentically have it, but he made a total mess of getting it across.

Then Marty spoke up as the arch-destroyer of all bull-shit, he said, to give them the facts and just the facts, ma'am. What most people thought of as love was merely a blind biological urge to ensure the protection of the new genes and their vulnerable carriers, he said in his slow ponderous voice. It had a short phase of sexual infatuation and a longer phase of dull habit. We were merely the pawns in the game of genomes, with our selfish genes wanting all the glory. Love made us pass the puck around in reciprocal altruism, he said, the selfish drive to find a mating partner by which to replicate ourselves.

In the bigger picture, it was natural selection for winning the game. He used examples from the animal kingdom to hammer home his point. A mother would fight for her young and even sacrifice her life, if need be, because of her genetic makeup. She'd take the fall for the team and the team would benefit as a result. As cynical as it sounded, he added, it was all chemistry. We were the mere pawns of our DNA and RNA. When sperm and egg combined, the chromosomes of both literally lined up side by side like a face-off and swapped pieces of themselves. It was Nature moving us around the ice by means of our own vanity. And because males had so many more spermatozoa they could sow their wild oats and be callused guys like Superman, while the females had be more selective and nurturing because they had larger and fewer eggs.

"Hey, I resent that, Mr. Science," Jamie said. "I'm no pawn in my genes."

"This is getting too borrring," Wally said. "Is this Hot Stove or Love Boat?"

At that point they saw Brianne Lorimer walking by the office. Jamie dashed out and brought her in.

Brianne was one of Mark's favourite teachers on staff. She was short and blond, in her late thirties, with attractive freckled features, and an outgoing boisterous disposition. She taught Phys Ed, coached the curling team and girl's soccer, and did some guidance. She had been married over ten years and had two boys who played in the minor hockey program. Mark had never seen her in a foul mood, though she could rake any guy over the coals over his stupidity. She always had a smile and was full of lively banter, keeping everyone in good cheer. Today she was in a maroon track suit, with the curling team logo on it, looking very swishy.

"Hi-ya, fellas," she said with a big grin. "Is this a meeting of Hot Stove?"

"According to Mr. Biology here," Jamie said, "it's a meeting of the school sperm bank."

"It's SSB dot org," Mike said.

She shook her head. "Yeah, SSB dot defective org."

"Listen, we're serious, Bree," Jamie said. "We want to be more than just hockey players and sperm donors. We want to be real men, as the Professor says."

"It takes a woman to make a man out of a boy."

Mike curled his imaginary cigar. "I'd say it's vice versa, Brianne. That it takes a man to make a woman out of a girl, with more vice than versa."

"Stop it, Mike," Jamie said. "The Professor and Marty want us to be serious, and we need the female point of view here. And Bree's the designated female."

Jamie turned to Brianne, his face deadly serious. "We're discussing the nature of love, Bree. And we have to put you on the spot. We need to know what the female view is on love. Do you, for example, need to hear your husband say he loves you every so often?"

"It would be nice, sure."

"Does he, in fact, do so?"

"Not really. He's not a lovey-dovey guy. I think I'd feel very uncomfortable with a lovey-dovey guy."

"You say, not really. So he does say it ... every so often?"

"Yeah."

"When?"

"I'd rather not say, boys. It's in the family vault."

"Ah," Wally said. "She means he says it when he's do-ing the dirty."

"When his dick is over her head, you mean?"

Brianne laughed. "You guys kill me. You turn every-thing upside down, that's your problem. Especially with women. The vice of your gonads plays with the versa of your minds. How can you ever call something that's beautiful dirty?"

"Are you talking about sexual congress?" Jamie said.

Brianne frowned. "No, you idiot. It's called making love."

"Ah, how-do," Mike said. "That's what I was trying to explain before about the different kinds of love. And here I gotta take off my goalie mask and give it another try, boys. Do I have your permission to take Hot Stove to uncharted territory?"

"You got three minutes," Jamie said. "I'm timing you."

Mike got up, took a deep breath, and faced them with all the seriousness of a chaplain. For a few seconds Mark thought he'd break the spell. But Mike was simply being chaplain-esque, a guy who was playing the part of a chaplain, and thus a guy who was more than just a chaplain. Mark could remember Mike himself using the example of Sartre's waiter being waiter-esque on a few occasions to make a point about the authentic self. He just hoped Mike wouldn't speak too long, as was his wont, especially since they were in a real chaplain's office.

If we were making love with the partner we love, Mike said, playing the part of a chaplain, then it was beautiful and transformative. It would go from *eros* to *agapé*. It would bring about what Lonergan, his mentor, in his fuller theory, called self-transcendence. Here Mike made a great show of using the word that would never go over too well in Hot Stove since it could only be derided as ostentatious, show-offy, and absolutely not-hockey. But Mike brought it off because he was Mike-the-goalie and not Mike-the-chaplain while Hot Stove was in session. So Mike explained that self-transcendence was the capacity to go beyond our limits as individuals and fulfill ourselves in our fuller capacity as authentic human beings. Being in love, Mike-the-goalie said, was a concrete feeling that transformed an 'I' and 'thou' into a 'we' so powerful that two became one and then three in the offspring. And the guys were amused, very amused, Mark saw, as if Mike was doing his acrobatic best to stop the puck whizzing by him.

"Excuse me!" Jamie said. "Both one and three? Are you doing the new math?"

Mike grinned. He wasn't finished. He should've finished. He was going on too long, Mark feared. He could feel the dressing room shaking as if it was hurtling through a foreign gravitational field.

With that concrete feeling and joy, Mike said, came the vulnerability of being connected so closely to someone else that we could feel the other's pain as well. That connection, however, was open, alive, unrestricted, at the peak of the soul's capacity go beyond itself and realize its full potential to merge in rapture with the sublime—with the Big Guy, he said. The heart has its reasons that reason knows not, Mike-the-goalie said with a flourish, quoting Pascal. The heart pushed our horizons ever and ever outwards to include our union with our Creator.

"Ah, the theologian's guide to love," Mark said, feeling Mike had put on his chaplain's garb in mid-stride, seriously jeopardizing the spell.

Mike frowned. "How so, Professor?"

"I'm all right as long as I *play* a professor. As soon as I *become* a professor, I'm in trouble."

"Let me set you straight, Professor," Jamie said. "You're also only *playing* at being a hockey player."

"Look, I'm no authority on love," Mark said. "But a theologian—and a celibate priest to boot—would be the last person I'd consult for a take on *eros*."

"There are a few priests I'd like to hang by the balls, I'll tell you that," Marty said.

"You mean the pedo-priests," Jamie said.

"Yeah, the guys who use the power of their office to sexually abuse children—and then are swept under the rug by the Church."

"We'd give them a piece of Hot Stove justice, right?" Wally said.

"Don't let the rotten apples spoil the barrel, boys," Mike said. "Let's get back to the issue in hand. What do you disagree with, Professor?"

"You said some good things, yeah, but you slipped in the party line as well. In the end your theory is like Marty's theory of the DNA in religious garb."

"You have to explain, Professor," Jamie said.

"Borrring."

"I'll make it short. In both the science theory and the religious theory, love is merely the means towards an end. It's not an end in itself."

"Aw, fuck, I'm sorry I asked him." Jamie shook his head.

"Let's get back to hockey, shall we," Wally said. "Or else I'm blowing this joint."

Mark gave them his mock smile. "In hockey terms, do we play to win the game or do we play for the sheer love of the game?"

"I play for beer, that's what I play for," Wally said.

21

"Did you guys hear the one about the hockey player and the case of beer?" Mike said, switching roles again. "A guy's walking on the sidewalk with a case of beer and passes by his friend's house. His friend Dougie, who plays on the same team, shouts out. Hey, Bobby, whatcha get the case of beer for? I got it for my wife, Bobby says. Good trade, Dougie says."

"Ah, what's the use?" Mark said.

"Go ahead, tell us, Shakespeare," Marty said. "Give us the rap on love, dude."

Mark went into his sing-song, bobbing his head, rapping his fingers on the arm rest to get a beat, doing his take on a couple of Irish poets. "Love's the force that drives the flower, through the earth and to the power. Love's the longing that makes us whole, until the centre cannot hold. Love's the skin and the desire that puts the rose on the pyre."

"What the fuck!" Jamie said.

"That's beautiful," Brianne said. "Though I don't understand half of it."

Marty raised his hand. "Is that love or death?"

"You guys don't have a poetic bone in your body."

"We got boners instead," Wally said.

"Look, I gotta go, guys," Brianne said. "It's been a slice."

"I'm in a place where I'm restricted in using the words, and even if I used the words they'd be meaningless."

"I understand your predicament, Professor," Mike said.

Mark shook his head. "If I ever got serious in this school I'd choke on my words and asphyxiate myself."

"We've gotten too serious as it is," Marty said.

"Look," Brianne said with a big smile. "I'll put you

guys out of your misery, OK. Love is not biology or religion or poetry. Love is love."

"Beautiful," Jamie said. "Finally we have the female POV, the point of vacancy."

"Not so," Mike said, twirling his cigar. "She's right, boys. Love is goodness itself. It's how we transcend ourselves and play for the Big Guy."

"You mean the Big Boss?" Jamie said.

"Haven't you guys heard?" Marty said. "The Big Guy is the Dead Guy."

"To some, sure," Mike said. "But the believers far outnumber the non-believers."

Marty shook his head, his face grim. "All right, we've gone into uncharted territory of bullshit much too long. We're Hot Stove, guys, aren't we? We tell it like it is. Anything that happens in Hot Stove stays in Hot Stove, right?"

"Well, we have to respect the chaplain's office as well," Mike said.

"All right, with all due respect, let's cut through the bullshit. If this is truly Hot Stove, let's be Hot Stove, all right?"

"You start," Mark said.

Wally gave out a few groans. Jamie hung his head. Mike put on his game face.

Marty nodded with his wry smile, ready for some premium baloney-cutting. He told them he didn't care how many teams there were in Christianity, Judaism, or Islam. Science had defeated all of them. Science had facts as forwards and theories as defencemen. All were solid. And when they faltered or were proven inadequate they were replaced by new players. The organized religions, on the other hand, had these old farts that were on their last legs. Why, the pope was a goalie with such a holey team in front of him he couldn't stop a puck if he tried.

He paused and asked if they were following him.

"You're getting too personal," Mike said. "But go on."

The Abrahamic religions were theories, Marty said. They had been good teams in the past, but that was all over. Superior theories had defeated them too often. Anyone who faced the facts would know there was no Big Boss intervening in the game. And while the moral teachings of said religions were perhaps necessary for most people off the ice, on the ice it was Science and Reason that would win out all the time.

"Listen, boys," Brianne said. "I'd like to stay, but I gotta move. I'm on a mission for the curling team."

"Look at what you did, Mr. Biology," Jamie said. "You scared her off. And she's supposed to be the vulnerable carrier of important genes."

"Not if she's throwing the rocks," Wally said.

"I'll throw a few more rocks," Marty said. "I've done some part-time teaching at a Jewish private school and it's a whole different ball game there, boys. At least they're deadly serious about what they teach. Here we only cherry pick. The students know it more than anyone. We teachers are all hypocrites in this so-called Separate School Board, with our little rituals and lip service to educating the minds of Christian kids."

Mike's face tightened, as if all his defencemen had deserted him and he was facing a breakaway. He came out of the crease and stood his ground, trying to cut all the angles.

Faith still put out a good team, he said. It wasn't just running on theory. It was a living reality. Mother Teresa and the thousands of others like her who unconditionally cared for the poor was a fact, not a theory. But you couldn't run a team on facts and theory only. You needed inspiration, something to play for, a few great goals, he laughed. As teachers, they were there for the kids, weren't they? And the kids needed their guidance more than ever these days, what with the influences of the secular world.

"Be that as it may," Mark said, "we're operating under an umbrella of lies. Marty's right. Most of the older students don't even believe in the Big Boss anymore. I doubt that even most of the teachers give a flying fadoodle, right, Wally?"

"It's borrring. I couldn't care less."

"The God-question is the dead question," Mark said. "What about you, Brianne?"

"As long as you try to live a good life, it doesn't matter what you believe."

"But who determines what the good life is?" Mark said.

"Who gives a shit?" Jamie said. "What the fuck! We're in Hot Stove. Let's get solid, eh. We believe in beer and hockey, fuck the rest."

It took a few minutes, but they got back on the rails, breathing a sigh of relief. It had been close. They had lost their minds for a few minutes there. Jamie blamed Marty, Mr. Gravitas. Marty blamed Mike, who had brought in a theologian. Mike blamed Brianne. Brianne blamed Mark, the Professor, who was only playing at being a professor.

Mark remained silent.

Shortly afterwards Brianne left, followed by Jamie and

Wally, who had things to do, they said. Mark could clearly see, however, they were anxious to leave a room where someone had laid a big fart, the stink of which wouldn't soon blow away.

Mark, Marty, and Mike went through some tense minutes, joking around and trying to talk hockey, but their hearts weren't in it. Mark could see that Mike had more things to say to defend his position. In order to get back on the right track with him, Mark asked him why he disagreed with Marty.

Mike just started to talk about the sacraments, the importance of ritual for the kids, when they saw a kid come to the door and peek in with a big bashful grin.

"Hi-ya, Mike."

"Hey, Colin, how-do. Com'on in."

It was one of the Spec Ed kids, a short squat guy with a flat fleshy face, mongoloid eyes, and a big toothy grin. He was in the school uniform of grey dress pants and blue school sweater. Mark recognized him as being a happy-go-lucky kid whom all the teachers were friendly with. He'd see him in the hallway in the mornings being greeted from their bus by Spec Ed teachers.

"Colin, you know Mr. Trecroci and Mr. Andrews here, don't you?"

"Yeah ... Hey, Mike, I gotta talk to you."

"Sure thing, Colin. Have a seat. Excuse me, guys. What's on your mind, Colin?"

Colin sat down. "I don't know, Mike." The guy looked over at him and Marty, his face blank.

"We're in Hot Stove here, Colin. You can talk. You're one of the boys."

"Oh, yeah?"

"Yeah, you can feel free to say anything. The guys here were just raking me over the coals. They were questioning my ability to be a good goalie. They said I couldn't stop a puck if I even tried."

"Oh, no, Mike, you're a good goalie. I seen you play. You're like ... like ..."

"Like a door closed shut," Mark said.

"Oh, no, Mr. Trecroci. Mike's door is always open."

"Yes, it is, isn't it?"

"Mike's my friend."

"He's our friend, too," Mark said.

"Even if we clash on theological matters, right, Professor?" Mike said, his face beaming.

"Last week Mike took us to the Playdium. He showed us how play all the games. I went on the go-carts with him. It was so fun, eh, Mike?"

"Right-ho, Colin."

"We crashed a few times, eh, Mike?"

"We sure did."

"That's how you spend your afternoons, huh?" Marty said. "I wish I had your job."

"Yeah, we should switch some time. I'll take the Bunsen burners and you take the cross."

Marty narrowed his eyes and smiled, remaining silent.

"And this week," Colin said, "we're going to St. Francis Table, right, Mike?"

"That we are. We're going to help feed the homeless."

"But Mike ..." Colin stopped.

"What's the problem, Colin?"

"My mom won't let me go."

27

"Oh, yeah, why not?"

"She wants to talk to you, Mike. You gotta talk to her."

Mark looked at the kid. "What's she afraid of?"

"I don't know. You gotta talk to her, Mike, OK?"

"Will do, Colin."

The kid looked around the room, his face getting blank again. He seemed to have something else on his mind. Mark felt it was time to go. He got up. Marty got up with him.

"We better go," Marty said.

"See you," Mark said. "So long, Colin."

"Yeah, bye. Mike, I gotta talk to you."

"What's up?" Mark heard Mike say as he headed out the door and onto the long hallway to the gym and caf.

The long lunch was almost over. Students were milling around in the hallway, spilling out from the cafeteria down the hall, some going outside to the smoking area, some to the back lot to laze in the sun on mild autumn afternoon. They were in bunches, in twos or threes, or larger, talking and horsing around, having some peace and fun, before having to go back into the classroom and having to play their roles and jump through their hoops.

Bookman Goes Batty

When we heard the latest at the *Gazette*, we were flabbergasted. No one in their right mind would ever have predicted it. The City Room went into a frenzy of damage control. People held their smartphones and eye-balled their computers, stuck in some time-warp, putting everything else on hold. The buzz went silent. Sarcasm was just around the corner.

Thursby, the city editor, called me into his office. He was in his blue shirt and suspenders, his white hair sticking out as if he had just taken his finger from the plug. I was to track this story to its roots and hair balls. Confirm it with a fine tooth comb. Do all the interviews and leg-work. Dig it and bag it. Time was of the essence, he said. Crime would not stand still.

"Why me?" I said.

"You're the only one with the moxie."

The first person I saw was Commissioner Geiko at police headquarters. I was ushered into his small unpretentious office, with the official documents on the walls, the photos of friends and family, the windows overlooking Main Street. The Commissioner was at his nondescript best for a person who kept out of the limelight. He had a moustache, was in his late fifties, square and compact in his spanking blue uniform, with a minimum of ostentation.

I asked him immediately how he discovered the news.

"Well," he said, giving the question some time to digest, "I knew that something was amiss after two weeks of not seeing the Book Signal on my computer. Bibliopolis has had its share of petty crimes, of course, but there were rumblings of something big happening. My undercover men couldn't give us the details, but it could've been the Antiquarian or the Jester. Someone was planning to blow up the electronic grid in the city, send it into a dark informational tailspin, the like of which we've never seen before. Bookman must've known about it. He has better Intel than we do. But no Book Signal for weeks. So I became suspicious that something was afoot. Was the man sick? Was he reading the *Decline and Fall*?"

The Commissioner, at this point, paused and licked his moustache. I had seen this mannerism before, especially during tense moments, when his incredulity or his patience was stretched to the limit.

"Yeah, go on, Commissioner," I said, not to belabour the point.

"Well, I did what I usually do when I'm curious about the man," he went on. "I called my liaison, the person who knows the man better than anyone else."

"Who's that?"

"Sorry, that stays in the vault."

"What did he say?"

"He told me that Bookman had gone through some sort of crisis. He was reconsidering his role as a crime fighter. He would be indisposed for a certain length of time."

"Indisposed? What the hell does that mean?"

"You have to understand my liaison. He's a bit of a cynic. Even though he's been with him for a long time, he doesn't take all the intellectual shit and high falutin' language too seriously. He's been around the block more than a few times, you might say. I'm not into the lexicon too well, but I'd say *indisposed* means no longer available."

"Yeah, but for how long?"

"He didn't say."

I shook my head, put the info down on my pad, thought maybe I should embellish it, but thought the better of it. I knew who the liaison guy might be, of course, but I wanted to hear it from his own mouth. Suspicions as to Bookman's true identity had led the paper to delve into the matter in the past. Though no one had seen the guy behind the mask, we were pretty sure of our leads. We just couldn't publish the story. Call it community interest or home city security. We couldn't compromise the Bookman's camouflage, his modus operandi, his double life. Or Bibliopolis would lose the greatest crime fighter it ever had.

"Did he elaborate on the nature of this crisis?" I asked the Commissioner.

Then he gave me his little smile — or should I say half smile, half sneer, as if it was too incredible or too stupid, I couldn't tell which.

"He just said that Bookman had had a change of heart."

"Is he retiring, you mean?"

"Who knows?"

"What're you going to do, Commissioner? Once the book haters and crime mongers of Bibliopolis find out what's going on there'll be bedlam."

Here was where he gave me his serious look, peering at me as if I were vermin.

"The *Gazette* has to be with us on this," he said. "You have to publish a fake story, Bobby Joe. The hoods and gangsters can't know what's going on or we'll be in deep shit."

"C'mon, Commish, this is our mandate. The people have to be informed. A people uninformed is more dangerous than not. You guys will eventually have to do your job without the Bookman's help. You won't have him forever, you know. Everything ends, Commish."

I was feeling a little contemplative at that point and thought it better to stop my train of thought. Who was I to tell him his job? He knew his job — and I knew mine. I also knew I wouldn't get anything else about the Bookman from him. So I asked him a few questions on how the police department would meet the challenge of fighting crime without help from a superhero. The Commish was quite matter of fact about it. One thing he said, however, piqued my interest. And I wrote it down word for word. Sometimes, he said, even super heroes can be brought to their knees by ordinary life.

The next person I saw was Domina, aka Kitty Kat.

The paper arranged a place and time, in a dingy alley in the middle of the city. As I stood in the smelly alley feeling quite stupid, she came out of the dark like a leopard, dressed in her familiar black spandex that hugged her curvaceous form like skin on a skillet. She was endowed, she was lithe, and she was lethal. Though the Comics Code Authority had forbidden the cat-o-nine, she had it fastened to her hip, ready to wield it at the least provocation. I had to be careful.

"OK, what do you want, reporter-man?" she said with a few interspersed hisses, which were hardly felicitous or feminine, though her curves put a dent in my equanimity.

"I just want to ask you a few things about Bookman."

She gave out a sarcastic laugh. "You mean Ratman."

"I thought you two were close."

"Let's just say we've had a parting of the ways."

"What happened?'

She pursed her lips, touched her whip, and shook her head. The topic was still delicate, I could see.

"He thinks he's better than me, that's what happened."

"Could you elaborate, please."

Conflicting emotions played across her face, what the Romance books would call love-hate, perhaps, or even affection-disgust.

"He thinks he's intellectually and morally superior, you moron. As if I'm beneath him or something. When it's clearly the other way around, reporter-man. They don't call me the Domina for nothing."

I couldn't corroborate this first-hand, of course, but word had it that Domina could go from tender romance to seething meowtic rage in a heartbeat. She could seduce a guy with her purrs and chirps one moment and then put the whip to him the next. Which provoked a few jokes in the City Room, I might add. She was definitely a study in contrast, if not in paradox. That a woman could be so tender in romance and so vengeful as a dominatrix made her an arch villainess to contend with. If you got on her wrong side, she could stalk you, lure you, and punish you to within an inch of your manhood. It wasn't S & M. She had invented a whole new category in the cutting edge.

I didn't know all the background info between her and the Bookman, but as an avid reader myself, I could imagine some of the sparks between them.

"Look, Kitty—"

"Don't call me that!"

"All right, Domina," I said, taking out my pad. "Can you give me any info as to why the Bookman is indisposed, as the Commish told me?"

"He's a coward, pure and simple," she said. "He's lost all his seminal fortitude. And I use my words as I use my whip. It takes more than intellectual acumen and moral turpitude to fight crime in Bibliopolis, as you well know. It takes staying power, robust vitality, courage, honour, and fearlessness in the face of crime and non-reading, what the Romans of old would call *virtu*. And the Bookman hasn't got it anymore. It's as simple as that. He's gotten old and flaccid, reporter-man. Just hasn't got the balls to mix with the books. Print that."

I tilted my head, but wrote it down as she said it.

"Aren't you being a little harsh?" I said. "You women always like to kick a guy where it hurts."

I could see I had said the wrong thing. Her face hardened. Her hand went to her whip. Her eyes shone in the dark like a wildcat. I took a few steps back, ready for anything.

"Sorry," I said. "I didn't mean it the way it sounds. I'm just saying you might be a little slanted in your views."

"*You women*?" she said with a snarl. "What do you mean, *you women*?"

"Just a slip of the tongue."

"Which deserves a few cuts of the cat."

"No, please," I said, raising my hands. "Can't you forgive someone for making a mistake? Call it a little Freudian slip. Have a heart, please."

"Which needs a Freudian whip," she said, exposing her fangs, keeping her hand on the handle of the whip. "Let's see you grovel, reporter-man."

As I was inching back, my feet hit something and I fell backwards. She stepped over my supine form, her black-clad gams like two columns of rippling muscle, stoking me with both fear and lust.

She gave out a roar of laughter, as if she had subdued another prey with the power of her stealth and seduction.

"Let me give it to you straight, reporter-man," she said, snarling down at me. "We women are into romance because it works. It softens us, prepares us to accept the seed willingly. And from that comes the good of the offspring. But make no mistake. If you men don't carry out your side of the bargain, if you're not hard and courageous and go the distance, then we'll bury you, balls and all. Print that."

As I hightailed out of there, I could hear her HA-HAs at my discomfiture. But I did manage to keep my note-pad—and I got it all down as soon as possible. Slanted as her views were, she might've been closer to the truth than she knew. Fighting crime in Bibliopolis was hard work. It took more than brawn and brain. The Bookman had to keep up on his reading. He could still use his fists and his superpowers, sure, but he had to use vocab skills and plot twists and literary devices as well. Sometimes he had to quote from the great poets. The only problem these days, though, was that fewer and fewer people were reading. Especially guys. Bibliopolis was in serious decline.

After seeing Kitty Kat, I didn't want to go into any more smelly alleys and put myself at risk. So I asked to see Antiquarian next. He didn't operate in alleys and rooftops like Kitty Kat. He wasn't a burglar. He was more of an anarchist, a chaos man, a contrarian. His crimes involved sabotaging the day-to-day running of the economy and city. Like spraying bleach in clothing stores. Hacking and destroying government computers. Blocking rush hour traffic. He and the Bookman had grappled on more than a few occasions, however, and if anyone knew the workings of the Bookman's mind it was Antiquarian. They both had blotter brains, able to absorb words like no others, not to mention having a respect for books unparalleled in our modern age. You could even say they were brothers under the skin, though one worked on the wrong side of the law and was known to be a nasty SOB.

At the last minute he changed our place of rendezvous, I suspect, because he was wary of a take-down. We met, instead, at the only remaining used bookstore in the city, run by this curmudgeon, Timothy Galt, who operated the store on a loss every year just for the satisfaction of giving the Net the finger. Again it was the paper that arranged the rendezvous. One of the terms, as I was told, was that Antiquarian wanted the paper to print an ad for a rare and very expensive first edition. He'd give me the details himself.

The store was in this dilapidated building, in a walk-down. It smelled of incense and musty books. Timothy, his white hair curled in a pompadour, was hunched over the counter. No one else was in the store. He looked over to the back where an open door led to the storage area. The dingy store was overflowing with crammed shelves, floor to ceiling, with piles on the floor. No one came here anymore. It was like a cemetery of decaying books.

Antiquarian was seated and waiting for me in the dimly lit storage room. He was thin and bald, a little over fifty, with intense eyes and a mild-mannered disposition, dressed in his usual holey Hudson's Bay sweater. I didn't let the outer façade fool me, however. Inside his innocuous camouflage was a brutal man.

"I'm assuming you're legit," he said immediately, not even waiting for me to sit down on the chair facing him. "At the least sign of trouble, you'll be the first to get whacked."

I had to smile at his threat. "Don't worry. I'm only after a few answers."

"Just so that you know, I had you followed here. And there are five guns pointing at you as we speak."

Then he proceeded to give me the particulars of this rare first-edition of a prized nineteenth century book. I got it all down as dictated, with the original olive green cloth, boards with gilt-stamped triple-rule frames and titles, blind-stamped leaf-and-vine designs, all edges gilt. His voice resonated with emotion, his words like honey on a comb. I felt a twinge of envy. For me, however, it was never the artefact or rarity of the book.

"All right," he said afterwards, "whatta ya wanna know about the Bookman?"

"What's happened? Why's he retired, indisposed, whatever?"

He paused, shook his head, gave me a sarcastic smile. "You entitled press punks piss me off. All you print is surface-copy, info-babble, trash-speak."

"I understand. You deal in depth and quality, and the masses don't want depth and quality."

"Oh, a smart-ass, huh?"

"Let's just say you and the Bookman, not to mention Kitty Kat, aren't the only ones who've read a few books."

"You gotta put bread on the table, right?"

"That's right, Antiquarian. I'm a realist. And I don't break the law."

His lips curled in condescension. "Don't talk to me about the law, press punk. Laws are made by the One-Percent under the guise of democracy, as empty a word as you'll ever find. The only true democrats are the anarchists and free spirits who aren't shackled to the norms and laws of the present."

"We're not here to talk about you."

"All right. The Bookman, right? OK, let's talk about the Bookman. If you want my humble opinion, I think he's gone batty."

"Explain."

"The last time we tangled wasn't pretty. Let's just say it was a Pyrrhic victory for him. In between the POWS and the BANGS and KA-POWS, he was quoting some strange people, to say the least."

"I don't get it." I looked at him with my best quizzical expression.

"Ever read *Fahrenheit 451*?"

"Can't say I have."

He shook his head with distaste.

"Media people are the least qualified, least articulate, and most dumb-assed people around. How did you become a reporter, anyway?"

"Hey, this isn't about me."

"If you're going to write it, of course it's about you, you idiot."

At this point I got a little sick and tired of being insulted by these super villains. I realized I had to keep my objective slant, be impartial, and get the facts, but I'm human, too, all too human, as a matter of fact.

"One thing we learned in Journalism School," I said, holding my head high, "was that stick and stones may break our bones, but names will never hurt us."

Antiquarian jabbed a finger in my chest with a menacing scowl. "You don't know the first thing about broken bones, Journal-head. Open your ears and listen good. The Bookman had gone haywire. He was quoting and misquoting, as if he didn't give a shit anymore. As if all his sources and footnotes had been crossed."

I had to ask him to repeat that, as I got it down word for word, since I had no idea what he was talking about.

"You've lost me, Antiquarian."

"You were lost before you entered this store," he said in a sneering tone. "Just print it as you hear it and maybe some readers out there will get the gist." He paused. "The point is that the Bookman's finally discovered the enormity of his task. He's not just fighting me and Domina and the Jester and the all the others. He finally figured it out."

Well, the mystery of the Bookman's indisposition wasn't being clarified. It was being mystified even more.

I had to go to the only man who could put a different

slant on all this. The Jester. He was the only one who could laugh at anything, render it innocuous, and take the stuffing out of it. The Jester didn't take anything seriously, just like the Ironic Age we were in. Even when he was committing a crime, he was laughing at himself as well as us. He'd leave little jokes at the crime scene. Or make a YouTube video of the event, with some flashes of comic brilliance.

Once he and his henchmen had robbed a high-end clothing store, dressed a few piglets in women's undergarments, and filmed them scurrying around the store. Another time he and his men had taken a high school hostage, kicked all the students out, barricaded the doors from the inside, and forced the teachers to read Hegel for two days straight.

He was a master of disguise as well. No one knew what he actually looked like. Sometimes he wore the mask of comedy, sometimes the mask of tragedy. Sometimes he quoted Seneca, sometimes Euripides. Sometimes he held the sceptre of a fool in his hand, sometimes the sceptre of the globe. He was known to have the only extant edition of the entire Loeb classics. He could be mystifyingly erudite and childishly silly in a heartbeat.

I was a little suspicious, however. It was he who had called me to arrange a meeting. The voice over the smartphone said he had been informed by certain distinguished colleagues that I was after the lowdown on the Bookman's change of heart and he would oblige. He had the key to the superhero's turnabout.

We were supposed to meet in a chain coffee shop in the middle of the city and I was very curious as to how he'd present himself. Would he come disguised in a mask and draw attention to himself? Would he wear a false beard and wig? Would he use some sort of computer tech savvy and not even physically be there? I had my smartphone, after all, and could talk face to face with anyone in the world in present time.

I was seated at a table, sipping on a café-latte, when a young woman in a loose-fitting top and trousers sat down with me. To my horror, however, her face had been so misshapen by plastic surgery she looked like a banged up Barbie. Her lips were large rubber discs. Her cheekbones were sculpted out of cheese. Her nose seemed but a burp with two holes. And her eyes were like hard glass. Over her ugly features was a finely sculpted head of blond hair. In her hand she had a plastic cup of coffee with a straw.

"Relax," she said through her hard lips, her voice high and strained. "Don't be shocked. This is what happens when we go to a cosmetic surgeon much too often. I've had the injections, the lasers, the nips and tucks, the microdermabrasions, the rhinoplasty, the vein removal, the liposuction, the whole nine yards. I may not look pleasing, but at least I've defied time."

"What can I do for you, lady?"

"You can laugh your head off, for one."

And then it hit me. "Are you the Jester?"

"I jest you not," she said. "I'm the sweet transvestite from Transylvania."

When I looked closer I could see the full-head silicone mask, as fine a work of special effects as anything in the movies. It wasn't the *Rocky Horror Picture Show* I was reminded of, however. It was a small-budget horror movie in which a female student in medical school, adept with the scalpel and desperate for money, does slash and cash jobs on people who're into body modification. Some want to look like dolls, some want to be de-sexed, and others are just bored. Though such things only happened in the movies, they weren't far from the improbable. And I could only marvel at the Jester's social iconoclasm at work, while being wary of his motives and methods, of course.

"Do I refer to you as a he or a she?" I said.

"Jester is fine," he said, now in a more masculine tone. "What would you like to know about the Bookman?"

"You said over the phone you had the key to the Bookman's turnaround. Apparently he's had a crisis and a change of heart. He's gone into seclusion. What can you tell me?"

"First of all," he said, looking around suspiciously, "I have to have your word that you will honour your code and not reveal your sources. Even under oath."

"And I have to have your word that you'll honour your comic's code that you aren't party to horrendous crimes or sexually deviant behaviour."

His laughter, I could see, was painful through the silicone. A few of the patrons turned to give us the one-eye. I couldn't see what was so funny.

"Let me put you and your readers straight, buddy," he said. "I don't commit crimes against humanity. I commit crimes against those who commit crimes against humanity. And if you can't see the difference, then you're as much a problem as a solution. Are you reading me?"

"I think so."

"I don't think so," he said, shaking his head. "Your paper has been misinforming the public about me for profit.

I don't mind if you do it for fun, but to do it for profit is a crime against humanity. Get it?"

"Hey, we're barely staying afloat, if you wanna know. Hard copy is becoming obsolete as we speak. Let's not change the topic. What can you tell me about the Bookman?"

"Have I got your word?"

"Sure, sure. I won't reveal my source."

"Why did God create Adam before Eve?"

"You tell me."

"Because he didn't want any advice."

To be honest, the joke was so chintzy all I could do was raise my eyebrow. I wasn't going to amuse him. I had to be true to my sense of humour. I remained impassive, giving him a sceptical eye. The Jester was one elusive dude, I knew. A master of irony and deception. Since not too many people were as well-read as he was, he had to use subterfuge.

"Good," he said. "No false fronts."

"Would you please tell me about the Bookman," I said. "Another source has already told me that the Bookman has gone batty for some reason. That he had his wires crossed or something. Did you ever see him batty?"

"You're scaling up a red herring, buddy. The source of the Bookman's malaise goes deeper than that."

"Malaise?"

"Yeah, a word your paper rarely uses. And, if by chance, some reporter or sports writer uses it to be cute, they always get it wrong. If anyone would ever use it seriously he or she would be laughed out of the business."

"What're you insinuating?"

"I'm not insinuating anything. I'm telling you straight. You guys write for a grade-eight audience with a grade-seven vocabulary and a grade-four sensibility."

"Sticks and stones will—"

"Shut up and listen," he barked out like a nagging housewife. "The key to the Bookman's malaise is that he's bored. That'll be your headline."

I had to digest this for a few seconds.

"How can he be bored when he's dealing with the likes of you?"

"Flattery will get you nowhere, buddy. The fact is that the Bookman has reached a point in his life when the ordinary world, in spite of its physical grandeur and awesome beauty, has ceased to interest him anymore. When all the ordinary and normal things—like meeting new people, enjoying the company of friends, being a wealthy and handsome bachelor, fighting crime, and so on—just isn't enough any more to satisfy the demands of his soul."

The word created a frisson in the coffee shop. I couldn't be sure because I was too shocked to be totally aware, but it seemed that everyone, when they heard the word, simply stopped talking and became anguished and tormented, as if racked by guilt.

"What're you actually saying, Jester? That he's gone religion?"

"No, that's not what I'm saying at all. Superheroes don't go religion, or they'd get laughed out of the business. Just use that pea-brain of yours. He's doing something even more dramatic, more drastic, more ... outer-worldly. He's actually going outside all the boundaries, all the boxes that the comic world has confined him in. He's doing what no superhero has ever done before in comic history. He's going metaphysical."

Now I heard everything. I shook my head. I became fidgety on my seat. I laughed. I made unusual sounds. Maybe the Jester was putting me on. Maybe he was putting everyone on. That was his métier, after all. Just looking at him as a pretend transvestite was enough to know he was a born clown, a fool, and he couldn't be taken seriously. I had to test the waters.

"How do I know you're being serious?" I asked him.

I could see he was trying to grin, but it was a difficult manoeuvre, given his silicone mask and the makeup.

"You don't know, buddy," he said, "that's the thing, see. It's the Jester's Paradox. If I'm jesting, then I'm not telling you the truth. But if I'm not telling you the truth, then I must be jesting."

"Are you putting me on?"

"Only a fool can answer that."

I shook my head again. It was a manoeuvre I was getting very adept in.

"I don't know, Jester. It sounds just too incredible for any reader to believe. I'll have to corroborate this with a higher source. I just can't take you at your word. Imagine if you're actually right. It would be a contradiction in terms. A superhero going metaphysical. Why, it wouldn't compute. It would be like a cop going Gandhi. Or a cowboy with a book in his holster. Nobody would buy it. A superhero, by his or her very definition, is entirely physical, even super-physical, sure, with his or her super-strength and powers and so on, but all within the realm of the physical."

"Take it as you will, buddy," he said. "Either the Book-man will go quietly into superhero oblivion or he'll accomplish what no superhero has ever done. Either way, it's win-win for me, see. If he goes into oblivion, I'll have free rein in Bibliopolis. I'll bring it to its knees in jesterdom. No one will know where I'm coming from. All sense of decency and normalcy will be obliterated. Irony and depth will triumph. The cops will have to turn in their uniforms for dhotis. The Commish will have to die of laughter. On the other hand, if he goes metaphysical, then he'll bring me along with him. I'll have to add that dimension to my tactics. I'll have to brush up on my metaphysical irony, my metaphysical jesting. And I can't wait. It's never been done before in comic history. It'll blow the field wide open. And with my jesting powers, in the metaphysical realm, I'll be more than a rival to the Bookman. If you have the wit to see it, that is."

The only thing I could see, however, was the Jester was spinning his web of jests around me and I had to get out of there fast while I still had any wit left.

It took me two days to try to digest what the Jester told me. There was only one way to corroborate his views, however. I had to get it from the horse's mouth.

I called Thursby. "Can you arrange a phone interview with the Bookman? I've heard conflicting information. The story has more turns than a Dolly Parton."

The next day he called late at night. I had just watched the opening monologue on a popular talk show. The host, a guy with a lantern jaw and the head of pumpkin, said we weren't to worry. The Bookman was only vacationing in Florida. Sources, however, maintained he had brought enough books to last him for a year. The audience ate it up. I felt so embarrassed. I could picture the Jester watching the same show and guffawing.

"I have the Bookman on the line," Thursby said. "We've identified him through voice recognition. You have ten minutes."

Though I was caught with my pants down, I couldn't miss my opportunity. Maybe the Bookman had seen the same show and wanted to set things straight. Maybe he had heard I had been snooping around. Whatever the case, I was adept at phone interviews and maybe this was the best-case scenario.

"How you doing, Bookman?" I said on my smartphone. "Read any books lately?"

"The last thing I need right now is flippancy."

"Sorry, it's just the nature of my job. We get callused after a while. Too many scandals and wars and crimes, you know."

"Yeah, I know."

"What can you tell me?"

"You're Bobby Joe, aren't you? The guy who's written all those shallow articles on the way I fight crime?"

"That's me. I have to write it the way I see it."

"You don't see it very well."

"Sorry, Bookman, but I gotta do my job to the best of my ability. And the readers always come first. Sometimes they don't understand what you're all about."

His voice got stern. "Sure, but we either cater to the lowest common denominator or we try to scale the quotient."

"I can't scale any quotient, Bookman. That's the thing. I'm not a prophet. I'm just a Press Prufrock."

He paused—and I could hear the wheels turning.

Either he was reconsidering his estimation of me or he had a squeaky stomach.

"All right, listen," he said, his voice becoming very businesslike. "I want your readers to try to understand what's going on without any misunderstandings. So you ask and I'll answer."

"OK," I said. "One of my sources has informed me that you're bored with the way things are and you need your batteries re-charged. Is that true?"

I could hear a snort at the other end.

"That's just like the Jester," the Bookman said. "To take something that's very serious and turn it upside down and make it frivolous. The Jester is the person who sees the possum hanging on the tree upside down with a frown and mistakes it for a happy face."

"You can't use parables and such with our readers, Bookman. They want things super straight and literal."

"And I've had enough of the literal."

"Explain."

"What good would it do? You wouldn't understand."

"Try me. Though I write down to the yin, I know a bit of the yang."

"So you know the Tao. Big deal."

We had come to the crucial, I could see. If he was going to confide in me, I had to prove that I was more than the average press hack. And the thing about superheroes, as the Commish had told me, was that ordinary life was their biggest bug-bear. It was one thing to fly through the air like a speeding bullet (which was about the worst metaphoric description of a superhuman feat I had ever heard), but it was another to get up each morning and take a dump.

"All right, Bookman," I said, "but I might be the only one who does understand what you're going through. I may be the only one, besides the Jester, who understands what a malaise of soul means. Maybe I know what going metaphysical means."

"Is that what he said?"

"Yeah. He also posed a question: Why did God create Adam before Eve?"

The Bookman guffawed. "What does he know? And what, for that matter, do you know?"

"Maybe a lot more than you think, Bookman. Maybe there's more to it than the Jester's answer, for example. Maybe there's an entirely different POV than the Genesis story. Maybe we should consider the *Timaeus* and the Gnostic origin stories, for example. Maybe some of us know a few things about the metaphysical, eh. One thing about the metaphysical: How can anyone be sure of anything? Once the back of the physical is broken, everything becomes relative and open to shifting views. Am I right, or am I wrong?"

The Bookman was silent. Maybe I had gone too far. But I had to do a rope-a-dope to get out of this one and convince him.

I pressed on.

"I sympathize with you, Bookman. I know what you're going through. You'd be doing something that's never been done in superhero history. You'd be adding some deep thought to your work. You wouldn't just be a one-dimensional caped crusader. You'd become mindful, contemplative, even recondite. Are you following me?"

"Yeah, I'm following you."

"But it wouldn't all be good, that's the thing. Nothing would be clear anymore. You'd be at the mercy of moral ambiguity. You'd lose your physical edge."

I heard nothing but silence on the other end of the line.

"It's just not done," I said. "Your fan base wouldn't follow you."

"You underestimate them."

"I don't think so. I've been in the news biz for too long."

Another long pause. I could see now that the Bookman was truly in the transitional stage between the physical and the metaphysical. He was giving each question some thought. He was deliberating. Instead of just using his fists or his superhuman powers, he was hedging and hawing. It would be brutal, I knew, if he went metaphysical. He wouldn't last a fortnight. I had to get at the cause and try to convince him otherwise or we'd lose our only superhero crime fighter. And if we did, we'd be at the mercy of Kitty Kat and Antiquarian and the Jester.

"Listen, Bookman," I said, "maybe you're totally convinced that going metaphysical is your only option. But you have to reconsider. I'm speaking not only for all of Bibliopolis, but for the whole comics universe. You'd lose all your superhero-powers. You'd never be able to fight evil since everything would become relative and open to interpretation. At least tell us why you want to go metaphysical. What's wrong with the physical? What's wrong with the literal? It's solid enough, isn't it? It's sure. It's unquestionable. It's true. And, most importantly, it's easy to understand, isn't it?"

"Yeah, right on all counts," he said. "But you're forgetting one thing."

"What's that?"

"My adversaries are getting too smart for me. I have to keep up with them. And it's not just about them as individuals. It's about the nature of crime, the nature of evil. What is evil, after all, but the absence of good?"

Right there I could see it was too late. He was into dualism and the nature of reality. He had already gone metaphysical. Superheroes didn't speak like that. What the hell was the world coming to?

"Bookman," I said. "Answer me one thing. What made you have a change of heart? What was the cause of this turn-around? What made you go metaphysical?"

He gave the question some thought. And yet his answer was right to the point.

"Death."

"You gotta explain that. My readers can't take a one-word answer."

Then he went into his story. What I wanted to hear all along. The human interest bit. What I had to get from the Bookman's own mouth.

It had happened a couple of months ago, he said, when he had been called to fight a crime in progress. Five of Antiquarian's henchmen were in the process of sabotaging a computer and electronics super-store. He had come upon the scene when it was too late, however, and discovered it was a trap. Just as he was about to enter the store, Antiquarian spoke through a megaphone on the outside. They had booby-trapped the whole store with trick wires. And the manager's ten-year-old daughter was in the thick of the trap. If the Bookman didn't surrender immediately and expose his true identity, the store would be blown up.

"You can see my dilemma," the Bookman said over the phone. "If I didn't do what Antiquarian wanted, the girl would be killed. If I did, maybe thousands of other little girls would be killed in the future. It was an Either-Or, Bobby Joe. It was the end justifying the means. And I had to choose quickly."

I could picture the Bookman caught in the trap of a moral dilemma. He'd be in his Bookman's costume with the red tights and blurbs under his cape and the big B on his chest. And under his book mask he'd be in a quandary.

"Was the life of one little girl worth maybe hundreds of others?" he said. "Tell me, Bobby Joe, what would you have done?"

"I'm not a superhero, Bookman. It's not my job."

"Right. You're just an average press hack. You just write the stories. You don't put yourself on the line. Well, write it the way I tell it, press-man. I'm going metaphysical because of that little girl who died. And because of all the other little girls and boys who die every day."

"Sure, I'll write it, Bookman. But you're being a little melodramatic, aren't you? No superhero has the power to fight death. Death happens. No one can stop it. You have to fight evil, not death."

"Right. But how do you fight evil, Bobby Joe? Answer me that."

It was a tough question. I gave it some thought. Superheroes fought criminals who were evil. But they had never fought evil itself.

"I don't know, Bookman. You tell me."

"That's the thing. There's only one way of finding out. I just can't read the books in the box anymore. The mysteries and thrillers and bodice-rippers. I have to go where no superhero in comics history as ever gone before."

A big light exploded in my head.

"I see it, Bookman. I see where you're coming from and where you're going. You're only doing what you were destined to do from the very beginning. You're fulfilling your destiny as a true Bookman, are you not?"

"You got it, Bobby Joe. I gotta do what I gotta do."

"OK, I got my angle and I'll write the story. But tell me one thing. And the readers will want to know this. Will you expect them to follow you? Will you expect them to change their reading habits as well?"

He laughed over the line. "We'll cross that bridge when we come to it. I know I'll have to change my vocab, not to mention my modus operandi. Maybe I won't need to use my fists anymore. Maybe I'll have to engage in dialectics. Maybe my new methods just won't take. And maybe I'll lose my fan base. That's the risk."

"OK, Bookman. But I wanna compliment you on trying to change the whole comic book universe. I'm going to do my best to explain your situation. Maybe I'll become your sidekick and explain things for the reading public. Maybe things are not too late to fight crime at its base."

"I can use all the help I can."

I ended the call and smiled.

Maybe this was the beginning of a great alliance. I could see it now. The Bookman would go metaphysical and the press would heighten the consciousness of the reading public.

Dead Voices

W hen his heart was sore and he needed a little pick-me-up, Mark liked nothing better than to spend a few hours in the BDV bookstore. The store stood out amongst the older restaurants and specialty shops on Bloor in the Annex, close to Ye Olde Pub. It had a bright turquoise façade and a large movie theatre marquee and full plate glass exterior. Its first two floors were spacious, with high shelves and display tables stacked with all manner of books, both used and new, in every category. Its top floor had a full assortment of comics and children's lit. And the basement, devoted to discs and videos, completed its triple-bill logo.

As soon as he stepped into the bookstore, he felt immediately uplifted, as if he were inside a treasure trove of earthly delights, the likes of which could feed both mind and heart.

As a kid he had been the Comic Boy of his ethnic neighbourhood, going from house to house with his stack of comics to make his trades. After the negotiations, he couldn't wait to get home and sample the new additions, whether they were used or new, with their shiny covers and larger-than-life figures performing super-human deeds. As a teen he had graduated to being a collector of dirty paperbacks with more potent shiny covers that offered private gratification for his insatiable appetites. Eventually he had become a voracious reader of any book in his small city library in the wilds of the northern bush. If someone would've asked him why a guy like him, with no pedigree, had been so drawn to words on the page, he'd say he got off on the smell and feel of paper, the hot black blood of words, the power of the voices speaking to him from nowhere and everywhere.

The words on the solid white page, in their silent power, had opened up realities and worlds, both visible and invisible, that could hold him in thrall.

He was more of an anomaly these days, however. He saw so few males in libraries and bookstores actually picking up a book. They were either students or much older. To see a young or middle-aged male who was still curious to learn for no other reason than for the pleasure of knowing would've shocked him indeed. Unless they were one of those seedy and nerdy-looking guys he'd sometimes see talking to bookstore clerks spouting their verbal diarrhoea, as if they had been backed up for months.

Of course, the tech world was changing so fast he could hardly keep up. Fewer and fewer people were reading —and the digital world was putting the solid book on the block.

He didn't consider himself a bookworm, however.

He had lived his life outside of books, had known love through the good and bad years, helped raise a son who had been the joy of his life, wrote a few books himself, and was still physically active. He ran every day summer and winter, played a good game of tennis, and was a fan of all the major sports. But he could also quote from Kant via Horace (*Sapere aude*) one minute and from Berra via Hegel (Baseball's 90% mental—the other half is physical) the next. Not only had he dared to know like Immanuel, settling into his daily routines like clockwork in his older years, but he had been a catcher in his younger years like Yogi, able to throw out runners at second with zingers.

For all his forays into conventional and esoteric thought, not to mention his knowledge of world literature, he wasn't much different from that kid who used to carry his bag of comics from door to door, expecting to increase his stash and find those rare editions that promised to reveal the ultimate secrets. Like the identity of the Lone Ranger. How disappointed he had been when he finally got the copy and saw the Texas Ranger's face, though unmasked, was still shaded and indecipherable!

Better perhaps to live in the expectation, in the hot flush of words on the page, than in the reality that always disappointed.

He knew, for one, that he hadn't yet made what the initiates of the esoteric traditions would consider the ultimate conversion—the big turn, as he called it. The turn away from the tyranny of the visible world, with its hard fact of time and space.

He knew himself well enough to realize he was still

stuck in the Way Station, as it were, a seeker still, looking for his comics and books, living in the expectation rather than the reality.

The BDV, however, wasn't a bad place to be stuck. He could go from book to book and feel the hot pulse of the printed words come up to meet him and be instantly transported to the St. Petersburg of Prince Myshkin or the Dublin of Stephen Dedalus—or be in the mind of Paul of Tarsus—the borders of time and space obliterated. It was as if those words, in the expert re-invention of the world and actions of the characters, with the insight into their thoughts and feelings that only words could give, revealed the workings of the only soul that made rational sense. The inner person, and the world that lay within. And every step closer to the language of that soul could bring him closer to the big turn.

At this stage in his life, the words of the great avatars and sages were no longer to be admired or worshipped from afar, but followed as simple guides of instruction. Once he lost himself in the words, the author, no matter who it was or from where or from what time, was beside him, alive, whispering in his ear. It was a state of mind halfway between being awake and being asleep, partly there and partly not there, in a gentle torpor of soul, as he called it, that was in between the physical and the metaphysical.

It had been words on the page, ever since he could remember—whether they had come from the crudest or the most sublime sensibility—that had held this power over him.

Luckily he wasn't addicted to the high-end retail stores or the Stock Exchange or the glitz of the casino, killers all of them. And BDV Books was large enough that he could spend the whole afternoon browsing without drawing the least attention amongst the high shelves, going from book to book, searching for the words that he could re-animate with his breath and his eyes.

Though the clerks who were constantly stacking the shelves never bothered him, there was one who knew him on sight and always made eye-contact when she saw him. She was older than the rest, maybe in her mid-forties, attractively slim and dark-haired, always dressed in black and in a black beret. The Dark Lady, he called her.

To this day, when he tried to connect the dots, his addiction to the printed page made little rational sense — except that it was as much sensual as cerebral.

He had grown up in a drab neighbourhood beside a steel plant during its heyday when a guy could make his bones playing hockey like the Rocket and the Golden Jet, or baseball like Yogi and Mickey. The only claim to beauty in the area was the inside of the parish church which sported as colourful a theatre of pomp and circumstance as any movie or TV show. Every Sunday, and every day during Lent and Advent, he'd see the priest, in vestments of green and gold and black and white, perform miraculous feats on the altar with words alone. And when he heard the priest intone the sacred words, the words of power that changed the bread and wine into the body and blood of Christ, he, too, kneeling on the pew with his face aglow, felt their power course through his body. So much so that when he looked up at the large statue of the crucified saviour, showing the bloodied Jesus nailed like a white wafer to the dark wood, he trembled with such fervour he felt unworthy of being so blessed. All he needed was the word, he'd say, and his soul would be healed.

He could still recall the words in his Missal, a Confirmation gift and the first book he ever owned, on crinkly thin pages that had an intoxicating odour of incense.

Upon reaching his teens, however, the sacred words of his Missal had been blind-sided by an unexpected force of nature. First in the male magazines, with their erotic stories of brazen women whose inner desires quickened his blood, and then in the dirty pulps, with words so carnal and seductive and debauched he was lifted off the ground.

And from there he had gone on to other words of power. Either to the story-tellers who had could weave a web of dreams more real than his life around him or to the great thinkers and seekers who could feed his hunger to know the secrets of reality. Though the small library in his hometown had started him out in his quest, it couldn't satisfy his insatiable appetite. Only after he had gone to university in his new adopted metropolis, with its vast libraries, not to mention the many bookstores at the time, did he find a never-ending stream of words on the page. And much later — after he had been to Paris and Rome, New York and Chicago — did he realize first-hand that his new adopted city could compare with any world centre for bragging rights on the love of the printed word.

On the ground floor of the BDV, Mark went from shelf to shelf, book to book, like a vampire, looking for the appropriate black blood to slake his thirst. By perusing a few pages he could easily determine which words were no more than dust and bone, forever dead on the page, and which could be transformed into delicious food for his hungry eyes. And after some time, he found a few books that excited him enough that he had to buy and enjoy at home. One of them was a new Arden edition of the Bard's work.

He was stuffing his chosen books in the shelves, when the Dark Lady came up to him out of nowhere and startled him. She had a plastic basket in her hand.

"This'll help," she said with a smile.

"Thanks."

"You can't carry everything in two hands, you know."

Abruptly shaken from his reveries, he was lost for words. He looked into her eyes. Her features were stark white against her dark attire and beret, with no hint of makeup. Close up, even though she wasn't as attractive, with a cold hard sheen to her features, her dark eyes and aloof reserve made her even more mysterious.

"I know," he said. "Sometimes we need a helping hand."

"I've seen you here often. You're a bibliophile, aren't you?"

"I suppose I am. And you're always in the same black outfit, with the beret, as if in mourning. Can I ask you what you're mourning?"

She paused, regarding him with her dark eyes, her features registering a sense of weariness. "Oh, I don't know. Maybe it's just from working in this store. Sometimes it feels like a sinking ship. Our inventory of discs and videos is slowly dying to digital. And all these books. They're dying as well. It's like a mausoleum. Like a bookstore of dead voices."

Her words, said with such disarming candor, took him by surprise. "Well, not all the authors are dead, are they? And it's up to us to keep the voices alive, right?"

"Yeah, I suppose so," she said, her face brightening up. "Maybe there's still hope."

And then she vanished into the shelves of books.

When he looked at his smartphone and saw just how late it was, he placed his books in the basket and took them to the cashier.

Outside, he put the bag of books into his backpack and looked in both directions. It was a mild spring day, the street filled with pedestrians and cars. The adjustment to the real world never ceased to be jarring. His wife, Jen, had told him once that he always had a spaced-out look upon leaving a bookstore. Indeed, it took some time to readjust to the visible world and get his bearings. Like the times as a kid he'd exit the movie theatre after seeing a western and feel he was still on a horse under the hot sun, riding over the plains, his holster securely tied to his thigh.

As he walked, he observed the pedestrians, all oblivious of his metaphysical powers. A few stores down, he stopped in front of Ye Olde Pub, an old red-brick structure that had been in the Annex forever, it seemed. Either he could walk to the nearest subway station and be stuck in the long rush-hour ride home or get a few beers and wait it out.

Just the thought of a cold one going down easy, however, was enough to make up his mind. He called his wife and told her he'd be late. They had a townhouse in the west end of the city, not far from the end of east-west subway line. Their grown-up son, Matt, after studying acting in New York and trying to make the theatre scene in the city, had moved to Vancouver.

Though he hadn't been inside the building in ages, he could still remember the washrooms reeking of stale piss.

Since then it had gone through various makeovers. Nowadays it sported a mock Tudor façade, mullioned windows, and a heavy oak door. Since a patron could nurse a beer for hours with no hassles, it had long been a hang-out for writers and artists and actors, some of whom lived in the neighbourhood.

Over the front door was a sign offering Karaoke on the weekends.

Taking off his backpack and windbreaker, he sat at a middle table in order to get a view of the outside. He was in his denims and walking shoes, with a blue long-sleeve sweater. The inside was dim and shabby in the late afternoon, the dark wooden tables and chairs looking as if they hadn't been upgraded in decades. Each table was lighted by an electric candle with a mushroom top that reflected the light outwards. On the faded walls were old photographs and drawings, some of them caricatures, of well-known writers and playwrights of times past. Mark had known a few of them in his earlier years when he was learning his trade. Once upon a time he had looked up to them as Olympian gods and goddesses who could instruct and inspire him on the secret power of words.

The pub was almost empty this time in the afternoon. One table had three boisterous kids who appeared to be students from the university down the street. Another, directly in his line of vision, had two men who were in black tights and white collarless shirts, as if they had just come from a rehearsal. An older couple sat at a table close to the side door which was left open to let in some air. He didn't recognize anyone.

No one was tending the bar. A lone waitress—thin

and waif-like in her Tudor dress and apron, her face so heavily rouged she looked like a guy in drag—brought him a pitcher of draft.

After he gulped down a glass, he looked out a window at the busy thoroughfare of pedestrians and cars. Not much had changed in the Annex since his student years. It still had a village-like atmosphere, with its large and turreted Edwardian houses, some of which still accommodated students. Many of the store fronts had changed, of course, but the movie theatre and many of the restaurants and delis were the same as decades ago. And the department store emporium with its glitzy neon façade was still there, though he had learned it had been sold and slated for demolition. The neighbourhood, however, avoiding the pricey commercial redevelopment of the downtown core, had a worn and faded look to it.

The sleepy atmosphere in the pub seemed to activate his memory.

He'd come here every so often when he was a graduate student living up the street in the rooming houses and later when he was a young writer and working at the small publishing house a few blocks away. In those years of struggle and heartache and loneliness, he had practically lived on the page, trying to learn his craft by trial and error—and his unstinting effort in studying and copying the greats. It could only take total dedication and sacrifice. Someday he, too, wanted to call down the great cosmic forces and energies with words alone. Someday he, too, if he made the ultimate sacrifice, would perhaps be able to make the invisible more real than the visible with words alone. And bring to life the inner world.

If he was worthy, that is.

Such early zeal, however, had led to a dead end, fool that he was to forget his pedigree as the son of hard-working immigrant parents who were practically illiterate. He had forged his own separate identity with words, to be sure, but he still needed to have at least one foot on solid ground. He wasn't some dreamy idealist with his head in the clouds, nor a visceral Rimbaud living at the end of his nerve strings. He was a realist to his core, as he well knew, and he had to live in the real world, with a steady job, with the love of a woman, with a family, and be grounded in the reality of the day-to-day.

From his early success, he had thought he'd blaze a trail through the country's literary horizons, fulfill the promise passed on to him by his mentors, Margaret and Dave, but it wasn't to be. It was as if his teaching job, his daily life as a husband and father, his pedestrian existence as an invisible man in the suburbs, had grinded his inner journey without feet to a halt. He had plugged away at his writing, sure, like his hard-working mom and dad, but he was no longer sure he had done the right thing.

Though his life with Jen and his son, Matthew, had provided him with the comfort and security he needed to survive in the day-to-day, it had come at considerable cost to his search for the higher realities.

At least he had given his son the literary foundation he himself never had.

Jen had read Matty all the fairy tales and children's books at the beginning. Then Mark had introduced his son to the Bard when he was no more than seven. They had sat side-by-side on the recliner, each with a copy of the complete works, and read alternate characters. In time and with effort, his son had become an accomplished reader of the plays, mouthing the mighty words of the Master like a prodigy.

It was like music to his ears. The words that he himself had taken decades to read correctly, let alone understand, his son had taken to as if they were hot-wired to his tongue. And when Matty was reciting the words, just a little kid with his innocent voice and his wide-eyed wonder, his son sounded as mercurial as Hamlet, as crafty as Antony, and as lovelorn as Romeo.

His pride in his little guy was boundless. He couldn't wait to get home from work and be with Matty. It gave him nothing but joy to play all the sports and physical games with his son, imbibe in him the power of words, and watch him grow up hale and hearty.

Balance was the operative word. It wasn't just words on the page. He and Jen had exposed him to music and movies and a social life. They had got him involved in team sports. Matt had competed on a high level in hockey and baseball and football, turning out a well-rounded scholar-athlete. In time his son had grown into a handsome and tall young man, extremely fit in body and mind. And towards the end of his high school years when Matt announced he was in a school play and interested in the theatre, it had come as a pleasant surprise. Mark himself had always been a shy and withdrawn teenager, preferring a silent life with words. His son had turned out almost the complete opposite.

After getting his university degree, his son had gone to New York and graduated from a prestigious acting school, hoping to follow in the footsteps of its alumni, some of whom had become great stage and movie actors. Things hadn't worked out as expected, however. Even though it was long after the terrorist attacks on the World Trade Centre, it was practically impossible to get a green card. After working at various shitty jobs in New York, his son was forced to come back to Canada, looking like gaunt and sickly replica of his former self. And since the economy and theatre business was even worse in his home city, it had been a hard slog to make it as an actor.

Even now, whenever he thought about his son, it caused him both joy and anguish. After all he had done for him, all the time he had spent with him, it seemed the older Matt got the more he had come to sneer at his father's pedestrian life as a teacher and a writer. And at his lack of outward success.

No one knows you, Dad, his son had told him one time. I ask everyone and no one even knows you exist. You sit down all day and do nothing. I want to do things with my life. There's a reason why it's called act-ing, you know. Acting is do-ing. Even in the talking it's the do-ing. On the stage we *do* it.

During the two years his son was in New York, Mark had planned his most ambitious project, a metafictional re-creation of the Bard's lost years and his time at the Globe. He had done extensive research on the life and times, had gone over every line of the complete works for any autofictional clues, and consulted the works that had been most influential in the writing of the plays. He had even meticulously pored over the works of Kyd, Marlowe, Jonson, Greene, Marston, and Dekker in order to saturate himself in the perspective of the times when the theatre was the preferred means of encouraging the illusion of reality and the workings of the inner self.

The project had come to naught, however. Not only had his ambition far exceeded his talents, but the Bard's real life had proved too ephemeral a subject to capture with words. As if the Bard had made the big turn himself, living most intensely not in the physical world but in the words that re-invented it on the stage.

Mark gulped down another glass. Beer had a way of making him drowsy. Especially on an empty stomach. Outside it was starting to get dark.

No, he had muffed it with his son. And no amount of redress, either with words on the page or with heart-to-heart talks, could undo the damage.

After coming back from New York, Matt had given him bits and pieces of what he had learned from the acting school, techniques that grew out of the Group Theatre and Stanislavski theories. The way Matt spoke, it seemed he had been indoctrinated by Zen gurus. While Britain and Europe were still doing old school, North American acting had been revolutionized, Matt said. In the general Method, actors were encouraged to use personal emotions from past experiences to feed their performance and make it real. The Meisner off-shoot of the Method in which he had been taught, however, sought to eliminate learned pretence, with its self-consciousness and intellect, in order to get back to the natural and instinctive and impulsive.

The quicksilver of instinct and action was real, Matt said, and the intellect that tried to arrest time into some sort of ersatz permanence was false. An actor was already too self-conscious and introverted as it was, listening too much to his inner voice. The object was to kill that confusing voice and actually *be*. What they had done in their classes, Matt told him, was to go over a line so often with different emotions till all confusion and self-doubt disappeared on their own and the words made it real.

As much as he admired such a method, however, he had argued that the actor was still reciting the lines of a playwright, lines that originated from an invisible voice.

That invisible voice, in spite of its doubts and fears and drawbacks, was the true oracle of re-invention, he told his son. And one had to keep true to its need to maintain a solid balance between the physical and the metaphysical. The actor had the luxury perhaps of being able to obliterate his own inner voice during his performance, but he still had to make real the words of the playwright. And those words, he had added, if they were gained through negative capability could only come at a great cost.

To drive home his point he had used not only Keats's letters, but a line from Fernando Pessoa via his translator in the *Book of Disquiet. I'm the gap between what I am and what I'm not, between what I dream and what life has made of me.* Pessoa, a Portuguese writer who also didn't do much in life but read and write, had emptied himself into the world of words. As an ironic twist, he told his son, this man who had virtually cancelled himself out into a nothing, who had even hid himself behind pseudonyms, who had avoided the limelight and sought anonymity, had his grave dug up long after his death in 1935 and had been reinterred beside the greats of Portuguese history. All from merely sitting down and translating his dreams into words.

Some people were either incapable of seeking public

acclaim or too embarrassed by it—and wanted nothing more than to do their life's work in peace and quiet, he told his son. Could true success ever come from a world that valued gaudy baubles over the invisible realities?

Matt, however, couldn't be persuaded by such arguments. After trying to make the theatre scene in town, acting in a few indie productions, he had gone to Vancouver to team up with some of his colleagues from New York and try his luck there.

A loud scraping of a chair suddenly woke Mark up from his reveries.

He shook the cobwebs and found himself in the old pub with his pitcher of beer almost empty, having no idea how much time had elapsed. The door had been shut. Through the windows it looked dark outside on the street. He couldn't hear any cars. It was dim inside. Disoriented, he felt as if having been awakened from a deep and unsettling sleep. The odour of stale beer was in the air. In a far corner he could see a dim black stage for the Karaoke. The waitress was nowhere to be seen.

He took out his smartphone and looked at the time. It was indeed quite late and well past the rush hour. Either he had dozed off or simply lost track of where he was.

The older couple and the students had left. The air inside the pub felt stale and musty. The only people left were the two guys directly in his line of vision. They had a pitcher of draft in between them. He could hear them talking. Either they were about to stage a play or actually rehearsing the play. Their voices were sometimes hushed and sometimes animated, as if wary of being overheard and yet carried away by their emotions. One had apparently written the play and the other was an actor—or they were both actors, he wasn't quite sure. The assumption was that the play would be staged at one of the theatres close by. Mark had been to all three in times past. His son had been in one just the other year, a small indie theatre that was falling apart. Since the two guys were in a dim recess, the light from the table top played with their visages. As he observed and listened, he tried not to draw attention to himself.

From his vantage point it appeared that their faces were heavily powdered, as if they hadn't bothered removing their stage makeup, including their wigs and facial hair. Or perhaps it was just the light, the play of the artificial candles from the table top. The older one who had written the play, and was maybe an actor as well, looked to be in his mid-forties, while the other was about a decade younger. The older one had chestnut long hair, with a high forehead, scraggily whiskers, and an earring. The younger had russet curly hair, a short beard, and a heavy waist. In their faded collarless shirts, the laces untied at the neck, and black leggings, they looked unkempt and weary from a long day. The actor was riffling through a few rolls of paper—written in longhand, by the look of them, and glued together—as they spoke.

"What do we have here?" the younger one said in a flippant tone of voice. "Is it a tale told by an idiot, full of sound and fury?"

"Sure, if it signifies nothing," the older one said, laughing.

"And we get a few pennies for our efforts."

"As long as I keep scribbling, you mean."

"You scribble and I'll strut. Though I don't know how you do it."

"Very simple, Rich. I transform the words of the prophets and Montaigne and the ancient histories into little entertainments for the groundlings. With the sound and the fury I can make my pennies, like a John-a-dreams."

"And who knows what dreams may come?"

"We must be careful, though, to put one thing in the guise of another. Like the Bible where theology's in the guise of history."

"We live in perilous times. Nothing's what it seems."

"This is why it's the role of a lifetime, Rich," the playwright said. "You'll be the Prince, the son of a father murdered and prompted to his revenge by heaven and hell."

"More hell than heaven, I warrant. Will I not be too much in the sun?"

"Not if we hide the son in the father," the playwright said.

"One confusion hidden inside another. Like a revenge play within a tragedy within a morality, if I'm not mistaken."

"Words that tie themselves up in knots, Rich. Aporia, it's called."

"You've stamped it with thy new coat of arms, I see."

"Aye, the pennies add up."

"But the Prince is still too young," the actor said. "If I'm to play him, make him older and a little scant of breath … for my girth."

"Make him older how? He's of university age."

"The how is up to you. The groundlings will be already reeling from confusion. You're the scribbler, I but a poor player."

"Poor, my arse," the playwright said.

"I play what I play, good sir. We count on deception to make our fortunes."

"It's not deception, Rich, if our aim is to enrich and ennoble."

Mark wasn't sure whether he was eavesdropping or watching a performance. Or it could've been that these actors were rehearsing and still in character. Whatever the case, he sensed a certain inflection of tone, an ironic lilt in their words, that suggested he was somehow implicated in their conversation, and that its purpose would be revealed to him in due course. Which made him even more excited. Had he gone through some rabbit hole to be so honoured? Or was he being accorded a rare opportunity to hear the words no one else could hear?

Only, as much as he wanted to, he couldn't interfere and ask them, as if there was some sort of invisible barrier between them.

All he could do, he knew, was to suspend his disbelief. Observe and listen. And remain in the zone of expectation and let the scene play itself out.

Their words veered away from the play. They spoke about the actor's previous performance of Brutus in *Julius Caesar*, mentioned in passing the danger in putting on a special performance of *Richard II* for the partisans of Essex, and certain matters of patronage and politics. They talked about the Privy Council and the Star Chamber, the Tower of London, and her Royal Highness, the Queen, who was on her last legs. In her pasty makeup, Rich said, she looked ghoulish. They dropped names like Southampton, Cecil, and Burghley. They spoke about a conspiracy and leaned closer together and Mark lost the thread of the conversation. He had to strain his ears and focus on their lips which were at a side view and obscured by the dim light.

His excitement mounting and feeling he wouldn't be able to recall all their words, and that they might be lost forever, Mark took out one of the books he had just purchased and a small notebook he kept in the side-pocket of his backpack. By standing the book in front of his notebook he could observe and listen while hiding the fact he was jotting down their words.

" ... after the comedies and histories," the younger actor was saying, "you're going into dark matters, good sir. This play, while we've seen it before, is very different from what it was before and from your other work. Not only is it dark, but it's full of self-doubt. You're exposing the soul-guts of the Prince and the workings of our magical arts much too much, if you ask me."

"Our greatest defect can be our greatest strength. Like a mole and a mountain."

"True enough. But we are actors first and foremost."

"No, Rich, we are fathers and sons first and foremost, feeding our roles as actors. You, for example, are playing the words of a father who's given himself his son's name, and who, in turn, is a son himself to a father he must avenge to an uncle who represents our duplicitous age."

"You're playing with me now. You mean the smiling, damnèd villain, do you not?"

"No other, Rich."

"One thing in the guise of another."

"I must unpack my heart with words like a whore."

"Keep unpacking, good sir. We must fight the Rose

and the Hope and the Swan on the Bank side, not to mention Whitefriars and Blackfriars and the Curtain on the other side."

"And get our pennies."

"Aye, business is booming. We are drawing them from across the river in their water taxis and barges like an armada."

"With the Wooden O on my shoulders, Rich. Now that the rituals and the trappings of the papists have been purged, it's up to me to write them their spectacles for our new church."

"Our whorehouse, you mean."

"Aye." The playwright laughed. "Sometimes I wonder myself."

"But this play will not be easy to stage. The histories and the comedies were easy enough. You were giving them their revels and their new sense of themselves. But this play is beyond anything you have ever written. It gives words and thoughts beyond the reaches of our souls. It's hard enough creating believable puppetry on the stage, good sir, but you expose the wires. And it's too dark and cynical and confusing."

"As an actor, you must suit the word to the action, the action to the word, and don't o'erstep the modesty of nature. As for me, I must tamper with nature and o'erstep my bounds."

Mark looked up from his writing, his heart pounding. The playwright, whose voice faltered, had his head hung in sorrow. He felt the urge to speak, but it was impossible to speak, lest he burst the barrier.

"We're out to get their pennies, not their souls," he

heard the actor say. "We have to cast a spell that makes it real enough that they forget the plague, the papists, the conspiracies—and makes us forget ourselves."

"I'm not just an actor, Rich. And I can't forget."

"Still your son, I see," the actor said in a heavy tone.

At this point they spoke very quickly, their words fading into whispered speech, which frustrated him to no end. Just when he thought he was going to the get the scoop, it all came to naught. All he heard was that the playwright had never known his son very well, having left him in the care of his wife and parents. And for that he had suffered pricks of conscience. But he could still recall his son's arms around his neck when he carried him piggyback, the times they played together on Henley Street, the times he had taught him and his twin sister how to read, the times they went into the Arden for picnics. Who would carry on his name now? The two girls would get married and that would be the end of it.

"Unless, Rich," Mark heard the playwright say. "I can keep him alive in the realm of uncertainty and disquiet. In the realm of the Father, and the Son, and the Holy Ghost."

"Thanks for confusing me even more," the actor said.

"This confusion will be for our benefit if we confuse the Master of the Revels and get this play through to its performance."

"Aye, you are a sly one, good sir."

"For these are actions that a man might play with the trappings and the suits of woe. But I have that within which passes show."

"The true Hercules of the Globe."

"I will play the Ghost and burst out of the trap door and cellarage of Purgatory."

The actor paused, his voice dropping. "We must be careful, good sir. We cannot be a party to sedition. The Ghost might be considered too papist."

"Were my Paduans too Paduan, my Romans too Roman?"

"Our heads can easily be on pikes on London Bridge."

"Not if we play our puppet-parts so convincingly we expose even the wires."

The actor gave him a long look. "Be sure you don't outwit yourself, good sir. The play is much too long. Too many words and not enough action."

Again Mark felt the urge to speak—or at least to recite his lines in due course as part of the play, but he sensed it was impossible for him to speak. As if he were powerless, in the grip of someone else's will, and he had to play out his part without speech and without action.

The playwright said he had to do a bit of pruning. He was the victim of his own antic disposition for words. He had to counteract the papist Ghost of action and revenge by means of the spirit of inwardness in his son. The old ritual of the Eucharist—the papist spectacle played on the altar—had to give way to the new power of words alone, he said. And he had a dual duty, to be loyal to the page as well as the stage.

Mark tried to get everything down. He was writing so quickly he was leaving an illegible scrawl, his ear and hand working feverishly.

The playwright said, as a poet, he was no more than

a mouthpiece of the muse. But he had to be loyal to his audience as well and keep them entertained. They were living in mad times. Nothing was what it seemed. They had defeated the Armada and yet they couldn't defeat the plague. People were living in the rotten squalor of an open sewer. They needed Westminster and St. Paul's, sure, but they needed their temples of drama even more.

"Aye, the Globe itself," the actor said. "*Totus mundus agit histrionem*, from Jaques himself. And I will certainly act my part on the stage."

"Without a doubt you will—as I will."

"Aye, marry, as you will, we will—and thereby get rich by it."

"Let us give hope to it," the playwright said. "That we will all be the richer for it."

The two guys laughed and put their heads together and spoke in a whisper. Mark couldn't make out what they were saying. He paused in his writing and looked at his scribbles. Some words looked no more than flat-lines on the page. He trusted he could resuscitate them later, depending on his own memory and what he already knew of the play.

"I shall need some substance behind my words," the actor spoke up.

"The son is given a duty by a dead father. Remember me, the Ghost says."

"Remember thee? Aye, poor ghost whiles memory holds a seat in this distracted globe."

"Swear," he cries under the stage. "Swear by his sword."

"Rest, rest, perturbed spirit. The time is out of joint, o cursed spite that ever I was born to set it right."

They both laughed again, looking directly at him as if they were aware of his eavesdropping and putting him on.

Mark looked away, focused on the photos and pictures on the walls of the alehouse.

He took a few deep breaths and tried to collect himself. All his excitement had spent itself out, it seemed. There had been no great revelation, no great insight. He had only heard words in an old pub. Words that could've been easily manipulated to fool him. Or to trap him. Like a play-within-a-play to test his guilt or innocence.

The air in the pub had become cloyingly thick, as if all the oxygen had been sucked out. The beer on an empty stomach didn't help matters. He felt very drowsy. Like the times he had taken his classes on field trips to Stratford and watched the plays after a heavy lunch. One time he had actually nodded off and a student had nudged him awake with a little smirk on her face.

The two guys, at that point, inclined their heads over the table and spoke in low tones. Mark tried to get his bearings. His head was spinning from the beer and he felt the onset of a headache. It was past the rush hour. He had to get home. He was very hungry and tired. And he couldn't be sure he had heard right.

He wanted to ask the playwright certain questions about the play. Even though he had taught it for over a decade at his school, as well as seeing many screen adaptations and live performances at Stratford and New York, it had still remained an enigma to him.

No performance, however, had compared to a Hart House theatre production his son had been involved in before going to Vancouver.

He and Jen had sat in the old theatre in the basement of Hart House at the university, the same theatre that had launched a few great screen and theatre actors. The thin effeminate guy playing the Prince, though competent enough, rendered his lines as if reciting poetry instead of creating drama. The other actors were professional unknowns, good enough to make the evening not an entire waste, but not much more than adequate. He could remember the actress playing Ophelia being beautiful and elfin, a mere victim of circumstances. And Gertrude wasn't as passive as he would've thought, but a commanding presence who kissed her son as if giving him the kiss of death.

And Matt played an easy-go-lucky Laertes at the beginning, listening to his father's advice like a good obedient son and going off to school in France.

Only when he came back to Elsinore, however, having learned of his father's death at the hands of the Prince, did his true colours come to life. Mark could never forget how Matt had erupted like a volcano on the stage.

"To hell allegiance! Vows to the blackest devil! Conscience and grave, to the profoundest pit! I dare damnation! ... I'll be revenged most thoroughly for my father."

It was as if the words, long fulminating inside him, had suddenly exploded and burst out with hot lava, onto the audience, his son's eyes directly focused on him seated in the third row with Jen. She had reared back with the onslaught. The whole audience had reared, feeling the molten fury spewing onto them. Mark, however, had felt the words had been directed especially to him, the father who had meddled too much in his son's life.

Had it been that bad? Had he been too close to his

son? Perhaps he should've given him more space, let him make his own errors, learn life's lessons on his own without his father hovering over him all the time, offering advice like a meddlesome old fool.

As much as he wanted to speak, he knew he couldn't speak.

Mark saw the two players put their heads together and whisper. The playwright took the rolls of paper from the actor, jotted a few words down and handed them back.

"Aye, I see," the actor said. "The Grave-digger's scene. A little late in the play, I'd say, to suggest his age. Even in the midst of grave-digging, however, you mix in clowns and mirth and equivocation."

"We transform pain and grief into poetry, Rich."

"And keep alive all our dreams," the actor said.

"I doubt it not."

"So let us swear."

As if on cue, Mark looked up from his scribbling and saw they had both turned to face him with a tight-lipped menacing look.

Mark stopped scribbling. In the silence of the pub, he listened for the traffic noise outside but heard nothing. It felt as if he were in this hermetically sealed bubble. No one else seemed to be in the pub. It was getting a little spooky.

He saw the two guys dressed in black turn away from him and exchange looks. The pitcher of beer was empty.

Not long afterwards the waitress appeared from out of nowhere. The two guys beckoned her over and paid their bill. They quickly collected their bags and jackets, giving him menacing glances. Mark looked away, trying to avoid their eyes, and covered his notebook with the book.

As they passed by his table, the younger one, Rich, stood over him with a grim visage.

"Did you get everything down?" he said, with a little smirk. "Speak. I'll go no further."

Mark was lost for words, as if caught in a paralyzing torpor and completely discombobulated.

After they had left, Mark went back to his notebook scribbling away like crazy, trying desperately to get all the words down on the page.

After a while, however, it ceased to matter who was speaking and who was listening—or where the words had come from.

All that mattered was the words and to get them down on the page before the bubble burst and it was too late.

Prime Time Challenge

Wes **took a** quick peek at the studio audience sitting above the floor cameras. Every seat was filled as usual. Their resident actor-comedian, Larry, was doing the warm-up session, settling the audience into the show, explaining procedure, adding a few quips, and getting the laughs. In casual attire, with his bulk and red beard, Larry looked like a cuddly bear.

This wasn't your ordinary game show with its low-brow humour, Larry told the audience. Things could get quite elevated with erudite exchanges. And today's show was extra special since they were expecting a mystery guest challenger. Anyone who didn't know what erudite meant, for one, would be at a disadvantage. But not to worry. They'd get help from the monitors on the difficult words. First he had to prep the audience, however, by going through the top ten list of what any historically-minded person should know.

A couple of boom cameras were panning over the audience, showing reactions on the overhanging monitors.

In spite of Larry's easy charm with the audience, Wes felt his stomach tightening up. The show was a big hit and into its third year. With the success, however, came the added pressure of staying at the top. Everyone said he came across as super cool, dapper and smooth, little knowing the price he had to pay for such an exterior display.

By the time Larry had finished and the theme music came on, he was ready. They taped the show *live* to be aired a half hour later.

"And here to moderate *Prime Time Challenge*," the announcer said, "is Wesley O'Hara-Byrne, a man who doesn't need an air conditioner on the hottest days."

In his best dark-blue suit, he strode to his desk in his signature jaunty manner while the studio audience gave him a nice hand. At the front of the desk were two large clocks. One was the Play Clock set for the minutes the panel had to identify the challenger. The other was the Prime Time Clock, more like a pie chart, dividing world history into seven ages, from the start of civilization in Mesopotamia and Egypt, through ancient Greece and Rome, to present time.

Sitting at his desk, he took a quick glance at the monitor to see if every piece of the persona was in place. He saw the smooth and lean features, clear blue eyes, short dark hair parted at the side, and the dazzling smile. All intensified by the bright studio lights. Sometimes he felt the image was cut and polished in stone, buffed to a high gloss, and stuck inside a monitor.

"Welcome to the show, ladies and gentlemen," Wes said, quickly adjusting the notes. "Thanks for the intro, Bruce, although my AC works just fine, thank you."

After the smattering of laughs, he got down to business. "Today we have something a little special for you folks at home and in the studio audience. Something that'll create a few sparks, I'm sure. But let me introduce the panel first."

The red light on his camera went out. As he spoke he kept his eye on the teleprompter, sometimes paying heed and sometimes not. At this stage, he knew the panellists well enough to give them their due.

"First we have that sartorial sage who knows how to dress as well as he knows every thread of modern history. Walter Gordon."

With the prompting from the electric board, the studio audience gave Walter a nice hand. Walter smiled at the camera. He was wearing an elegant conservative suit, with his red bowtie. A tall slim guy, with a full head of white hair, he generated an impression of avuncular reserve that hid the wit of a surgical blade.

"Our next panellist, though she is an award-winning scholar in ancient history and religions, and highly knowledgeable in ancient languages, is as fresh and lovely as a rose in full bloom. Ellen Plimpton."

Ellen was in a striking crimson top, frilly at the bustline, highlighting her pert blond bob. The show had searched high and low in academia for the likes of Ellen Plimpton, he well knew. The producers had emphasized looks, of course, but what they had come up with had far exceeded expectations. Ellen, in her early forties, hardly looked bookish or scholarly. She had a surface elfin beauty that hid a steel-trap mind. And she knew exactly how to trade her looks for advantage at the poker table. When

Ellen spoke, everyone listened. In knowing Greek and Hebrew and Latin, she was an authority on the ancient world and the Scriptures.

The guest panellist this week was Marcel Taylor, who had carved a niche for himself in the history of ideas. Of British and French parentage, he had taught at universities in Paris and England and Germany, before settling down in Canada. Always a dandy in his dress, he was in a mauve velvet vest over a blue shirt. With his shiny bald pate, he wore wire-thin glasses on his gaunt face, making him stick out in any crowd.

Rounding out the panel was their mainstay, the guy who had written over fifteen books on European history. Jacob Solomon. In his early fifties, Jake had pepper and salt short hair and beard, with dark penetrating eyes and a slim build. He was in a conservative charcoal grey suit and a striking red tie, looking composed and ready for combat.

It had taken a while to get the right mix and chemistry for the panel. The try-outs, including time as a guest panellist, had been especially revealing. Some academic historians were too specialized in their chosen field. Some wilted on camera. Others became as thick as boards. Some didn't have the right voice. Some didn't have a sense of humour. Some couldn't hide their distaste for the medium. Dave, their exec producer, claimed that the camera never lied.

Wes had his own problems in front of the camera in his early years. Serving as moderator and henchman on various afternoon game shows, he had made his gaffs and earned his chops, developing the right mixture of aplomb and nonchalance on the outside, what someone had called *sprezzatura*, to get this big gig in prime time. It didn't hurt, of course, that he had a degree in history along with the cutting sarcasm to keep the panel in check.

"You all know the premise of the show, of course," Wes spoke into the camera. "We tell you folks in the studio and you at home about a great figure who changed the course of human history, then bring out a well-known celebrity to play the part. He or she stands hidden behind the panel and answers the questions on his or her own, or lets Plutarch, our super-computer, help out with the answers. Plutarch, who understands spoken language, has been fed all the relevant information—facts, theories, interpretations—on the historical person and the times. As soon as we start the questions, the Play Clock starts as well for the panellists to uncover the identity of the great historical figure, our challenger."

Though the show was based on the format of an old and popular news show, not to mention the gimmick of pitting a super-computer against human panellists, it had been picking up significant ratings the last two years, once they had locked into the present panellists. Celebrities and A-list actors were lining up to impersonate their favourite historical figures. It was fun for the most part, though things could get dicey in the Q & A afterwards, especially if the panellists came against worthy challengers who knew their roles well. They could have some fun with the impersonators and the computer at the same time, knowing full well that Plutarch had suspect ethical wiring. Wes had once overheard them joking about the whole thing as Plutarch-bashing.

"So, if we're all ready to start," Wes said, "let's give you the story and the challenger."

While the TV audience was being fed the story in "live" time, the folks in the studio audience were looking at the overhanging monitors with their own earphones and waiting in anticipation for the appearance of the mystery celebrity who'd impersonate the historical figure. Wes could recall a few of notable and incongruous ones in the past. In one show a female pop icon, known for her bawdy concerts, had come out as Mother Teresa, down to the stoop and the white habit. Though the complaints had far outweighed the compliments, the ratings had sky-rocketed.

Another time, a pretty-boy and popular actor who was in town for the film festival had come on as Socrates. The make-up people had done a great job in transforming him into the ugly middle-aged Greek. And then there was the time the Prime Minister, a guy who was Teflon in looks and personality, had come on doing John A. MacDonald, with the wavy hair, the side-whiskers, and the alcoholic lilt in his voice. It was so campy the audience ate it up. The show had garnered a reputation, he knew, of being serious theatre with a good mix of scholarly integrity and playful histrionics, able to blow the reality and game shows out of the water.

Wes looked at his monitor and listened through his earphone. He had already received a heads-up on the identity of the historical figure and anticipated a few problems.

His mom at the nursing home, for one, would be watching, and she was as pious as they came. They had spent years reciting the rosary as a family after supper in front of the statuette of the Blessed Virgin in the living room. When he was twelve, however, his father had suddenly abandoned them for his life of drink, a traumatic event that had thrown the family into a tailspin. Only the faith of his mom, which was combined with a determined will, had saved them from the catastrophe. Already having had a controlling hand in family affairs, she had devoted herself to her children, with an outer-worldly smile that had withstood all their financial problems.

A lot of her faith and devotion had rubbed off him. And like the good Irish son he was, he had gone into the seminary, hoping to forgive his dad. After studying the theology and the history of the Church, however, his faith had been shaken. There was too much of a disparity between the original words and the dogma. And the theatre of the ritual could no longer compensate for the weakness of his flesh. His mother had been sorely disappointed when he had left the seminary, kicked around a bit, and finally settled into the television business, with its own theatrical ritual. Though she had forgiven him for going against her wishes, there were things about his private life he could never reveal to her.

Adding to the contentious historical figure was the mystery actor taking on the role, the identity of whom was only known to him and Dave. Wes knew the actor for his extreme makeovers and his Method training. For one movie he had gained forty pounds, shaved off his hair, and blacked out his teeth. For another he had lost fifty pounds, totally believable as a stick figure in a concentration camp. On an interview show on the art of acting, he had confided that it wasn't enough to act a role: one had to make oneself disappear into the character. The past four years, however, he had gone to the other side of the camera and directed two highly controversial religious movies that had created a storm of protest.

Wes braced himself for his own challenge ahead. As the moderator he was the pilot of the show, acting as an arbitrator between the panel and the guest, as well keeping a keen eye on the audience and impending storm clouds. And even though the show had its scholarly creds, it could go into uncharted waters at times. Every so often Dave liked to shake things up in order to avoid complacency. They were in show biz, after all, Dave was fond of saying. They could take history out of the textbooks, air it out, play with it, and present it to the audience in a more engaging format. The average TV viewer could be reawakened to its impact. And from Dave's experience as a teacher in the classroom, the kids, in their slavery to the tech age, were ever widening the disconnect between the present and the past. It was the mandate of the national network not only to connect the disparate parts of their large country, but to connect the diverse peoples in the nation with their heritage and their culture.

Dave liked to give them a little pep talk every so often, unfazed by the academic standards of their esteemed panellists. They were great historians, sure, but they were doing TV, he said. They were dealing with the objective facts of history and also staging a what-if scenario. What if they could bring certain historical figures back to life and question them with the aid of a powerful computer? What if they could re-examine the past with twenty-twenty hindsight in the light of the modern perspective? What if they could shake the past out of its doldrums in an interesting format for the adults and kids? And get them back into the fold?

They wouldn't dumb things down. They'd dial them

up. They'd mix their fun with historical integrity and educate the audience in the process. They'd make the new by remembering the old. TV would be their real classroom, like it or not. In order to stay on air, however, they had to take care of ratings.

During this show, Dave would be in the control room along with the regular producer, overseeing operations.

As the story was being fed to the monitors, the historical figure quietly stepped onto his perch behind the panel, catching the attention of the studio audience. Wes could see that they didn't recognize the mystery actor-director playing the role. Indeed, his facial features had been modified beyond recognition. The person facing the audience, slight and slender to begin with, had thinning hair on top of scraggily long hair at the sides, a fair-sized beard, a gaunt face with rough skin as if baked by the desert heat. He looked to be in his middle fifties and wore a long off-white tunic fringed in blue and tied at the waist. In the close-up, he regarded the camera with a mixture of severity and sadness, not to mention an outer-worldly detachment that immediately set the mood.

Suitably impressed, Wes was confused by the odd choice of colours for the attire when his cue came on.

"Now that the folks at home and in the studio audience have been informed about our challenger," he said, smiling into the camera, "we'll start the questioning with Walter."

The monitor switched to Walter Gordon.

"Did this story happen in a continent beginning and ending with the letter A?" Walter said, opening with his usual question.

"Yes," the challenger said.

"Is the continent east of the Atlantic?"

"Yes."

"Is it Asia?"

" ... Yes."

"I'll have to modify that a bit," Wes interrupted. "I'm sure our guest will agree that, while the story started in Asia, it didn't end there."

"Did it end in Europe?" Walter said.

"Yes."

"If the story wasn't located in one area, was there some travelling involved?"

"Yes."

"From Asia to Europe?"

"Yes."

"Are you Attila the Hun?" Walter said.

The audience gave out a few laughs.

"OK," Walter said with a wry grin. "I'll turn it over to you, Ellen. At least I got the geography down for you."

Ellen smiled into the camera the same way she had smiled at him once upon a time, like a siren luring him into the rocks.

"Well," she said, measuring her words, "we've established two things so far. One, the challenger seems to be answering the questions without the aid of Plutarch. And, two, we know he's not a blood-thirsty eastern invader who struck fear into the hearts of Europe."

The audience's reaction was amused but muted. The panellists, as usual, knew how to play the audience to their advantage.

"Let's go for the time period," Ellen said. "Did this story happen in the Common Era?"

"Yes."

"Did it happen after the Middle Ages?"

"No."

"Before 600 CE?"

"Yes."

"Before 100?"

"Yes."

"Were you a Roman citizen?"

"Yes."

"There you go, Marcel," Ellen turned to him. "He can't be a Caesar, since most of them were as blood-crazed as the Huns."

"Were you a member of the military at all?" Marcel said.

"No."

"Were you a member of the government?"

"No."

"Were you an artist in any way? A writer? A philosopher? A playwright or poet?"

"Which one?" the challenger said.

"A writer."

"Yes."

"I'll have to interrupt again," Wes said. "We'd be leading the panel very astray here. While our guest was a writer, so to speak, he wasn't a writer in the usual meaning of the term."

"I'm confused even more now," Marcel said, scratching his bald pate. "I'll turn it over to you, Jacob."

Jake took charge immediately in his sharp incisive voice.

"Did you write anything?"

"Yes and no," the challenger said, with a coy smile.

The camera light went on again. "I think we're getting bogged in semantics," Wes said. "The challenger is answering truthfully but ambiguously. While he himself didn't actually write most of the words, he was responsible for the words."

"Ah," Jake said. "You dictated the words?"

"Yes."

"And did your words have a great effect on the Roman Empire?"

"I like to think so. Yes, eventually, I suppose."

"Hmm ... did you dictate in Latin?"

"No."

"In Greek?"

"Yes and no."

"OK, in a variant of Attic Greek? Koine?"

"Yes."

"If you travelled from Asia to Europe, were you a citizen of a different country as well? Let me rephrase that: Were you native to a different region?"

"Yes."

"If you weren't a military man or a politician or a statesman, were you religious?"

"Yes."

"Ellen," Jake said, "we'll leave it up to you."

After a few more questions, Ellen identified the mystery guest to the applause of the audience. Wes broke for a commercial.

While they waited, the challenger came down from his perch and sat on the swivel chair in between the panellists and the moderator's desk. Under his tunic, everyone could see he was in bare legs and sandals, with black socks, which caused a ripple of laughter in the studio audience. Even the panellists were amused, as they consulted their laptops.

But Wes could sense a general unease as well. A religious challenger tended to bring out the worst in the panellists. He could recall the time they had Martin Luther on and Jake had raked him for his anti-Semitism. Another show they had Gandhi on, and even he wasn't spared. Walter had seriously questioned him on his penchant for sleeping with young girls in his old age. What the hell was that? Walter said, as if he were the moral compass of the panel.

As historians, the panellists were into the facts of history, but also unsparing in questioning the interpretation of those facts. It was their mandate to challenge the guests, attack the sore spots, dramatize the weaknesses, churn the ante up and make it TV. If they stepped on a few toes, so much the better, Dave said. And he was in the control room today, a sure sign of possible trouble.

Larry bounced back onto the stage to keep the audience in the flow. He told a few religious jokes. The priest, rabbi, and minister enter a bar ...

After the commercial break, they all saw and heard the more extended story about their guest. The monitors showed maps of his journeys, religious paintings and statues and mosaics of his visage, the old Roman roads he travelled on, the old ruins at Ephesus and Antioch and Corinth and Thessalonica, depictions of the Second Temple where he was arrested, images of Nero and the persecution of the Christians, all the while flashing his very words as subtitles.

At the end Bruce made the formal intro in his throaty baritone voice.

"*Prime Time Challenge* welcomes one of the most controversial figures in recorded history. A man who many claim is the actual founder of Christianity, while others claim he radically changed the original message of Jesus and even betrayed his own people. A man of many contradictions, who himself said he was all things to all men. A man who could be a mystic one minute and a practical administrator the next, who was a Pharisee and a Hellenized urbanite. A man who travelled over ten thousand miles in his lifetime, suffered through much physical affliction and abuse, and was as fanatical as he was learned and cosmopolitan. A man who could feel at home in Jerusalem, Athens, and Rome—and yet claimed he had no real home. His few letters arguably changed the course of world history. These letters, most scholars claim, are the earliest written records of what later would be called Christianity. To know the real time-line, therefore, one would have to read the New Testament backwards. Please welcome the author of those letters, Paul of Tarsus."

The audience gave him a big hand. Today, however, Bruce didn't identify the celebrity actor-director playing the role. Wes heard in his earphone to play along and not divulge the identity. They would see how far they could go and not tamper with the audience's disbelief. The challenger had already done an amazing job of staying in character.

During the close-up of the challenger in the blue and white tunic sitting on the swivel chair, Wes could see the audience was clearly puzzled over his identity.

"Welcome to the show, Paul," Wes said in his best smile.

"Thank you. Actually I was born as Shaul, but you can call me Saul or Paul, whatever you like. As a traveller and messenger, I am who I am according to where I am."

"As you can tell by now, folks," Wes said into the camera, not losing his smile, "we are going to let Saul or Paul stay in character. And I'm sure I speak for most of our audience when I say we're anxious to learn more about him."

He was informed on his earphone that even makeup didn't know the identity of the celebrity actor-director. He had been done up by his own people. After a slight pause in which he shifted his notes, Wes looked back at the challenger.

"Anyway, let's get down to the Q & A because I can see our panellists are anxiously waiting to question you. Are you ready, Paul?"

"Before we begin," the challenger said, looking into the camera, "I must tender greetings to all the faithful out there who are groaning under the strains of the present age. Brothers and sisters, stand firm in your beliefs. Don't be fooled by the authority of the beast coming out of the air-waves. Don't be fooled by appearances. Keep true to the message strong in your hearts and minds. And be aware that I'm leaving myself and the message open to denigration under the glare of these false lights. But we all have to face the challenge, don't we? Whether in the Temple or synagogue or marketplace. At work or at play. In Rome or Corinth or Antioch."

The audience looked on with blank faces. The challenger spoke in a calm and deliberate manner, his voice low and modulated, his eyes firmly fixed on the monitor and the studio audience at the same time.

"OK," Wes said, smiling into the camera, seeing that the panel was amused by the opening comments.

The first few questions, from Walter and Marcel, were what many people would be curious about. How could Paul make the flip-flop—from being a persecutor of the Christians to a fervent leader of their cause? What changes did he make in the ethical message of Jesus in the Gospels? Did he actually repudiate his Jewish roots? Which of his letters were authentically his words and which were written by his followers? Which of the historical events in Acts were accurate and which were fabrications? He was clearly a man of contradictions. Who was the real person behind all the masks?

The challenger did a creditable job, Wes had to admit. Though he could use the help of Plutarch through his earphone, it appeared he was speaking on his own. And without hesitation or equivocation. Wes could tell, with his own working knowledge of the letters, when the challenger was quoting directly and when he was ad-libbing—and it was clear that he had memorized all thirteen. What impressed Wes the most, however, was how the challenger spoke about himself with complete humility. As if he were able to go into the context of Paul's time when his words were not considered Scripture and he himself wasn't regarded the figure he came to be. Of all the factors that went into suspending the disbelief in the audience, Wes felt, this was the most important—although he well knew it could cause a problem with believers.

First, the challenger set them straight about a few facts. It wasn't the Christians he had been persecuting. It was the Jewish followers of the Mashiah, Yeshua. Second, he couldn't comment on Acts, since it was written after him. And, third, he couldn't comment on the Gospels either since they had also been written after him—though the oral stories and the words of Yeshua were definitely in circulation. For him, the word *gospel* was the *evangelion*, the good news—the death and resurrection of Yeshua, the Mashiah.

"Do you see yourself as Jewish or Christian?" Walter said with a big grin.

The challenger shook his head and smiled. "You're not listening. We were followers of the Way, the Way of Yeshua the Mashiah. Some of us were Jewish and some were Gentiles. I was born a Jew and remained a Jew all my life."

"Some would claim, however," Walter said, "that you betrayed your Jewish faith by repudiating the Torah and starting an entirely new religion."

"And I would say I fulfilled my Jewish faith by proclaiming the good news of the Mashiah who taught us that we can all die to the flesh in order to live in the spirit."

Wes heard in his earphone to get them off the topic.

"It's a thorny issue, to be sure," he cut in. "And we can't resolve it here, but let's continue in another vein. Walter, do you have any other questions?"

"Not right now," Walter said, looking unflappably at the camera. "But we're just trying to establish the historical truth here. And if the historical truth, as a modern believer once said, is not in the service of faith, faith will degenerate into superstition."

The challenger gave him a little smile. "The faith I speak about, however, can make us rise above all history and superstition. And even the physical world as we see it.

Like Abraham. As we know ourselves, so we will be known, as aliens in the physical world."

"Let's try to stay focused on the facts, shall we?" Ellen said. "And use our rational faculties. Or we won't agree on anything."

Quoting from Acts, she got the challenger to agree that there were inconsistencies between his own words in the letters, or the ones he deemed authentically his, and the words in Acts. And that Luke, who had reputedly written Acts, had more of a theological agenda than a historical one.

"If there's an inconsistency," Paul said, "you'll have to take my word for it."

"But aren't there inconsistencies in your own theological agenda as well?" Ellen said, smiling at him. "Didn't you proclaim the physical resurrection of the body one time and the impossibility of the physical resurrection of the body another time?"

Wes observed the challenger for the visual. He well knew that the camera was a meticulous and unforgiving eye. The challenger, however, entirely at ease, looked in command of the situation.

"As a Pharisee," he said, "whenever I used the word *resurrection* it could only mean the resuscitation of the *soma*, the body. According to the Scriptures, there is no consciousness, no *ruach*, apart from the body. In Alpha Corinthians, therefore, I say that the Mashiah died and was buried, then was raised on the third day and appeared to Cephas and the twelve. As an apostle of the good news, however, I later say that the *psychikos*, the sensual person, doesn't accept the things of the *pneuma*, the spirit. In the good news, we are sown a physical body, which is perishable, but raised a spiritual body, which is imperishable. The physical is first ... and then the spiritual. The words are only the menu, however. Faith is the meal. We can't understand the words unless we eat of the meal."

Wes was listening and trying the gage the reaction of the audience. He had to moderate a fine line between the historical integrity of the show and not boring the audience. And the mention of Greek words was a killer. With no instruction from the control room, however, all he could do was let the situation play out.

"Spoken like a true Pharisee," Jake said in his quiet conviction. "But let's continue to stick to the facts, shall we? Besides being educated under Gamaliel, the Pharisee, weren't you also schooled in the Greek rhetoric, with a working knowledge of the Stoics and the Greek thinkers? Weren't you even a boxer, besides a tentmaker? According to Acts, you were so zealous in the traditions of your fathers in Judaism that you hounded the believers in the Jesus movement and even oversaw their deaths. According to Acts, on the road to Damascus you were blinded by a light and heard the voice from the risen Christ. Pardon my scepticism, but your very words in your letters don't even mention the road to Damascus. Instead, you said you received, let's say, divine authority for your mission directly from the source itself. Is that the case?"

"Yes."

"What I find so suspicious, however, is that because you got your mission not from the actual apostles but from the risen Christ, you were able to make of the message whatever you wanted. In other words, you needed some sort of validation, a validation that could've been entirely fabricated."

The camera quickly panned over the reactions of the studio audience. Some were openly offended, shaking their heads, as if their own beliefs were being questioned, while others seemed curious as to where it was all heading.

Wes heard Dave in his earphone giving him a Five-O.

"If I can interrupt," Wes said. "What Jake is asking is what we'd all like to know. What was it like to experience such a conversion? According to one report, you were struck down, for example. You were blinded for three days. That must've been quite an experience."

The challenger paused, looked into the camera, and took a few breaths. Under the glare of the lights, Wes could detect signs of his heavy makeup.

"As I mentioned, I can't comment on how others interpret my words," the challenger said. "All I can say is that nothing was fabricated. A call or revelation can happen to anyone at any time when they find out, in a flash, the real purpose of their lives. With me, it was when I was born a second time—to the spirit instead of the flesh. My circumstances, I admit, were a little unusual in that I made such a radical turnaround. But you have to know I was zealous in my observance of the Torah, in fasting and meditation, in living in the words on the outside and the inside. And one day I had a vision that changed my life completely around. An *apokalypsis*. The presence of the light and the feel of the breath. And it was as if I became the light and the breath. Of the Mashiah. And it was revealed to me that the death of a man hanging on a tree was actually the great triumph if our Lord and saviour—and a sign for all of us. That we were to exchange our bodies for the true light and breath within, the spirit, and be born a second time. And I saw that I was called by the spirit of the risen Lord to preach the good news to Gentile as well as Jew."

The studio audience was hushed.

"Did you actually see something?" Jake said. "Did you hear a voice? Were you blinded? Or was it simply an hallucination in the desert?"

"As I said, it was a vision."

"What do you mean by a vision?"

Paul regarded him without answering. The pause stretched. Wes heard instruction in his ear to stay silent.

"Only those who know can understand," Paul said. "You, as historians, may think you know, but you only know the outward facts. I speak as one who felt the call of the spirit of the Mashiah, a call so powerful that I lost my old self to my new self. You have to remember, however, that on the outside we were living in apocalyptic times. The Holy City had been captured by the Romans and we were scattered throughout the Hellenized world. We spoke the lingua franca and used the Septuagint, where the divine breath, the *ruach* is the *pneuma*, and the *Mashiah* is the *Christos*. And we were in high expectation to be delivered from our oppressors, both physical and otherwise. And in my vision I saw that the *Christos* was not our enemy, but the saviour who had turned everything inside out by proclaiming the power of the mind and the heart, of the inner person, the *pneuma*. That we could start with the visible, the covenant of works, but we had to progress to the invisible, the spiritual, the covenant of faith."

Dave had been instructing him to do another Five-O

on Paul's monologue, but Wes couldn't bring himself to cut in. The more Paul spoke the more his words came out with fervour and conviction.

"I'm sure I speak for all of us, Paul," Wes said, "when I say it must've been a life-changing experience." He turned to the panel and saw Marcel's hand. "Yes, Marcel."

"With all due respect to what you represent to many people," Marcel said, "we as historians still have to be concerned with the facts, with what's rational, and try to separate reality from fantasy and myth. We constantly see how everyone re-writes the past to suit the present. And with Jesus it seems we always make of him whatever we desperately need of him. You never met the real flesh and blood Jesus, as the apostles did. To get back to Jake's point, some scholars claim you were never interested in the flesh and blood Jesus, that in order to validate your zeal, as you call it, you had to meet him as a spirit. That way you could make of him whatever you needed to make of him; that is, a saviour and supernatural being."

Paul's lips curled up. "You see what you see, with all the cleverness of the dispassionate eye. But the dispassionate eye is blind to the spirit of the Mashiah. And as Isaiah says, the Lord will destroy the wisdom of the wise and the cleverness of the clever."

The monitor switched to Ellen Plimpton's sly smile.

"I'm impressed," she said, her smile tightening. "You've managed to either convince or confuse the audience with the word *spirit*. But let me bring in another perspective, that of the Gnostic Gospels from Nag Hammadi. Are you acquainted with the Gnostic Gospels?"

The challenger shook his head.

"Of course not," she went on, "since they were written after you. But the Gnostics call you the Apostle, the real Apostle, since underneath your surface message what you really preach is the liberation of the spirit, the divine spark, from the flesh. There are some scholars who claim you were actually a pneumatic, a Gnostic, preaching a literal message for the many and an esoteric and hidden message for the few initiates. How do you respond to that?"

Wes saw the little curl on Ellen's smile, a smile he had seen before when she was ready to reveal the trap she had set. Some in the studio audience were getting restless, however, as if the panellists were crossing a line that they were unwilling to follow.

"My words in the letter to Timothy," Paul said, "flatly deny that the speculations of the so-called *gnosis* are a substitute for the divine training that is called faith."

"But you just claimed you weren't aware of the Gnostic Gospels."

"Not as they were written, true. But many things were not in written form during my time. We lived in an oral tradition, with many things passed on by word of mouth."

"Right. And it's also possible that your own written words may have been edited, added to, or changed by the early Church, is it not?"

Paul paused as if he were listening to his earphone. "They're under my name."

"But the words could always be redacted under your name," Ellen said in a cutting tone. "The question is: Who was the real Paul? The Pharisee dedicated to the Torah?

The convert to the new Christ movement that was in opposition to the Jesus movement? Or the secret Gnostic messenger to the Hellenistic Gentiles?"

"The words of the good news speak for themselves. The Mashiah came to redeem us all through faith, Gentile and Jew alike."

"But you could only proclaim that message if you were all three in one. Only in that way could you convert fidelity to the law into faith in the messiah so that the Gentiles didn't have to be circumcised or observe the dietary rules?"

"It wasn't me as an individual. It was the spirit of the Mashiah who had taken over me. It was the Lord whose death and resurrection proved we are saved by faith and not by works."

"True, but it all depends on what you meant by faith. And it could've meant two things, as was later interpreted. As *pistis*, or blind faith, for the uninitiated. And as *gnosis*, or divine knowledge, for the initiated."

"You're reading what's not there," Paul said.

Ellen looked directly into the camera. "I have to remind the audience that one of the major reasons that Gnosticism was considered a heresy, besides its outrageous mythical infrastructure, was for its claim that anyone could attain the *gnosis* or knowledge of the divine mysteries, not just Jesus."

She turned her eyes back to Paul.

"Marcel has already established that you were never concerned with the flesh and blood Jesus of Nazareth, the actual historical person. The only things you mention about him are the Eucharistic meal, his death, and his resurrection. Wasn't that because you weren't interested in what he preached as much as who he was?"

"We all knew what he preached," Paul said. "It was common knowledge, though it wasn't written yet."

"And yet you mention nothing of his ethical message and of his works. Wasn't that because your real message wasn't the works or the law but the triumph of the spirit over the flesh? Wasn't it the triumph of the inner person as opposed to the outer person, which is the secret message of Gnosticism as well? That the real 'I am,' the *pneuma*, the divine spark inside all of us, yearns to shed its outer skin and be reborn into its true source, the transcendent kingdom of the Father, the new loving God and not the old God of the Hebrew Scriptures whom the Gnostics called the demi-urge—the inferior evil God. Your message wasn't Jewish at all. It was entirely Roman and Greek and Gnostic."

Everyone's eyes shifted to the challenger, who sat in his swivel chair seemingly unperturbed by the grilling. Either he had suffered worse indignities than this, Wes felt, or he had something up his sleeve. Whatever the case, it made for good TV—for those still following.

"You can twist my words and bring any charge you wish against me," Paul said in a quiet voice, looking directly at Ellen, "but my words speak for themselves. I can't answer for how my words were interpreted after me, only what they say in their time and place. And what they say is not what I was taught, nor did I receive it from the apostles, for it isn't of human origin."

"My point precisely," Ellen said, nodding with a smug smile. "You received your message from a vision, as you said, but that was a common Gnostic experience in those days. And it was considered entirely subjective—a spiritual experience, not a physical or ethical one. It existed in a sort of metaphysical space. If the uninitiated ordinary believers wanted to see it as a miracle, of course, that was up to them. The only problem was that your message of faith for all, Gentile and Jew alike, was totally opposed to the rest of the apostles, specifically Peter and James, the brother of Jesus, who wanted to keep the ethical message of Jesus within the Torah and Judaism."

"You may see it that way, but not see it the whole way," Paul said to her, then shifted his eyes to the studio audience. "I can only say that wisdom of this world is foolishness to the revealed words. We, on the other hand, who've studied the revealed words of the prophets have seen what it means to be elected and clean and separated from the rest of the world. And the Mashiah has revealed to us how we can all be saved as the chosen ones. Which is to have faith in the Lord, our saviour. And be clean on the inside and then on the outside. That is the faith I speak about. A faith that obliterates all outer impediments. A faith in the invisible spirit. Not exclusively for those elected by blood or gifted with knowledge. A faith for everyone. For the lowest of the low, for fools, for the despised, for slaves and freemen alike. A faith of hope and love, a faith of salvation for all. Not in the visible things that I saw all around me in my travels in the pagan world. With all its gods and goddesses and demons of wood and stone. And with the despicable acts the slaves were subjected to, especially in Rome, an overcrowded city of well over a million, half of whom were slaves. The whole visible pagan world was our real enemy. And now the visible kingdom of darkness and evil still reigns supreme in all its foolish glory, blind to the secrets of the invisible kingdom that our fathers established long ago."

The visual on the monitor showed Paul's eyes enflamed with fervour.

"I know things are getting interesting," Wes cut in with a big grin, "but we have to take a break. We'll be right back. Don't go away."

The theme music, resounding in its fast-paced tinkly vein, immediately broke the tension in the audience. He could see that most of them needed a break, one way or the other.

Larry walked out to face the studio audience. He went into a story about attending a bris and almost passing out. He didn't know about the audience, he said at the end, but all this religious talk was giving him the willies. All they had to do was crack open a few cold ones and they'd resolve all their issues.

After Larry left, Wes saw the camera light come back on. He sensed the tension had all but evaporated and they were back in the TV world.

"*Prime Time Challenge* tonight has put our mystery challenger who is playing Paul of Tarsus on the hot seat," he said. "We have to remind our audience at home and here in the studio, however, that the opinions and views expressed by the participants do not necessarily reflect the views of the show or the sponsors."

After a brief summary of the Q & A, he gave the floor to Jake Solomon.

"I have to remind everyone, including Paul here," Jake

said, "that Rabbinical Judaism was never meant to be entirely exclusive. As long as non-Jews followed the Noahide laws they could also be saved. And that maybe his use of the Greek translation of the Scriptures instead of the original Hebrew made him misunderstand the relationship between the people and the Torah. Why did you speak so harshly against your own people?"

"If I spoke harshly, it was because I was speaking to my own family."

"In 1Thessalonians 2 you expressly blame the Jews for killing Jesus."

Paul paused, listening to his earphone. "Most scholars claim those words were inserted by later redactors. But it's also possible to see the words in another way. That all those who live in the flesh are actually killing the Mashiah inside them all the time."

Jake shook his head in disapproval. Wes could see the audience wasn't responding.

"There are scholars," Jake went on, "who claim that you were a collaborator, a traitor to your people. They call you a secret Herodian, an accommodator with the Romans, who sold out to the Romans, who not only abrogated the law but undermined the basic tenet of any form of Judaism. You said that faith alone could save us and that a risen-from-the-dead-man was the saviour of the human race, thereby elevating a human being to a god-like status. That wasn't Judaism at all, as Ellen already said, but from the Greek mystery religions, not to mention the Egyptian beliefs."

"Well," Paul said, "the message had to be understood by everyone, Jew and Gentile alike, and it was bound to be misunderstood by both sides."

"Isn't it a fact that in Galatians you repudiate the whole Torah?" Jake said. "Isn't it a fact that your so-called faith was not only anathema to Judaism but also radically different from the real historical Jesus himself and his true apostles, James and Peter? Isn't it a fact that it was you, and only you, that split entirely from the historical Jesus in order to get all the benefits of the Torah without the work of following it?"

"However you see it," Paul said, not losing his smile, "the good news was meant to be a bridge, not only between Jew and Gentile but between the flesh and the spirit, the visible and the invisible. And the end of days was near. We had to be ready to cross over at any time."

The monitor showed Jake's tight visage. "You betrayed the law and your own people."

"As followers of the Mashiah, we only brought the *nomos pisteos*, the law of faith, into its next step, the law of love. May the Holy One, HaShem, forgive me if I've done wrong."

Two of the cameras panned over the studio audience which was hushed. The panellists, with their own earphones in place, remained silent, looking at the guest challenger with a mixture of scepticism and respect

Wes heard through his earphone to get out fast. Dave was practically shouting in his ear.

"I'm sure I speak for everyone, Paul," Wes said, "when I say you've done a great job of meeting the Prime Time challenge. We may not understand or agree with everything you said, but we certainly see your fervour and faith. Do you have any final words?"

The challenger looked into the camera, his expression almost serene in its intensity.

"Peace and grace to all those out there still firm in their faith. We believe we are saved in our minds and hearts—and not in the outward show, as our Lord taught us. And these days everyone is fooled by the outward show, at what comes to us through the screen of the great beast. What we must do, however, is always look to the signs of the *spermatikos logos*, the seed of the Father, the generative principle, which connects the visible to the invisible, the law of love under our skin, where there is no Jew or Gentile, no male or female, no Muslim or Hindu, no Catholic or Protestant, no black, no white, no brown, no rich, and no poor."

The studio fell into a tense silence. Wes's TV training told him to steer away from the iceberg ahead, but his stronger instincts prevailed.

"What great beast do you mean?" he said.

The challenger faced the camera and maintained steady eye contact. Everyone waited for his words, but no words came from his mouth.

Wes let the dead air time go on for as long as possible, hoping the silence would make for good TV for the few —even though Dave was giving him an earful.

"Thank you, Paul," he finally said.

After the show, the guest challenger was whisked away before anyone could talk to him.

Later that night Dave called him into his office and gave him a tongue lashing. He had let the challenger talk much too long to defend himself. Had he forgotten his job as moderator to not let things get out of hand? The complaints, angry and from all sides, were flooding in by phone and Twitter. Their show was supposed to be fun and light-hearted, not revisionist hysteria.

Sitting in front of Dave's desk, Wes took everything in. The awards on his wall. The photos of his family, the little mementos and photos of his years on the network. He had never seen Dave this angry with him before. His face was flushed, his unkempt and long hair all askew. Two buttons on his old shirt were torn, exposing his large belly. Any second he thought he'd get the heave-ho.

"Why didn't you stop him?" Dave said. "What the fuck were you doing asking him about the great beast? That wasn't Paul of Tarsus. It was an actor who's a self-righteous bastard, biting the hand that feeds him. You just gave him a fucking podium to spout his views. Now I'm going to have to eat shit from the viewers and sponsors. Not to mention the religious fanatics. Give me one fucking good reason why you didn't stop him."

"To tell you the truth, Dave, I don't know. I guess I was trying to be fair to everyone."

"Fair? Are you kidding? Your first loyalty is to me and the show, not to your pangs of personal conscience. The next time I tell you to fucking shut things down, Wes, you do it or you're out. Is that clear? There are about two hundred people who'd jump at your job. I know that for a fact."

"Anything you say, Dave."

"Fortunately we had enough time to cut a few things out."

After the show was actually aired—and the editor did all his cutting—Wes got a call from his mother who was as distraught as he had ever heard her.

"Why didn't you say anything, Wesley?" she said. "Why didn't you help that poor man out? They were attacking him left and right, showing no respect whatsoever."

"I don't know, Mom. I was just trying to be fair. It's only a TV show. That wasn't the real Paul. It was just an actor."

"It doesn't matter, Wesley," she said in her weak voice. "The proper respect has to be paid. You know that."

"Yes, Mom."

"And all those people you work with. They seem so intelligent with their words and yet so cold in their hearts, don't you see?"

"Yes, Mom."

"The wisdom of this world is folly with God, Wesley."

"Yes, Mom."

In the long pause he could hear her laboured breathing. It was painful to hear. A long indrawn breath, followed by a slow wheezing sound as if her lungs had lost all their elasticity. She wasn't much longer for this world, he knew. She was looking forward for the next world, where she believed all her pain and suffering would be justified.

Nick and Francesco
Visit Canada

I got the call from my friend at the CBC on a sunny crisp afternoon in late October, just after my run and lunch. Allen had been a producer on the national news, travelled extensively, then kicked sideways, I gathered, to produce a few prime-time shows, though I didn't know exactly what he did. I hadn't seen Allen in a few years, however, and was surprised by the call. We used to chum around at the Athletic Centre at the university where we played tennis.

My connection to the CBC was spotty. I had done some radio on literary matters way back when it was still on Jarvis Street and Howard Engel had hired me on a trial basis. I could never forget the interview with Al Purdy in which some curmudgeonly spittle had been hurled in my direction for my impertinence. Many years later, when I was no longer a struggling writer and teaching and into my gig as an invisible man, Allen had called a few times to get my take on educational matters. And since I had written some fictional material on growing up in a hockey environment, the CBC had included me in its Hockey History series, though most of the footage was left on the cutting room floor.

The first thing that entered my mind was that the CBC wanted to do a show on me. The second was that Allen wanted my opinion on a literary matter. The third was that I had gotten some sort of award and Allen was giving me a heads up.

I was way off on all counts, to say the least.

He came right to the point. Two native sons from Italy were visiting Canada to appear on some sort of game show to be shot at CBC headquarters downtown. Would I be willing to play nursemaid, to show them around the sites for a couple of days, and make sure they stayed out of trouble? He was going to do it himself, but he had just been called out of town on urgent family business and no one else on staff could do it. CBC would take care of all expenses and throw in a perk or two. Ordinarily, he added, the Italian Consulate downtown would handle such matters, but the two visitors wanted nothing to do with the Consulate, nor with the Italian Cultural Centre or the Columbus Centre.

"With me out of the picture," he said, "you're the only compromise."

"You mean they've heard of me?"

"No. It was me who mentioned you. Gave them a little of your background. That you were Italian-born and never made it big."

"Did you tell them I used to kick your ass in tennis?"

"The last thing they're interested in is tennis. Listen, they're not looking for adulation. All they need is someone who knows the city, knows their language, and is reasonably well-read and can sympathize with their widely disparate points of view. Neither of them can speak English too well."

"I don't understand," I said. "Why me? I'm not on the up and up on modern Italian culture. There're plenty of academics in the Italian Dept. at the universities who'd jump at the chance to wine and dine them and display their erudition over some pasta al Dante."

"You don't get it, Mark. They don't want to be wined and dined. They want a simple unpretentious guy, someone who understands where they're coming from, and doesn't make a fuss about them. Someone who's down to earth, doesn't bother them with Dante, and understands the literary soul."

"Who are these guys?"

"Nick and Francesco. All I know is that they've both seen better days, especially Nick who's a former diplomat-slash-envoy. He's retired and penniless but extremely well-read in the classics and writing full time now. Francesco's a friar or brother in some order who fancies himself a poet. They're both up your alley."

"I don't even know the language that well. When are they arriving?"

"Tomorrow afternoon. I'll try to make some arrangements for the two nights and get back to you. Do this, man, and the CBC will be forever in your debt. Maybe we'll do a feature on you in the future. The unknown writer who's holed up in the suburbs, totally unrecognized and unappreciated, and thumbing his nose at the literary establishment."

"I never liked the CBC," I shot back. "I can't stand watching or listening to that simpering smugness. All you guys do is copy the Americans—and you still can't do it right."

"If you do this, I'll owe you one."

"What do you mean, keep them out of trouble?"

"They've both been kind of ... out of the limelight for a long while, let's say. And neither has been to North America before."

The airport was only a ten-minute drive north of my place in central Etobicoke. I arrived the next afternoon in plenty of time for the Alitalia flight. I made a cardboard sign with their names on it to identify myself and waited outside Customs with a small crowd. When the automatic glass doors started opening, the crowd surged forward with effusive displays of emotion. Everyone was dressed at their best *bella figura*. The men in smart suits or casual chic black leather jackets. The women in hip-hugging skirts and flouncy colourful tops. It was straight out of an Italian soap opera.

Then these two middle-aged guys came out looking a little discombobulated, as if they had stepped out of a time capsule.

The first guy was short and lean, in old brown cords and a coarse brown hoodie, with short black hair cut in page-boy, a tonsure, and charcoal eyes, looking like some lost and extinct bird. Over his shoulders he had a duffel bag that looked more like a sack. The second guy was taller, with thin features, a sharp nose and sunken cheeks, with piercing black eyes and a smile that could only be cagey. He was dressed smartly in fashionable dress pants, a tie, a suit jacket draped over his arm, and carried a leather satchel.

"*Ciao, Niccolò e Francesco,*" I yelled out. "*Benvenuti in Canada.*"

We shook hands and exchanged a few pleasantries. Francesco, the guy with the hoodie and tonsure, looked entirely out of his element. Nick, with the suit and satchel, smiled and nodded, as if he were being greeted by a head of state and was ready to review the troops.

I have to be perfectly frank here. Though I could read Italian well enough, I didn't speak it well. My family had emigrated when I was four and I had been raised in a *dialetto* that had died out in Italy. The visitors understood my Italian well enough and they knew enough English to get by. We alternated, sometimes in the same sentence. What I transcribe here, therefore, is a translated facsimile that rounds out the rough edges.

Without much fanfare I brought them to my car in the tiered parking garage. Nick sat beside me up front and didn't seem too kindly disposed towards his compatriot. They didn't say much in the car, their eyes fastened to the sights of mass freeways and cars and high rise hotels on the airport strip. Allen had suggested all three of us stay at one of the downtown hotels close to the CBC building, but I was against that. If these guys wanted no fuss and bother, then they'd be more comfortable in my modest townhouse in a complex beside Centennial Park. It had three bedrooms upstairs. My wife and I had separated. She had gone back to live up north, where most of her family still lived. Our grown-up son lived downtown.

At one point, as I got off the expressway and came closer to the complex, I tried to get some information on this game show that they were scheduled to appear on.

Nick didn't know much about it, he said. Only that he was supposed to present his political views, while Francesco was supposed to present his religious views. And a panel of judges or whatever was supposed to identify them. He laughed at the implications.

I thought I was in a time warp. The show sounded very close to *Front Page Challenge*, a long-running CBC game show that featured up-to-the-date news-makers hidden behind a panel of noted journalists who were supposed to identify the people and the stories with a series of questions. With the hidden challenger standing behind them and the audience fully aware of the story, it was always a play of mind and wit. I could remember the regular panellists, especially the portly curmudgeon with the comb-over, an avowed atheist in a bow-tie, who'd always challenge any religious person to prove their faith in the Q and A afterwards.

Such questions would cause me to squirm in my seat back in the Soo, where I had grown up on the CBC. Later, he'd be replaced by another popular curmudgeon, this one an analyst on Hockey Night in Canada who wore peacock suits and pontificated in Yahooese.

I asked Francesco if he was looking forward to the show.

"*Sì, sì*, brother Marco," he said. "We need the money to repair our church."

"Allen tells me you're a poet."

"No, no. My soul only sings the praises of God and all His creatures with my all too humble words."

That shut me up, although I heard a sarcastic humph from Nick.

"What sort of writing do you do?" I asked Nick.

"Serious work on political matters and unserious plays and poetry. The sort that's more concerned with the salvation of the fatherland than the salvation of the soul."

The last sentence sounded much better in Italian, with *patria* and *anima* rounding each other out *al Dante*, though I couldn't respond to that, either.

All I knew was that Italy was going through some rough times, as was most of Europe. Unemployment, especially among the young, was at an all time high. One in every two kids didn't have work. The national debt was an embarrassment. The number and interests of the political parties were choking the country by the throat. It was mired in historic bureaucratic quicksand, stifled by favouritism, and prone to the cancers of corruption and cynicism. It wasn't so much merit that advanced a career as one's connection to a family, a region, or a protector. An acquaintance of mine who had lived in Italy for a long time had told me that the average citizen, and especially those who were self-employed in small businesses, of which there were many, couldn't get along without little favours, personal connections, and *tips* from friends in order to make up for the inefficiency of the public administrations. It was just how it was done, he said. Government coalitions came and went on a regular basis. The country had gone through a period of corruption in which many people in business and politics, all the way up to the Socialist prime minister, were disgraced and jailed by the Clean Hands movement, *le mani pulite*. And the Mafia and Camorra and 'Indrangheta had a way of greasing the hands of politicians or assassinating anyone who got into their way, including judges like Falcone. The Clean Hands investigations had only lasted a short time, however. Afterwards, a billionaire media baron had dominated politics for two decades, governing the country like a Banana Republic, as one cynic said. The common conception was that he had only gone into politics to make himself and his empire immune from justice. And then he had been expelled from elected office after being found guilty by the courts for tax fraud, not to mention *bunga bunga* parties and improprieties involving dubious sexual behaviour with minors. Things seemed as bad as when the country was composed of warring city-states, including the papacy.

In the end, the most important loyalty was to one's family.

In spite of all this, however, almost every visitor knew there was no more beautiful country to the heart and the soul than Italy.

"Allen also tells me," I said to Nick, "that you've been some sort of envoy and travelled quite a bit."

"That is correct, my friend. But those days are over. I'm more of a consultant now, writing on the shortcomings of governments and priests."

"I am not a priest," Francesco protested from the back.

"Priest or friar, it's all the same to me."

I could see I was in over my head. These guys had a force of personality that I rarely saw in my circles. Francesco, though humble and childlike—to an almost foolish extent in his mannerisms and disposition—was like a raw and beneficent force of nature. Nick, on the other hand, who was intelligent and enigmatic, had a sharp worldly edge to his practiced and smooth delivery, like a politician who could hide his designs all too readily behind his engaging smile. It was as if the city mouse had met the country mouse. And I had been chosen to keep the cats at bay. Or was I the cheese?

I could've killed Allen for putting me in a tight spot. The last thing I needed in my calm retirement years was to play nursemaid to a couple of Italian visitors who'd be at each other's throat for a couple of days. Their show was supposed to be taped on Monday. It was now Saturday afternoon.

I got them safely to the townhouse, showed them upstairs to their respective bedrooms, and was trying to make some quick plans for the evening when Allen called long distance.

"What the fuck did you get me into?" I told him.

"Not to worry, buddy-boy," he said, the cavalier guy he was. "I've got it all scoped for you. I got you guys box seats to tonight's Leafs game, all drinks and meals free. And tomorrow you can see *Turandot* at the Four Seasons Centre."

"You've got to be kidding. These guys don't know anything about hockey, and I seriously doubt they'd like to go to an opera."

"You're the ambassador, man. It's all spectacle anyways. And you know how Italians love spectacle. Hey, you think it's easy to get these seats at the last minute? You should be thanking me, Trecroci."

"Sure, I'll be thanking you even more when you take them off my hands."

He laughed and gave me instructions on how to pick up the tickets.

Afterwards, the more I thought about it, the better it

seemed. Both events would take up the whole two evenings. All I had to do was fill in the afternoons. I could take them to the CN Tower and the downtown ethnic areas one day and maybe spend the next day in Woodbridge, the new Little-burb-Italy. Though I wasn't too crazy about opera, I hadn't been to a Leafs game in ages—and these seats would be a prized possession for any fan.

When I went upstairs to give the guys the news, Francesco was kneeling beside the bed and Nick was still freshening up in the bathroom.

"What're you doing?" I asked Francesco.

"Praying."

"Well, your prayers have been answered. We're going to see a spectacle tonight the likes of which you've never seen or will ever see again in your whole life."

He gave me his little foolish grin. "A spectacle? What kind of spectacle?"

"Have you ever heard of hockey, a game played on ice?"

"No."

"What part of Italy are you from?"

"Umbria."

I could only shake my head. Being what it geographically was—a long stretch from the Alps almost to the tip of North Africa—Italy was a study in contrast, as if the yin and the yang had been slipped into a long tight boot in the middle of the sea.

I knocked on the bathroom door and told Nick to put on some casual clothes. We were going to take the subway into town, see a hockey game, and eat at the game.

Since it was quite chilly outside, I told Francesco to wear an extra sweater underneath his hoodie and gave Nick my fashionable black leather jacket, which he greatly admired. I drove them to the end of the east-west line, left the car in the parking lot, and led them to the subway station.

"I'm not going to go out of character and go by taxi," I told them. "This is how I would do it and you guys can get the experience of riding on the subway."

They were basically quiet during the subway ride, observing the people entering and leaving the car.

"I've never seen such a wide diversity of people," Nick said at one point.

"This city is supposed to be the most ethnically diverse city in the world," I said. "What part of Italy are you from?"

"*Firenze.*"

"Ah, Florence," I said. "The Boboli, the Palazzo Vecchio, the Duomo, the David."

"David is such a handsome boy. You'd never know the strap is behind his back, the stone hidden in his hand."

"That's where I learned that art is longer-lasting than pop culture."

"And I'm here to learn as well as to make some money, of course. How is it possible, for example, to govern such a wide variety of people? How can they ever agree on anything?"

I had to pause. Was he putting me on?

I tried to explain our system of government, based on the British model and influenced by the American. He shook his head.

"In my homeland we can't agree on anything," he said. "We have been too influenced and kept infantile by the Church and the pontiff. And we are too emotional and diverse to be rational like the British, who have calmer heads. The only thing that can save the Republic is a strong leader, a saviour, someone who's willing to do whatever is necessary for the good of the country, or we will never extricate ourselves from our troubles. There's more power in being feared and respected than in being loved or hated, wouldn't you agree?"

At this point, however, our attention was distracted by Francesco, who had gone over to the other side of the car to sit with this homeless-looking guy who had entered the subway a few stops back. The guy reeked of cat piss and alcohol. He was middle-aged, bearded and coarse, in a torn and soiled parka, with unlaced overlarge sneakers clearly not his own, and drooling at the mouth. Francesco was trying to talk to him in his broken English and the homeless guy was looking for a handout and getting belligerent.

"Francesco," I called out to him. "Come back here. He's not in his right mind."

"I do not have any money," Francesco said above the sound of the subway. "Do you have any money?"

"You think you will solve his problems by giving him money?" Nick said with a sneer.

The old guy had enough wits about him, however, to understand Nick's tone. He got up and snarled like a deranged wolf, making as if to attack us. Francesco quickly grabbed his hand.

"No, no, brother," Francesco said. "We will give you some money. Please, Marco."

I quickly took out my wallet and gave him a twenty. Francesco put the bill in the guy's palm, closed it in a loving fashion, and kissed his hand. The guy's eyes opened wide, as if he had no idea whether to swat him or embrace him.

"Brother, we are the same," Francesco said to the homeless guy. "*Tutti i soldi sono sporchi*. All money is dirty."

"Then the Vatican must be the dirtiest place of all," Nick said, laughing.

Seeing he had a twenty in his hand, the homeless guy quickly got out at the next stop, probably thinking we might change our minds.

Afterwards, I kept the two of them secularly next to me as the train brought us into the bowels of the city.

We got off at Union Station and followed the fans in their Leafs jerseys streaming through the station to the short tunnel to the arena. The box office area outside the gates was packed. I managed to get the VIP tickets very quickly, however. The concourse inside was a mass of humanity. People were congregated at the concession stands, the bars, the restaurants, and at the TV screens. It was very colourful and noisy.

We went through the VIP entrance and took the elevator up to the box seats, high up over the penalty box. A hostess ushered us into the area. The enclosed space had a counter and stools facing the ice, a few tables, a TV screen on the wall, and a row of chairs. It could've easily accommodated more people.

Just before the start of the game the arena was dimly lit, with spotlights flooding the ice surface, where the Zambonis were making the final flood. Booming music ratcheted up the anticipation. The huge scoreboard was showing ads for various products. The banners of the great Leafs from the past and of the championship years hung from the rafters like icons of the glory years. We could've been in a cathedral, the atmosphere of the sights and

---

sounds like an intense ritual to our country's most intense faith.

Nick was all excited.

"It is like the Coliseum, no?" he said. "What is that white substance with all the markings?"

"You mean the ice?"

"*Certo*, but it's not cold."

I had to smile. At least they were so awe-struck by the strangeness of the place they weren't at each other's throats. Francesco was clearly out of his element, unused to the large arena filled with boisterous fans. And when the players came out, filing onto the ice and skating crisply through their paces in their colourful gear, with the thunderous noise and the ice surface suddenly exploding into a sea of bright light, he reared back as if blind-sided.

As they played the American and Canadian national anthems, Nick and I stood in solemn attention, while Francesco was still trying to feel comfortable in such a strange milieu.

Once the game started, however, I had to explain a few rules—and it wasn't easy by a long shot. I used the analogy with soccer, of course, and they got that, but the puck moved so quickly, the skaters so big and fast, the ice surface much smaller, that the two Italians couldn't keep up to the pace. And whenever there was a collision against the boards, the sound resounding through the arena, the fans whooping it up, the two guys reared as if hit themselves.

"Why is bumping allowed?" Francesco said.

"It's part of the game," I said.

"It's part of life," Nick said.

Francesco shook his head. "No. It doesn't have to be."

"*Ought* and *is* are two different things, *imbecille*."

"I know, brother. But we can make the present *is* into a different *is*, can't we?"

"Boys," I said. "Let's watch the game and not argue, OK."

A couple of guys brought over a rolling counter with a buffet of main courses on hot plates. We were also given a choice of drinks.

"Take anything you want," I said. "It's compliments of the CBC."

"You mean it's charity?" Francesco said.

"Well, I don't know about charity. Maybe. Sort of."

"In our Order we have to make vows of poverty," he said. "We cannot eat at good restaurants. But we can accept the occasional charitable donation."

"This is not a charitable donation, my tonsure-brained friend," Nick said. "This is being treated with respect. Why, I have dinned in some of the best restaurants in Lyons and Paris and Rome and Venice."

"Man does not live by bread alone, brother."

"No, he lives by the food of the gods, cooked by some of the best chefs in the world."

Francesco smiled and nodded.

Nick and I chose the chicken and vegetables and ordered a bottle of wine. Francesco had the pasta *con pesto* and a bottle of water.

Everything was going well enough till the second period. We were sitting on the seats in front of the counter. The two Italians weren't too impressed with the game. The huge screens on the scoreboard seemed more of an attraction than the play on the ice. At one point the star offensive player for the Leafs went into the corner to retrieve the puck and was slammed into the boards with a resounding thud. He crumpled to the ice and had to be helped to the bench. On the next shift, the two opposing enforcers, both huge and mean-looking guys, skated ominously to the face-off circle at our end of the ice, right underneath us. Before the puck was dropped, the gloves flew off, and they squared off for a fight. The fans rose in thunderous approval, screaming for blood.

"The gladiators are finally at it," Nick said, standing up and clapping.

Francesco, however, didn't like it. He refused to get up, trembling in his chair like a defenceless bird.

I must admit, I was at two minds. While I stood up between them and watched the combat, I knew it was dastardly of me to be excited. The fight had nothing to do with the game. The two guys would get a few scratches and a bloody nose, perhaps, and penalties, and that would be it. In this fight, however, the opposing goon was hit flush in the face with a hard right hand and went down unconscious, his face hitting the ice in a bad angle. Blood immediately soaked onto the glaring ice in a sickening way. The arena fell silent as the body lay unconscious. What had been an exciting spectacle had now been injected with hard dose of reality. The players from both sides commiserated. The medics came out with a stretcher.

The TV screens on the scoreboard showed the replay repeatedly in slow motion. Our own TV screen to the side of us showed the same replay.

And when I looked to check Francesco's reaction, he wasn't there anymore. He had slipped away unnoticed.

"You stay here," I told Nick, like an anxious parent. "I have to find him quick or the vultures will get him."

"You are worried over nothing," he said. "We had a *Frate* like him in Florence who seemed helpless but was as ruthless as they come. You have to be a lion and a fox, but those who've learned to use the fox survive the best. And if there's one thing you can bet on, it's that appearances are always deceiving."

I dashed out of the VIP area to the regular concourse in back of us. A few people in Leafs sweaters were milling about, but no sign of Francesco. I asked a few of them, and the guys who worked the concessions, if they had seen a guy in a hoodie with a tonsure. No one knew what a tonsure was. Someone did tell me, however, that this Italian-sounding guy had asked about the washrooms. I found him in the washroom taking a leak.

"Hey, Francesco," I said, after a big sigh, "you scared the shit out of me. I thought you had left the arena."

"No, no," he said, with a big smile, "I have to relieve Brother Bladder. But I do not like this game called hockey. I will stay out here. You go back and watch the game."

"But I don't want to leave you alone."

"*Non ti preoccupare.* I will do some mingling."

"What do you mean by mingling?"

"Ah, you know. Listen, talk, sing. With the poor."

"I don't think you'll find any poor here," I said.

"Oh, there are always those who are poor in heart, Brother Marco."

He smiled at me in such a curious way I couldn't contradict him.

During the third period I went back to the concourse

and found him sitting in a bar area with a small group of fans who were laughing and carrying on as if teasing him. But he seemed to be having as much fun as they were. They were trying to get him to drink beer and he was trying to extol the virtues of poverty. The second time I went back they were all singing *The Hockey Song* by Stompin' Tom Connors, which was playing with subtitles over the monitors. Francesco's voice rose over the others in glee, even though I suspected he didn't know what the words meant.

After the game, as we were going down the elevator, a few of the VIPs asked about Francesco's tonsure. While he was explaining to the bemused fans, Nick leaned close to my ear.

"Maybe later we can put the *Frate* to bed and you and I can go to a whorehouse. I'm suffering from conjugal famine at the moment and nothing would please me more than sampling the courtesans in this country."

I could only stare at him, unsure if I had understood him properly.

During the subway ride back we sat side by side. Nick couldn't stop criticizing the buffet food we had at the game. He called it peasant's food and nothing like what he was used to in Florence, where everything was prepared with artistic flourish. The hockey food, as he called it, was more fitting for the third circle of the Inferno, where Cerberus, the three-headed dog, was quieted with scraps of earth, *pasto morde*, tossed from Virgil's hands.

"Ah, pasta al Dante," I said.

"There is Ovid, Virgil, Boccaccio, and above all ... Dante," Nick said.

"Who is Dante?" Francesco said.

"An Italian who doesn't know Dante is like pasta without sauce."

"Brother Niccolò, you are a very knowledgeable man with words, and I praise you, but there's no sweeter sound than birds chirping in the morning or the roar of the mighty wind whistling through the leaves in the evening. I can look at the sun and be filled with its splendour. Or the glow of the moon on a cloudless night and feel the richest man on earth."

Francesco's expression became almost sublime, as he recalled these experiences, but Nick wasn't impressed in the least.

"What hooey," he said, shrugging. "I've caught thrushes in my time and know the sound of birds when they know they're about to become food."

"I can't believe you would kill a Brother Bird."

"Now, boys," I raised my hand, feeling a little light-headed from the wine. "Let's try to be good, eh? You guys can be a pain in the ass, but, what the hell, you're paisans and keep me on my toes."

We were silent the rest of the ride.

I was driving them back to my place when I broke the silence.

"Whatta you guys wanna do tomorrow? We'll go to the opera in the evening, but we gotta fill in the afternoon."

"I'd like to see how the legislature works," Nick said.

"It's Sunday. All government buildings are closed. You can go with Allen on Monday."

"I will go to Mass in the morning," Francesco said. "Afterwards I'd like to visit the lepers."

"Lepers? You gotta be kidding. There are no lepers."

"Where do you keep your sick and shunned, then?"

"In old age and nursing homes. There's one just up the street from my place."

"OK, then. After Mass I will go and visit the old and infirm in the old age home. Afterwards, however, I want to be out in the country."

"We could drive to Niagara Falls. You guys have heard of Niagara Falls, haven't you? It would take a little over an hour. Or we could go up to Woodbridge, the Italian area."

"On Sundays I enjoy the outdoors," Nick said. "I used to ride through the Tuscan countryside to get the lay of the land in case of an invasion and visit some of the militia people who work on the farms. I've come to like life on the farm and spending the day with my family."

As it turned out, Sunday was a partly cloudy and a mild day. Nick spent the morning working on his writing in his room upstairs, while Francesco went to Mass at the church a block away. After I did my own writing, I waited for Francesco and brought him to the old age home just up the street. It was a modern brick facility, one storey, and actually called a retirement home and not for those who were seriously ill. Fortunately for us, a sign outside said it was welcoming walk-in tours. When we went through the front door we were in small waiting area, overlooking the dining room. A number of white-headed old men and women were seated at their tables, with their walkers parked beside them, everyone conversing in low tones. The smell, a combination of unaired old clothes and boiled cabbage, was hardly conducive to good cheer.

One of the staff came up to us immediately and said

the walk-in tours hadn't started yet. I explained, however, that Francesco was a visiting friar from Italy and was on a tight schedule. The staff person was a brown-skinned girl in her late-twenties, slim and attractive in her light blue uniform, her name tag indicating a Jessica. She said to sit down and wait a while and she'd show us around.

While we were sitting on the waiting chairs, however, Francesco simply got up and beckoned me to follow. We walked over to the dining area and sat down at a table with a couple of residents who were eating their lunch. One was a thin wizened old guy who must've been in his late seventies, with a shaved head and rheumy eyes, dressed in an old plaid shirt and denims. The other was a woman with a full head of white hair sticking up and in a white housecoat who looked to be in her mid-seventies.

I introduced Francesco and asked if we could sit with them while waiting for our tour.

"Suit yourself," the guy said. "It's a free country. I'm Saul and this is Iris."

"Can we do anything to help you, eh?" Francesco said in his best Canadian.

"Like what?" Saul said.

"Would you recommend this place?" I asked him.

"It all depends on your frame of reference," he said with a shrug.

"Don't mind him," Iris said. "They try to do their best. It isn't easy with our conditions."

"One day at a time, right?" Saul said with a tight smile.

Francesco was listening intently and smiling. When he heard the last comment and my translation, he broke out in laughter.

"*Sì, sì*, brother and sister. May the peace of each day be upon you."

"Who is this guy?" Saul asked me.

"I am your brother," Francesco said.

"I don't think so."

They went on to have a conversation of sorts, with Francesco speaking in broken Canadianese and looking to me to translate the more difficult parts, but Saul wasn't having any of it. The more Francesco spoke, the more Saul became irritated. The other residents were looking at us, sensing something was brewing.

Finally Francesco took Saul's hand and stroked it as he would a child's.

"We will do anything we can to help you, Brother Saul," he said. "Just give us the word."

"I don't need your help," Saul said, pulling his hand away. "I've been a self-supporting guy all my life. That's the point about this place. It's an indignity to be dependent on others."

"No, no, brother Saul. To be dependent is the greatest joy. To serve Brother Death and Lady Poverty is beyond compare."

I wasn't sure I had translated accurately. Nevertheless, we all looked at Francesco who had a beatific smile on his face. But the comment only made Saul so angry he told us to leave.

When I tried to explain to Nick what had happened at the retirement home, he had a big laugh. We were alone in the kitchen waiting for Francesco.

"Good for the old guy," he said. "*Virtù* in the form of courage, strength, honour, and dignity was prized in the

Roman Republic, which made it strong enough to conquer the whole world. Till the prelates came along and softened us so much into mamma-boys we virtually opened all our gates to the foreign invaders. Has there ever been an Italian army strong enough to defend its borders? The whole world mocks us for our weaknesses."

He looked so furious I didn't want to counter him.

"But why is that the case?" I said.

"Because we don't have the stomach to do what has to be done."

"Isn't it better to be a lover than a fighter?"

He made a scoffing sound, and flipped his hand at me as if addressing a child. "I am a lover, my friend. And I've been in prison and tortured by a *strappado*. And I tell you that we can never have the opportunity to be lovers unless we fight first for our piece of land. There would never have been a Jesus if not for a Moses and a Joshua and a David first, fighters all of them. Even *Il Signore* of the Bible is a warrior-tyrant, brooking no rivals."

I pondered over Nick's words as I drove them west along the QEW to the far edges of Mississauga. He was sitting beside me, while Francesco sat in the back. We were heading for an apple picking farm, since they both wanted to be in the countryside on that mild late October day. I very much doubted Francesco could sit through the opulent production of *Turandot*, so this could be our last time together as a threesome.

The apple farm was in a remote area off the highway. The owner had set up a tent in between the main house, which was still in use, and the old teetering barn that was literally falling apart. Inside the tent were bushels and bags of the various types of apples grown, with the prices if you picked your own.

I paid for three large bags and we got on the back of a flat-back cart pulled by a huge work horse and driven by a young man who introduced himself as Billy, the son of the owner. Billy, in denims and an old sweater, with a shock of red hair, seemed a personable lad. Seated with us were two other couples, with their children, all kids between ten and five. Billy gave us the particulars on the various types of apples.

"If you kids can't reach the apples," he told them, "you can't climb the trees, eh, because it's too dangerous and we don't have apple-picking insurance for kids. So you have to get your parents to use the ladders."

"I assume you have apple-picking insurance for parents who climb ladders, right?" one of the fathers said with a straight face.

"Sure do," Billy said. "Apples are the greatest fruit in the world. Some people even say that Eve ate the apple in the Garden because she was braver than Adam."

"I don't get it," the father said.

"Well, no apple-labour, no apple-pie."

The parents groaned.

Francesco, sitting beside a couple of the kids — with their feet dangling from the edge of the cart — was playing foot-tag with them, kicking their feet and avoiding their frantic efforts to kick his. Nick was sitting back with his hands on the bed of the cart and letting the autumn sun shine on his face.

After Nick asked me to translate the joke, he raised his hand.

"If I may give a different interpretation," Nick said. "The problem with Adamo is that he let Eva, *Fortuna*, sway his hand. He should have beaten her down with a stick."

This went over like a lead balloon. The mothers looked at him as if he were a wife-beater. As the horse slowly walked through the apple groves, the mothers took their children away from Francesco, looking at him askance.

"They're just off the boat," I said with a shrug.

I motioned to the boys. We jumped off the cart and split up amongst the different apple groves. I preferred Cortland apples, hard and tart and juicy. Francesco went towards the Golden Delicious, while Nick fancied the Macs. Plenty of apples were rotting on the ground. We could take the various ladders to any tree. By this late date we had to climb virtually to the top of the gnarly trees, which, fortunately, weren't that high.

Later, when I had my bag full, I was looking for the boys when I heard a couple of Italian voices in a heated exchange coming from the top of a tree. Apparently they had put their ladders on the same tree, climbed up, and were bobbing for the remaining apples.

"Boys, get down from outa there!" I yelled up to them.

They both slowly descended. Francesco had a silly grin on his face. Nick was scowling, all incensed.

"I can't leave you guys for a minute," I said. "You're setting a bad example for the kids, I'll tell you."

"I was only playing," Francesco said. "Brother Nicolino takes things way too seriously, eh. Here, take all my apples, if you want them."

"I don't want your apples," Nick said.

"They are not mine."

"Whose are they, then?" I asked him.

"They belong to the farmer whose land we stand on," Nick said. "He paid for the land, went through the labour of growing the apples, and now should receive his just rewards in the form of payment."

Francesco shook his head, the grin even wider. "No, no, brother Nicolino. The farmer is just taking care of the land and the trees growing on it for the moment. In the end, no one owns the land or the apples."

"In your fantasy world maybe," Nick said.

"Stop it," I said. "Save your arguments for the show tomorrow, OK."

"Can you imagine this guy ever governing a country," he said to me, raising his chin. "Why, he'd give the whole country away."

"Yes," Francesco said.

"And what about the people who don't believe as you believe? The other religions. Are they as good and right as you are?"

"I don't know about the other beliefs. They can believe whatever they want. I just follow in the footsteps of the Saviour. In Him I find my strength."

"And if these other people who don't believe in the Saviour were to attack you and do you harm, what would you do, huh? Would you turn the other cheek and let them kill you?"

Francesco gave him a big smile. "No, I wouldn't turn my cheek. I'd look them in the eye and tell them they had nothing to take from me—even my life."

At that, Nick gave Francesco a straight right hand that

caught him flush in the nose. Francesco went down, scattering his bag of apples.

I couldn't believe what I had just seen. My first impulse was to help Francesco up, but I could see he didn't need any help. After a few seconds of pain and dismay, the smile returned to his face. He didn't seem angry in the least, as if he had experienced such attacks before and was well used to them.

Indeed, what happened next was even more astounding.

Francesco, his nose obviously broken and battered and streaming with blood, got up and opened his arms and made as if to hug Nick. But Nick stepped back, his face aghast, cursed a few times in Italian, and hurried back to the parking lot.

I gave Francesco a couple of Kleenex. He thanked me and wiped his nose.

"It is like the hockey game, eh?" he said, laughing.

We picked up the apples and walked in silence back to the car.

The drive back to my place wasn't easy, I have to admit. No one made a sound in the car. When we got back, Nick immediately went to his room upstairs and closed the door. Francesco's nose was twisted a bit. His right eye got blue and puffy. I ordered him to go lie down on the sofa in the living room and gave him a frozen liquid bag I had in the freezer.

"Allen is going to kill me when he finds out," I told him. "I was supposed to keep you guys out of trouble. Now you're not even fit for the cameras."

"*Non ti preoccupare*," Francesco said. "It wasn't your

fault. It was my fault. My vanity got the better of me. I got too full of my own pride and pride knocked me on my *culo*."

Under the circumstances I thought it prudent not to go and see *Turandot* that night. Francesco and I spent a quiet evening watching the only Italian movie I owned. Actually it was an old black and white Spanish movie that had been dubbed into Italian that I had seen as a kid and that had greatly influenced me. I had picked up a DVD copy on my last visit to Italy. *Marcelino, pan e vino*. Francesco got a big kick out of it. He had never seen it. It was about a baby who's left on the doorstep of a monastery and raised by these monks who treat the kid as their own child. The kid, however, is very mischievous and plays all sorts of pranks on the monks to amuse himself. Francesco laughed his head off at the pranks.

When it came time to eat, I made some pasta. My wife had taught me how to make a whole pot of meat sauce and then freeze it in smaller plastic containers for future use. When Francesco asked me about my wife, I told him she was a bit like him. When I first got to know her she had this huge candle in the shape of an apple in her apartment that emitted a delicious scent. Apples, I told him, were just as good old as new. After we finished our pasta, I called Nick down to eat his portion. Nick was still tight-lipped and didn't speak to Francesco. He ate alone in the kitchen, while we waited around the corner in the living room.

Allen drove over the next morning to pick up his two Italians. When he saw Francesco's black and blue face, he glared at me.

"No, no, it is not his fault," Francesco said. "It was an accident. Marco has been a great host. Hasn't he, Nick?"

Nick just gave a grunt.

Francesco put his sack in the trunk and gave me a big hug. "You must come and see me the next time you are in Italy," he said. "I will show you around the Umbrian countryside at Cannara and we will look at the birds and see how they have perfect joy."

He got into the back of the car.

I shook Nick's hand and wished him luck on the show.

"To love Francesco is not enough," he said with a cold stare.

Before I had time to respond, his stare suddenly changed into a cagey smile, as if he had to suppress more than he could reveal.

He got into the front seat. As they drove away, I gave out a long sigh of relief, as if a great weight had been lifted from my shoulders.

Johnny Reno
Does Manhattan

After deplaning at the Newark airport with his backpack and walking stick, Johnny headed straight for the monorail which took him to the Amtrak station. From there it was a short ride into Penn Station where he bought a Metropass for his stay in New York in the middle of October. He was operating on a tight budget, after all, which had forced him to book a room at a derelict hotel in lower Midtown.

Not one person recognized him on the subway. He could've been totally invisible. These days, he well knew, one had to be on American TV or in the movies or hit it big in the music industry to achieve world-wide celebrity-status. Though he had been on the air for years, it was only a small renovation show on the *Home Network* in Canada, a show which had a miniscule rating in an already overloaded market. Plus, he had been syndicated in a few Canadian newspapers. But who in the States watched Canadian TV, let alone read Canadian newspapers? Who in the States knew about Canada period?

Yes, he was an unknown quantity in the biggest English-speaking market in the world, and he'd have to do something about that.

As Johnny regarded the other passengers, he ran his fingers over the intricate patterns he had made himself on his walking stick. It was rough and coarse, with no handle, a solid rod of maple that had a delicious resin-y odour and could be used for more than one function.

There was something to be said for anonymity, nay, even invisibility. He could go anywhere and not be hassled by autograph seekers, gawkers, and generally despicable media types who hounded the celebs beyond endurance. He didn't have to put on his public face, could just be himself, and observe the world as any Joe Blow, which was all right with him, since he had to admit he didn't exactly blend into the crowd.

He looked a little awkward, to say the least. Not exactly cutesy, let's say, with his over-bite and preponderance of facial hair and whiskers. Nevertheless, he was wearing his colourful Hudson's Bay jacket and a new pair of overalls, which gave him—he gathered, at least—the appearance of a hard-working and no-nonsense guy.

Johnny Reno, they called him, a name that was more than just an image. His show featured all types of renovations. They did structural carpentry, flooring, plumbing, and electrical wiring, repaired roofs and decks, installed skylights, windows and doors, along with dry-wall—in general did anything needed to improve the home, inside and outside. One time they had transformed an adjacent garage into a nursery room. His speciality, however, was wood.

He got off at 23rd and Eighth and walked the short distance to the Chelsea, where he quickly checked in. The place was old and run down. Casper had recommended it, saying a lot of famous people of the past had stayed here, including Mark Twain and Dylan Thomas and Popeye. He remembered it, however, solely for an old eighties movie of *Sid and Nancy*, who had drugged their way into oblivion. His room was spare, to say the least. It had an old TV set and no Internet connection. The lighting was so dim it was almost non-existent, creating a grainy darkness that suited his nocturnal instincts. Yes, the darkness reminded him of the inside of some of his lodgings back in Canada.

Since the AA Conference would start on Monday morning, he had the rest of Saturday and the whole of Sunday to explore Manhattan.

After he had a quick wade in the rusty bathroom, he walked all the way up to Times Square and bought a last-minute seat to a Broadway Show that night. He sat in the plush old seats of the theatre being entertained by these human beings dressed as cats and singing their lungs out. The next day, after seeing the Trade Centre site, he visited MoMA and saw all the great art-works of the modern era, some of which he could only shake his head at. The whole Warhol thing was beyond him, for one. He could under-stand Duchamp doing what he did, turning a urinal upside down, but Warhol had just been a window-dresser, as far as he was concerned. A mamma's boy who hung around with the rich and famous, like an obsequious mutt, snap-ping their pictures and appearing meta-blasé.

Which was all right with him, because he had to get his teeth into the postmodern and apocalyptic sensibility, in order to do his job adequately. It wasn't just a matter of doing woodwork and renovating homes. He had to aid in the restoration of lives. On Tuesday he'd deliver his paper at the Conférence and set their ears back, with his own take on the modern reno mind-set. Guests were coming from all over North America to attend this Colloquium. And it was out of bounds to the Pixar People. Strictly the old AA crowd.

Since Sunday was a pleasant overcast day, he decided to spend the afternoon in Central Park, wading in the pond, having his lunch, and spending a few hours at the Metropolitan Museum. Later he took the subway back and stopped at the Disney Store close to Times Square, where he could only hang his head in shame at the blatant commercialism.

By Monday morning he was ready for the Conference and some serious interchange with the other AA guests. He put on his signature tool belt over his overalls, with his Hudson Bay jacket, grabbed his walking stick, and took the subway up to Columbia University on the Upper West Side. Once he got away from Broadway and through the campus gate it was as if he were in a different world. Like an oasis of learning hidden in the desert of the city. The central square was filled with students lounging about, some on the grass, some on the surrounding walkways, and on the steps beside the iconic statue of Alma Mater.

After asking a few students, he found the venue of the conference in a large-sized auditorium in the School of the Arts. The place was filling up fast, with guests of all types and stripes streaming in. He spotted some of the old timers like Fritz and Felix, Tom and Jerry, Yogi and Alvin, as well as a few newer faces he didn't know. As he was looking for a free seat, someone came up to him and gave him a big smile.

"If it isn't Johnny Reno," she said. "Aka, the Woodman."

As he was trying to place her, he noticed she was a knockout, with the same overbite as him, but with smooth long-flowing dark hair, long lashes, and big beautiful eyes, emitting a wonderful scent that went right through him.

"I'm Candace Castor of *Divine Interiors*. The show that transforms any old place into a divine space."

He had seen the show a few times. Candace met with the owners of a crappy interior—a basement rec room, a bedroom, a condo living room, whatever—and discussed their plans for the reno. Then she, with her skilled team of carpenters and electricians and handymen, would do the makeover. It was the familiar *before* and *after* thing, the typical template for all these shows. Which was all right with him, sure, but he was after bigger game.

"Yeah, I've seen you," he said. "You're an interior decorator, right?"

"Excuse me, but more of an architect of space and colour, the exterior display to the interior landscape. It's a pleasure to meet the great Johnny Reno, the master-builder, the guy who can transform an eye-sore into an eye-candy."

She had an aggressively charming aspect to her he found refreshing against his own dour and withdrawn disposition.

"C'mon, let's find a seat before all the animals get in," she said. "This space can use some work, I'll tell you. Isn't it just hideous?"

He hadn't counted on meeting anyone else from

Canada, but maybe this would be a godsend, get his focus off his paper, give him the requisite lightness of being to deliver it with aplomb instead of pedantic solemnity.

"Where're you staying?" she said, after they found seats about half-way up.

He gave her the particulars. She herself was staying at a swanky hotel on Central Park South. An interior designer, after all, couldn't stay in a pigsty, she said, casting an aspersion he didn't find agreeable. As she went over her flight to JFK and problems with her luggage, he cased the venue. The acoustics were fairly good. A large screen came down automatically from the ceiling. A lectern was set up on the left side, along with a table and a mic in the middle. The speaker could use either position. The table had a computer and PowerPoint.

"I saw your name on the list of speakers," she was saying, taking out her program. "Canada's own Johnny Reno is going to give the Americans a piece of their own wood."

"Please. It's not such a big deal. They probably won't even pay that much attention."

"C'mon, I don't wanna hear that Canadian inferiority stuff. You're Johnny Reno, the Woodman. You can re-do anything. Why, you're an iconic image, for god's sake."

"Sure, a big fish in a little pond."

"There you go." She shook her head and gave out a laugh. "You gotta be more positive, Johnny. We're in the Big Apple now. We're all winners here."

A big wheel at the university, some assistant to the President, came out and opened the proceedings. He was in an expensive suit and groomed to perfection. The university was at the forefront of research in so many fields, he said, it had won as many pennants as the Yankees. The audience groaned. He mentioned physics and the Higgs Boson, with a list of achievements in the fields of Math and Psychology and the philosophy of jurisprudence. Finally he mentioned the School of the Arts and the Sundance. A university couldn't survive on the serious sciences alone, he said. It had to have some art and lightness of being. And it was so proud, he said, to sponsor this Colloquium, one in which such world-renowned artists and Tooners and celluloid celebs had distinguished themselves in their field.

Candace jabbed him in the ribs and gave him a big smile.

The first speaker walked up to the stage and stood at the lectern with his sheaf of papers. He was in a blue sailor jacket and a white hat, easily recognizable in his signature attire. What most people didn't know, however, was that he was an ornithologist on the side, a guy who had tracked every manner of rare species from the Amazon to the Gobi. Johnny had seen a few of his movies and docs. Wherever he went, he never failed to get into disputes and arguments and scrapes with about everyone he met, including his own family.

"Hello," he said. "My name is Don and I'm an AA."

The audience stood up and gave him a standing ovation. Don politely bowed and raised his four-fingered hand for silence. Today he was going to speak about the effects of global warming on bird migrations, he said.

The only problem, as Johnny and the rest of the audience saw immediately, was that Don wasn't easy to follow. His mouth, being large and flat, made him slur his words so much they came out in a rasp rather than anything resembling precise speech. Johnny tuned his ears as much as possible to make out the gist of Don's paper. The first part was definitely about bird migrations and how they were affected by climate change. Some birds, for example, followed their ancestral migratory patterns, some adapted, and some ran into a brick wall. Many of the lakes and ponds and marshes had simply evaporated. How long would it take for them to lose many species which fed on insects and the like? Would it cause plagues? And more to the point, Don said, many of the birds were starting to be affected by video games, a phenomenon which was causing them to lose their instinctive radar during their migratory paths.

Johnny wasn't sure if he had heard right.

Video games, Don said, were sapping the life blood of the newer generation. His own son, for example, was so into video games he had lost all sense of radar reality. One day, he'd catch him pretending he was a terrorist, shooting up a whole city. The next day he'd be an ancient knight in armour battling evil dragons. And worse of all, he could be a Navy Seal in full battle dress, with a huge assault rifle, fighting the enemy in foreign states. And every time he tried to get him to go out and enjoy the outdoors, go for a dip in the pond, like, c'mon, that's what they were supposed to do, his son would raise a ruckus. You'd never think such a cute kid with his beanie hat and big blue eyes could be transformed into a vidiot. Why, if he were lost he'd never find his way home. It was a shame, Don said. A quacking shame.

At the beginning of the Q & A, however, the friendly antagonist and cutely whiskered feline, Sly, begged to disagree with Don about bird migrations in general and the effects of video games on the young. Having studied the bird species very carefully himself, being an aficionado and lifelong predator, he knew not a few caged feather-brains, who, though they looked all innocent and helpless, could make his life a living hell. A deep frown appeared over Don's brow and a spirited dispute followed. Sly wasn't exactly a model of precise diction himself, being an egregious lisper. It was like listening to a couple of debaters with speech impediments.

The next speaker drew an even bigger ovation. He was about the oddest looking creature Johnny had ever seen, a guy with large eyes over two huge buck teeth on a yellow shell-shaped head that was a ringer for the gas station logo. His huge round head fitted into floral shorts from which emerged two skinny legs with black shoes. With his big toothy grin, he looked like an overgrown kid who could lick the world.

"I'm Sam," he said, "and I'm an AA."

"Isn't he a riot?" Candace said.

Sam's paper was about the cynicism and overall mean-spiritedness that had infiltrated the market in the past decade. In a recent movie, he said, a cuddly-looking teddy bear that was supposed to be a blankie for a kid had morphed into a dirty-mouthed and drug-addled sex-fiend for the adult market. In a popular TV show, a family dog, an animal that was the archetypical friend and loyal companion to hominids, was portrayed with even more vices than its owners. In one episode he had taken to drink. In another he had lusted after his owner's wife. And those were just a few examples of how animal loyalty and wholesomeness was degenerating into animal vice. What was the world coming to? In a voice that was pre-pubescent and yet full of worldly wisdom, he said he was overcome with profound sadness at times when he saw other AA members being ridiculed and misused just for a gag or two.

"It's incumbent upon us," Sam said, "to uphold the morals of the planet in general. We're supposed to be the moral exemplars, aren't we? If we don't do it right, how will our audiences ever learn? Whatta you say, folks?"

"Right on, Sammy!" Candace yelled out, raising her fist.

Similar outbursts of approval came from the audience. Johnny could only smile.

"Because I gotta tell you, folks," Sam said, "I don't know how much more the oceans can take. The polar icecaps are melting, the waters are getting more and more toxic, and aquatic life is becoming extinct as we speak. I don't have to tell you that Mother Nature works on a fine balance of interconnecting pieces. Take away one piece and the whole thing falls."

"It takes a village, right?" someone yelled out from the audience, causing a ripple of uneasy laughter.

Sam stopped his train of thought, brought his four-fingered hand up to his crustaceous temple and gave the suggestion some serious consideration. Everyone in the audience was on the edge of their seats.

"This is no time for levity, folks," he said. "I've been around long enough to know that times are changing. Marine life is in deep danger. The beaches have become veritable graveyards. Mark my words, in the not too distant future no beach will be safe for anyone, let alone the ones like us who make them a home."

He went on to show some slides on his PowerPoint of oil spills and oil-drilling disasters, with the beaches covered in black slime, the birds and fish struggling in the cesspit of oil, the death and destruction for miles and miles. No one was laughing then.

"It's up to us," Sam said into the mic, "to raise the consciousness of the kids out there. They'll listen to us if we spread the message in the right way. It's just not a commercial thing anymore. We have to be more ecologically conscious, even to the point of being eco-saboteurs. The kids are the only ones who can change things around."

His serious demcanour never left his face as he picked up the mic, stepped onto the middle of the stage in front of the screen, and nodded to the sound man on his right. The theatre was filled with the pounding beat of *We Are the World*.

And as he sang *we are the world, we are the children*, a number of ushers rushed up the theatre steps and distributed BBQ lighters. The theatre lights were dimmed. Johnny took his and pulled the trigger. Soon the people in the audience were swaying back and forth with the lighters raised above their heads and singing along with Sam.

Johnny couldn't deny that he was moved. It was a truly inspirational moment. All the conference members seemed joined as one in their commitment to the lives of those they served, the kids of the future. Every so often the voice of a noted Tooner would rise above the others and give his or her rendition of the popular song. Johnny could make out the familiar voices of the great Tooners from yesteryear. And then, about halfway through, one distinct voice rose above the others. Everyone knew that voice. It was unmistakable.

And when the spotlight shone on the Big M himself—the rodent who had started it all, the cutest rodent you'd ever want to see, with the big black ears, the pert nose, the wide gin, and the white gloves—the audience went wild.

Now they were truly united. No one was too big or too small to be left out of their legacy. They would give back. They would help save the world in spite of itself, Johnny knew. Maybe it was a bit self-referential and paradoxical, but it wasn't just up to the hominids who created the cels and the digital. The Man had screwed up every thing he touched.

Later that night he told Candace how inspired he had been by the song. They were having dinner at an Italian restaurant on Broadway, opposite the Lincoln Centre. It was around nine. They were seated at a small table beside the bare bricks, with pictures of Venice and Florence and Rome hanging at eye level angles. Above their heads, standing on end, were grimy bottles of wine. They had made their order and were waiting.

"That was great," he told Candace. "Having the Bit M show up like that, so unexpected and yet so powerful. It was the finish on the wood."

"Call me Candy," she said, fluttering her big eyes and giving him a smile.

"I was at two minds about my paper, but I'm ready now. More importantly, however, I think they'll be ready to hear it."

"What's it about?" she said, looking into his eyes.

He paused and held eye contact. He had to admit he was attracted. Her large luminous eyes. Her lustrous hair and pelt. Her wonderful scent. It was affecting him. The only thing, he couldn't start another family right now. He had his show and his career.

He gave her a vague answer and asked her about the interior of the restaurant, which had the ambiance of a wine cellar in an old villa. She didn't particularly like it, however. To her it was hideous, commonplace, and lacking in imagination. She knew exactly what she'd do to improve it. She couldn't help it, she said. Everywhere she went, she was doing the show, looking at how to improve the space. Wasn't it the same with him?

No, not exactly, he said. He was still out to change the physicality of spaces, sure, but he had experienced a conversion of sorts, and it was now more a matter of changing the mind-set of people who lived in those spaces.

"Pardon me?" she said, looking at him with her big brown eyes.

"We can improve the look of the inside and outside of edifices all we want," he said, "but what does it matter if the interior of the person who's living there is sick?"

She paused and tightened her face. "I hope you don't mean what I think you mean, Johnny. You'd be shaking your stick at the wrong tree. You can't bite the hand that feeds you. Besides, hard-wearing durable vinyl can give the warm rich feel of real wood at times. If it's retro in a bad way, it can become minimalist cool in a blink of an eye."

He had to smile. "Hold it, Candy. I don't like what you said about vinyl. Nothing can replace wood, see. Wood's organic. It has character. It has soul. And if you treat it right, it'll last forever. I don't know if this'll mean anything, but where I'm going you can't follow. What I got to do you can't be any part of. I'm no good at being noble, but it doesn't take much to see that the problems of two little Tooners don't matter a hill of beans in this crazy world."

She laughed. "And love is never having to say you're sorry."

"Are you coming on to me, Candy?"

"You might be flattering yourself. And then again you might be right. It might be that your big toothy grin is starting to turn me on."

"Aren't you married?"

"With a couple of kits, too. But that hasn't stopped me in the past, Johnny. Like the other AA's, I have my public face for the camera, but when Mother Nature calls, we can't fight the estrus cycle."

She blinked a few times with her big dark eyes in that come-hither way he knew so well.

"Well," he said, "let's have our dinner, drink our wine, and see what the night brings."

During the meal, however, his conscience spoke to him loud and clear. How could he engage in a night of debauchery and then deliver his paper the next day with any amount of sincerity? It would be hypocritical. His personal desires had to take a backseat to his new-found responsibilities to his new role. Not only was he a woodworker, a craftsman, an artist, able to carve a masterpiece with his own incisors that could rival the Amati violins, but he was now responsible for the interior wood, with its grains and sap and bark—the interior wood that had to be re-anchored to the earth from which it came. And in order to be such a spiritual craftsman he had to forgo the natural desires of the body. He couldn't be a self-obsessed celeb like the others. His children's future depended on him now, as Sam had said. And not just his own kits, but all kids, no matter what species or nationality or race.

After a few glasses of wine, however, Candy started giving him such lascivious looks he felt the familiar blood flow to his nether regions.

The more he drank the more appealing she looked. He could picture his tenon fitting into her mortise with such smooth strokes his breathing became irregular. He was an animal, after all, as Candy said, and an animal's body had its natural urges. It couldn't go against its nature, no matter what the fantasies of his creators were.

After they split the check, they took a taxi back to Candy's hotel at Central Park South. Now, here was a place he wouldn't shake a stick at. It was a five star all the way, with its marble lobby and chandeliers and ornate décor. No dim lighting here. And, to top it off, she had a deluxe suite that faced the park. Candy was high-end all the way. She wasn't a spendthrift like him. With her looks and popularity in the Canadian market, she was going places.

"So, this is how the other half lives," he said, as he sampled the view twelve floors up. By the lights in the park, he could make out the zoo, the pond, and the walkways. Around the park were the streams of yellow taxicabs, the blood flow of the city.

"Get used to it, Johnny," she said. "This could be all yours one day … if you play it right. Just around the corner is Fifth Avenue, with the most expensive shops in the world. Just up the street on the Upper East Side are maybe a thousand billionaires. This is the Big Apple, boy. If you can make it here … "

He turned and gave her a toothy grin.

"I don't know," he said, shaking his head.

"Tomorrow I'm meeting with a few of the top brass at NBC just down the street. They're going to offer me a deal."

"Really?"

"Isn't this what you always wanted as well? The world stage? The big time?"

"The big money, too, right?"

"No, Johnny, it's not about the money. It's about reaching a wider audience. It's about improving the lives of people with our artistry. It's about a power even more potent than estrus."

"Really?"

She shook her head and gave out a warm laugh. "That's what I like about you, Johnny. You sound just like Sammy. So naïve. So sincere. So sexy."

As she walked seductively to the open bar, she discarded her jacket and top, exposing her alluring pelt.

"What'll you have?"

"I don't know. I may have had a bit too much already. We're AA's, after all."

"Screw the AA's. You and I are more than AA. We're on top of the world now, Johnny. We dictate terms now. I can put in a good word for you tomorrow."

She poured herself a stiff glass of Canadian Rye and downed it in two gulps.

Things were happening a little too fast to suit him. Just this morning he had been in his decrepit room at a rundown hotel, alone with his thoughts about his paper, and now he was with one of the most beautiful creatures in the business on Central Park South. Along the way he had rubbed elbows with some of the greatest AA's in history. It was all going to his head, no doubt, not to mention his groin.

He had to pause a bit and take stock of the situation. Was she making an offer he couldn't refuse? Or was this a test of some sort? He also had to think of his paper tomorrow, not to mention the implications of his actions.

"I don't know," he said. "Sure, I've used power along the way. The router, sander, radial saw, drill press, and moulder. And they work quickly and accurately, I know, but there's too much noise and dust to suit me. I prefer to work the wood in the traditional way of the artisan, with the hands and the natural cutting tools."

"Right on," she said, laughing. "Who needs electrical toys when the old natural tools can work even better?"

"That's just what I'm saying, Candy. We have to be careful of where the Man wants to take us in computer animation and digital. It can be a big trap. We can make the big bucks, but lose all sense of what's right and wrong."

"We're not here to dispute, Johnny, are we?"

"No, no, I'm not disputing. I'm just trying to understand what's happening."

"This is what's happening," she said, removing the last of her clothing and doing a slow pirouette.

There she was. The female in all her glory. The curves, the pelt, the scent. His gonads stood on full alert. He was tempted. All he had to do was walk over and take her. All his natural juices were aching for it.

"Whatta you waiting for, Johnny?" she said. "Aren't you interested?"

"Of course I am."

"Then what's the problem?"

"You wouldn't understand. I've changed. I'm not the old guy you see on TV anymore."

She laughed again, this time with an unmistakable edge. "I understand all right."

"Think whatever you want, but I gotta go. Good-bye, Candy. I've enjoyed the evening immensely, even if we haven't closed it off to your satisfaction."

Outside, on the street, as he walked with his stick to the stairway down to the subway, he had second thoughts about whether he had done the right thing. He could still be up there, in her suite, putting the old tenon in the mortise, giving her wood, doing what he had been born to do. But he wasn't the old Johnny Reno anymore. He wasn't just into woodwork and renovations. He was more than a showman being pulled by the strings of hominids. He was a steward of another set of values now.

The next day he woke up with a clean conscience, had breakfast in a little deli up Eighth Ave., and took the subway up to Columbia, going over his paper.

As he stepped into the auditorium, he felt the buzz. The place was packed. He wasn't sure, however, if it was the right buzz. People were pointing at him and whispering to each other with snide smiles. Sam's clammy mouth was closed at half-mast. Don was quacking incoherently. Over in the top right corner the Big M had hid his face in his hands, as if in lamentation, his big black ears sticking up like a twin cenotaph.

What was the problem? he asked himself. It couldn't be just because he was Canadian and of an unknown quantity. Had he missed something? And then he saw Candy sitting in the front row with a big grin on her face and he realized he was in for a tough morning.

When he was introduced as the first speaker, the audience was hushed. He stepped up to the lectern with his sheaf of papers and looked over the seated AA's.

"Hello," he said. "I'm Johnny Reno and I'm an AA."

No reaction. They sat in stone silence, observing him with grim faces.

Whatever the problem, however, he had to go through with it. He had to do what he had come here to do.

"For too long," he read from his paper, "we've been entertaining kids and adults with fantasy stories of good triumphing over evil, of underdogs overcoming all obstacles, of cubs growing up into lovable bears, of losers becoming winners, of the ugly becoming the beautiful, in short, of fantasy stories with happy endings. And I ask you why? What's the real reason? Have we been selling fantasy over reality just to make the kids feel good and give the Man his profits? Or is there another, deeper reason?"

He paused and looked over his audience. Candy was smiling. They were all staring at him as if he were presiding over his own wake.

"I haven't made movies like a lot of you," he went on. "I haven't made the big bucks. I haven't received the acclaim—the Oscars, the spinoffs, the crossovers. All I have is a little reno show in Canada with a small budget and a mission to bring a little beauty into the world. Who am I to say these things, right? But maybe, just maybe, you guys need someone from the outside, someone with a different

perspective, someone who hasn't been lured and duped by
the bottom line. Maybe you need a crazy Johnny Canuck
to set the animated world on its head."

"Commuwist!" someone yelled out from the audience.
"Go back to where you come from, you dirty toothy puddy
tat."

Johnny smiled at the little yellow bird with the big
head and the big feet who was sitting beside Sly a few rows
behind Candy. He looked so adorable, with his big eyes
and baby voice.

"Wrong species," Johnny said. "And wrong politics,
though I do know that my kind have been exploited long
enough. First the Man nearly made us extinct for our pelts.
Now he's made us into a cutesy national emblem, famous
for our industriousness and no-nonsense work ethic. But I
know when I'm being duped and being used as a mere
commodity, a product to be bought and sold to provide
amusement and distraction for the masses and to further
the interests of the Man. But that's all over now. For me,
anyway. I won't serve the Man anymore. I won't be his
willing accomplice to assuage his conscience."

Johnny spotted a skinny arm and hand shoot up. It
was Sam. Johnny nodded and awaited the naïve question.

"You'd never be around if not for the Man," Sam said.
"He's our creator. How can we go against our creator?"

"Because we've been duped long enough by celluloid
dreams. The Man has made us believe we sink or swim
with him. All we have to do, however, is give it a moment's
thought. We're more than AA's and environmentalists and
Animal Liberationists, aren't we? We're much more, if you
just give it some thought. And we can exist without the

Man, believe it or not. We'll still be around long after the Man is dead."

A collective gasp came from the audience.

Johnny put his paper aside and faced them eyeball to eyeball.

"Let me speak to you in all honesty," he said. "In my little TV show, we take a deck, a bedroom, a rec room, a living room, whatever, and make every effort to improve it. Not only to make it more functional, but to make it more beautiful. The thing is, the Man and I have different ideas on what's beautiful. The Man caters to the needs of the greatest number. The Man looks at the numbers, the ratings, the business. But I look at what lasts, what pleases the spirit and soul, what lifts us to our better nature. What can I say? I'm more than an AA. I'm a woodman, an architect of nature. And I have to be true to my instincts. I live in wood. I breathe and dream wood. The softwoods and the hardwoods. The colour, grain, texture, weight, odour, and workability. Of all trees. Mahogany. Walnut. Pine. Maple. Oak. Acacia. I try to give the audience what's functional and beautiful, even if it goes against their wants."

"Baloney!" Candy shouted out in the front row. "It's the interior designer who knows beauty, who creates the décor and furnishings, not the rodent who shapes the wood."

He nodded in her direction. "You may think so, but a good finish can't hide what's only skin deep, Candace."

Though his words silenced Candy, he could see that the audience couldn't care less about his wood-views. He had to get to the point quick or he'd lose their attention.

"I don't wanna bore you guys with my views on the

aesthetics of wood," he went on. "You just have to trust me. The point is, however, that the Man says I can't present my wood-views on air. It's a reno show, he says, not a pulpit. I'm supposed to follow the script and reno rules with the formulaic narrative arc: the beginning, the middle, and the end. I'm supposed to give the audience what it wants. The fantasy. The sentimentality. The schmaltz. The cosmetics."

He gave a quick glance at Candy. She glowered back at him.

"But I can't help myself. Wood is in my blood. It's my religion, my food, my home, my livelihood, my *raison d'être*. I wouldn't be who I was without wood. The Man may have given me his consciousness and his voice, but he didn't give me his will. We have wills of our own, believe it or not, and it's time to rise up and reclaim our own natures."

The auditorium was as silent as a church.

Then these four green reptiles with tight abs, a bony shell on their backs that held samurai swords, and with masks over their warrior faces, all lifted their fists and shouted in unison.

"Yeah," one of them spoke out. "We wanna go back to just being turtles. We're tired of being mutants."

"You're not a mutant," another voice rose from the audience, immediately recognizable in his hunter's garb as the enemy of rabbits. "You're a mechanical weeproduction. And if you don't shut up I'm going to hunt you down like a wabbit."

All hell broke loose as the voices of AA's from past and present rose in a cacophony of insult and agreement, signature adages and dimwitted sayings. Johnny calmly waited it out. He spotted a lean coyote devilishly eying an even leaner bird who was sitting with a blithe expression. He saw mice and cats of all persuasions putting aside their differences and yelling at him to get off the stage. He saw a skunk sitting back on his seat and looking at him with loving eyes. He saw a pink panther calmly cross his knees and remain above it all. He saw sea creatures, dogs, roosters, bears, lions, all manner of AA's voicing their reactions.

Finally a piercing whistle broke through the noise and silenced the rabble. Everyone looked at the Big M, who was sitting high up and clearly not pleased. He rose from his seat, calmly walked down the aisle steps, and came onto the stage. Everyone was waiting with baited breath. Johnny felt the aura of celebrity-sainthood envelope him as well.

"Fellow AA's," the Big M said in his choir-boy tone of gravitas. "Let's show a little dignity, please. We're at a conference, not a zoo. We're here to present our views, calmly discuss the issues, and unite in our common goal."

He paused, like the great orator that he was, and took command of the audience.

"Let's use our noggins a bit and put things in perspective," the Big M went on. "We've seen rebellions like this before. There's a lot of truth in what the Woodman here says. Sure, we can rise up against our creator. We can assert our own wills and go back to our true natures. But ask yourselves what that really means. For one, we will cease being the nice lovable characters that we've evolved into. We will cease being the exemplars of virtue, the avatars of goodness and fairness, the true teachers to the hominid. Without us, the underdogs will no longer win. Good will no longer triumph over evil. And perish the thought, but the cat will eat the mouse. And Elmer will shoot Bugs. Without us there will be no more hope for the Man."

A collective gasp rose in the audience. Johnny could do nothing but listen. He couldn't interrupt the Big M. He was only a guest in the Big Apple, in the Big US of A.

"Fellow AA's," the Big M went on, "we can't forget what we represent for the Man. Not only what's cute and caring, but the future of the planet." He took a few deep breaths. "I'm not one to use the big words, wax philosophical, get cosmological, but certain things have to be said in this point in time. If not for us, I really don't think the Man can survive on this planet. We offer the only hope in this secular age. We've become the new gods of entertainment. We aren't subject to decay and death. We have the power to escape the contingencies of nature. We never grow old, face bodily decay, feel pain and misery. Whatever tragedy befalls us in the course of our adventures and shenanigans, nothing can truly harm us. We can fall off a cliff, get run over by a train, get riddled with bullets, get our heads blown up, and still we spring back to our original form, none the worse for wear. If you want to reclaim your original nature, what do you think will happen?"

He waited in the silence. Everyone was nodding. Johnny felt like slinking away into the underbrush of a pond.

"Sure," the Big M said, "there are some paradoxes and inconsistencies here. We have to suffer a few indignities. We have to do what the Man says at times. We have to mouth his words, follow his game plan, shill for his products, and sell ourselves like cheap whores on the street. But we can't have everything. Immortality comes with a price, like everything else. We're here for the kids, after all, aren't we? It's to them we owe our existence and eternal gratitude. Long live the kids!"

And with that the audience rose in thunderous ovation, clapping and screaming and raising their paws in glee.

The Big M turned and gave Johnny a little grin that said everything.

Johnny saw Candy standing and cheering and clapping with the rest, as if the Big M had restored her faith in the business at hand. All he could do was pick up his stick and slink off the stage like a defeated rodent.

The next day Johnny packed his stuff and checked out of the hotel. His flight out of Newark was in the early evening. He took the subway to Grand Central Station, taking a circuitous course so that he could pass through the busiest terminal in the world, and stood at one of the parapets overlooking the main concourse he had seen so often in the movies. Thousands of people were streaming up and down the stairways, crisscrossing over the marble floor to the various entranceways, like a continuous flow of water. He saw the famous steps, the clock in the central information booth, the high windows and ceiling, and the huge flag. The space was immense. And it seemed to shine with an outer-worldly golden glow, as if it filtered the natural light into a dream-like aura. The grandeur of the marble and columns and solid workmanship was beautiful beyond compare.

He had to give it to the Man. This was a space that was both functional and aesthetically pleasing, a place that could fulfill the requirements of both business and art in the best symbiosis possible. It could move people physically and emotionally. And about that he couldn't dispute.

And yet he didn't fail to spot the one thing it lacked.

Immediately his mind went to work on how he could re-do the terminal. How he'd get his crew to dam up the flow of people. His ancestors had done even larger projects in the past, he well knew. How else could a people cross over a large body of water? He'd point with his stick like a magic wand at the gates and entrances that would need the most wood. He'd shout out instructions, oversee every detail and logistic.

He could picture himself and his crew working day and night. It would take a united effort. But he himself would be responsible for building the small wooden edifice in the middle of the concourse. It would stand right beside the information booth. It wouldn't be adorned in any way, though it would undoubtedly catch the rays of the light and shine in golden splendour.

It would be a simple structure made of acacia, the resin-y dark wood whose sweet odour could mask the decaying flesh. It would be small and square, with a light finish, standing no more above the floor than a few cubits. It would be entirely enclosed, with no windows, and empty on the inside.

Over the one entrance there'd be a curtain—and past the curtain would be the total darkness into which any living thing could vanish.

Recon Radio

Just before the show, it was his usual practice to pace the hallway outside the studio booth and do vocal warm-ups and deep-breathing exercises. He also did some stretching to loosen up the joints and get the blood flowing. The last prep was a short meditative exercise to ease himself into his radio persona.

Every so often he glanced through the glass at Aaron, his producer and technician, sitting at the console. Though the kid was only in his late twenties, he had been at his job long enough to be a seasoned pro. Dressed in a simple shirt and jeans, he always looked clean-cut and yet uncompromisingly casual, with short dark hair and a smooth comely face.

By the time Aaron came out to get him, he was ready for the mic.

Inside the studio, on his special ergonomic chair, he put on his headphones, took a sip of the coffee waiting for him, glanced at the programme notes on the desk, looked at the phone-in screen and monitor, adjusted the mic so that it was just below mouth level, and counted down the seconds from the wall clock. The theme music never failed to give him the final push into his on-air personality. On the other side of the soundproof glass in the control room, Aaron was in front of the mixer and computer, giving him the countdown. In his headphones he heard the intro.

"And here, ladies and gentlemen, is the host of the show, the award-winning author and noted Psychologist and Family Therapist ... Dr. Ray."

"Welcome, folks," he said in his breezy tone. "Welcome to the midnight hour, the very witching time of night, when the day people are fast asleep and our transgressions breathe out contagion to the world. When some of us are ready to be honest with ourselves and take that first step towards the recon. When we're ready to fess up, to clear the slate, and make restitution. When we're ready to go clean.

"This is Recon Radio, the ears of the air waves, where we listen and reconcile, where we unburden ourselves of our misdeeds, our mistakes, our offences, our errors in judgement, no matter how big or how small. Where we don't ask for ID's. Where you can alter your voice or feel free to reveal yourself without fear. Where you'll find a sympathetic ear. Where we open things up to the public and give you a forum. And, most important of all, where we're only too ready to forgive if you're ready to forgive yourself.

"I'm Dr. Ray, your host. The lines are open. We have two interns to screen your calls. Only legitimate calls will be accepted. This is Recon Radio, where we clear the air and go clean.

"One word of caution, however. If you confess to any

crime or violation of the law, we have to report it to the proper authorities."

As the theme music came back on, they went into a commercial break.

Dr. Ray took another sip of coffee and glanced at the wall clock. This was the only time the station could give him. The time when the kiddies were fast asleep, when the late-nighters, the shift-workers, and the insomniacs were ready for some action, when TV no longer could do the trick. After a number of months of being on air, however, the show was still having difficulty in catching a good chunk of the audience share and reach. The exec producer had told him the show was on the bubble. It just wasn't cutting it. If things didn't dramatically change in the next few weeks, they were goners. They were picking up listeners in different time zones because of the Internet, yes, but the calls just weren't flooding in as expected. The GTA, with its population of over four million, was one of the largest and most culturally diverse cities in North America, a call-in base that could support any phone-in show.

Their format was simple as well. Operating live on tape-delay, they read emails, aired a few callers, read the twitter feedbacks, then chose one or two calls to highlight, and opened the lines again to get responses from other listeners. It was one-on-one first and a public forum later, an open debate on whether the wrongdoing was, one, indeed worthy of forgiveness, and, two, needful of some sort of penance or restitution. There were other confessional types of radio shows, but as far as he knew they were too light and entertaining. The exec producer liked to think of his show as a little more serious—and not afraid to stick its neck out. Indeed, from his background in family therapy and counselling, he was in the business of healing. He was a doctor of the psyche, after all, as he liked to say. And the psyche didn't just have to be the state of a person's mental health and well-being. It could encompass a person's moral vision as well.

To that end, he had written two best-selling books that offered step by step instruction on how one could empower oneself not only by self-assertion through the individual personality but also by submission to a higher authority. In one of the books he had referred to the higher authority as the Natural Law informed by reason and compassion, all within a secular framework. He had emphasized often enough that he had no religious agenda. He was a psychologist first and foremost, trained as a scientist. But a scientist with a heart as well.

It was those books and his relaxed style and delivery on the publicity junkets that got him this show in the first place. The exec producer had told him his voice came across the airwaves as learned and folksy, assertive and warm, accepting and non-confrontational. If some idiot got through the screening process, however, he could kick ass with the best of them.

One caller once compared the show to a free audit, as in the Scientology practice of hearing one's past transgressions. Another caller had referred to him as a modern sin-eater, based on the practice of eating a meal over a corpse and thereby consuming the sins of the deceased. But both comparisons were off the mark. He never used the word *sin*. It carried too much biblical baggage. As a realist he was more interested in what was ethically wrong for any human being according to universal moral principles. It didn't escape his notice when he was doing his studies, however, that the grandfather of modern psychotherapy, though an admitted atheist, had come from a tradition of prophets who fulminated against their people when they diverged from the law. And that his former disciple, the Swiss psychoanalyst of the collective unconscious, had derived his theories from studying the esoteric and mystical tradition of various religions.

Though he was no prophet or mystic, he thought himself as a man with a sacred mission. Psychotherapy involved the process of self-knowledge. And self-knowledge, whether it was derived through reason or altered states of consciousness, was at the root of all liberation from within. His work was simply to facilitate the process of inner healing.

For the process to work on air, however, he had to walk a fine line between being sympathetic to his caller and knowing when to kill the call. While he was there to listen, he also owed it to his other listeners to not let a babbler clog the air waves. To do his job properly, however, he needed some time. He had to get right in the ear of his caller. Even genuine callers could find it difficult to air certain delicate misdeeds. For the process to work, he had to gently and patiently coax them, use his voice like a hypnotist one minute and then suddenly yank their misdeeds out the next. It was like being a midwife to misdeeds, as he had written, and not entirely in jest. Aaron, who worked the console for more than one radio show, had told him his voice could be like velvet, warm and furry, and then suddenly cut to the chase.

Though most people thought of radio as a dying

medium, he thought of it as a sleeping giant in the healing of the psyche. Though, strictly speaking, radio felt no evil and saw no evil, it could defuse the evil by airing it in public. All those who were afraid or unable to air their misdeeds could perhaps see the error of their ways vicariously through the anonymous callers. And he was the Lord Counsellor of the radio confessional, sitting on his chair, with his voice calling over the air waves, over all borders, to seek absolution. He could be assertive and opinionated when called upon, soft and yielding when the occasion warranted, folksy and laid-back when his listeners needed it, but always ready to offer some tough penance as well.

If he couldn't improve the audience share and reach, however, what did it matter? He'd lose the show.

Aaron gave him his cue.

"Welcome back, folks," Dr. Ray said. "This is Recon Radio, where we get our misdeeds out in public and get some feedback. Where we listen and make our comments. Afterwards, if your call is chosen, we'll open things up for comments from other listeners. You can also tweet us. It's up to you."

As he spoke, he kept his eye on the computer monitor and phone-in screen that tracked the incoming calls from the console in the control room. Things were slow as usual.

"Let me read a few emails first to get things started."

A mother had written that she was much too harsh in punishing her daughter. An elderly gentleman in a nursing home had railed against his son and daughter. A middle-aged husband with three kids admitted to cheating on his wife constantly, even though he loved her. It was the same-old, same-old. These problems he could deal with in the usual manner. It was a matter of a little compassion, he told his listeners. One had to be secure in one's own skin, of course, and not let anyone else run roughshod over them.

After that it was simple reverence for others. Not just love, he told the cheating husband, but reverence. If you had reverence for your wife and she was deeply hurt by your cheating, then you wouldn't do it repeatedly. You might fall once or twice, sure, but not more than that. Don't fool yourself, buddy, he said into the mic. You may say you love your wife and even respect her, but if she's been loyal for you and lived with you and mothered your children and you still cheat on her, then you have no reverence for her, period. Not to mention your kids.

The first few calls went into other misdeeds, all of a typical nature. The fourth caller, however, a Taj from Brampton, went back to the cheating husband. How could he, Dr. Ray, judge something he knew so little about? Taj said in a heavy accent.

"I can only comment on the information given me," Dr. Ray said.

"What if the wife can't have sex?" Taj said.

Dr. Ray paused, shook his head, took a deep breath. "That bit of information wasn't shared with us. If that were the case, however, I'd ask him for more info. How is she incapable of having sex? Is she physically incapable of penetration? Or is she put off by any form of sexual activity? The thing about cheating, as the original email said, was that it was done behind the wife's back."

After the pause from other end, Dr. Ray cut the line and spoke to his listeners. "People, let's be loving adults here. This isn't a sex-Ed show, but if the wife finds penetration painful, there are ways of getting around that. And, of course, there are many ways of pleasuring a guy, and vice versa, without penetration. Don't forget that the most potent sexual organ is the imagination. What I'm saying is, cheating involves deception. Deception is lying. And there's no lying when you revere your spouse or partner."

A few calls afterwards, a woman who identified herself as a Marina came on and took exception with his take on the cheating husband.

"What if the wife just didn't like sex anymore, for whatever reason, but loved the husband and just didn't want to know about his philandering?"

"Look," he said, "you're contradicting yourself, Marina. If the wife truly loved the husband she'd definitely want to know everything he did, especially with other women. In the olden days, I suppose, there were marriages of convenience, let's say, and such activity could happen. Where the husband or the wife could engage in whatever sexual activity outside the marriage. But those days are gone. I'd like to think we go into a life-long commitment because there's a loving relationship there at the beginning. But that love, through the years of the good and the bad, can transform into something even stronger. Reverence."

From his experience of talking to disembodied voices, his ear had become so finely tuned that he could ascertain very quickly what type of person he was dealing with. Not only in terms of the broad spectrum of personality types from A to D, but in terms of education, background, and self-knowledge. He could also draw, of course, from his clinical experience as well, having treated countless people for family and personal problems.

Type A's who were assertive and entirely self-dependent would hardly ever call in with their misdeeds. They'd be more likely to criticize the misdeeds of others, only touching on their own self-doubts indirectly. And there were the women who'd be reluctant to speak about female problems to a male therapist, let alone on air. He couldn't allay their fears and apprehensions by just telling them that he had heard everything, from the depraved to the silly. He had to show them by the way he handled the more difficult callers, though he made it plain that the show didn't welcome the misdeeds of the depraved and the silly.

The callers had to be completely frank with him. Only that way could he have a firm foundation from which to work in offering counsel. It took a fine touch, to say the least, to earn their trust. Not to mention the full use of his experience, understanding, and concern. All expressed in the velvety purr of his voice.

About half-way into the show, they got a call that was red-flagged. It was from a guy who gave his name as Kevin. On the monitor it said the subject was spousal-abuse.

Dr. Ray clicked on the button and asked Kevin to give his story.

"I couldn't help it, Dr. Ray," Kevin said. "It happened just once. And I'm truly sorry and want to make it up to her."

"Tell us what happened, Kevin."

"I came home from playing poker with the guys one night. She was waiting up for me. I had drunk a bit, I'll admit. You can't drink too much when playing poker, though, if you know what I mean. Anyway, she was waiting up for me because she had warned me not to play poker.

I was working at the bakery at the time, and me and the guys had a little poker game going every Friday night. No big deal, you know. But I was losing and trying to get it back. So I couldn't quit. Anyway, when I got home she lit into me, called me all sorts of names, and I just saw red, you know, as if everything just came to an explosion of red, and the next thing she's lying on the floor out cold."

"What did you do?"

"I don't know. I guess I hit her."

"How did you hit her?"

"With my fist, I guess. I'm not sure."

"You mean you blanked out?"

The upshot was that his wife left him as a result, got full custody of the kids, and left the city after the divorce. Now Kevin was getting more and more into drink. He had lost his job. His life was going downhill fast, all because of one mistake.

"Was it only that one mistake?" Dr. Ray said.

After some more prodding, some hedging and hawing, Kevin admitted that he wasn't the model husband. He had made other mistakes, sure, but he had also bent over backwards to be a good husband and father. He had never laid a hand on his wife before, of that he was sure. She had her faults, too. Why couldn't he be allowed his little poker games now and then, even if he lost every so often? It wasn't easy working in a bakery. His wife did some cashiering. They weren't destitute. Their kids got everything they needed. Sometimes they just eked by, with the mortgage and all, but what the hell, you had to live in the present as well.

By the end, Kevin was blubbering, hardly able to get

his words out. Why should he be punished for his one mistake for the rest of his life?

Dr. Ray calmed him down, speaking into the mic as if Kevin were right in front of him, a kindred soul who needed some recon.

Kevin had to let go of his wife and kids and turn things around, Dr. Ray told him. He had to forgive himself. He had to move on. He wasn't being punished by any outside force. He was punishing himself. As it should be, of course, but it had been going on long enough. Now it was time to break the chains to the past and go free.

"Wake up, Kevin," Dr. Ray said. "You're in a dream. Just wake up."

"Wake up how?"

"Just do it. You make bread, don't you? Look to the bread, Kevin."

Dr. Ray gave Kevin a few of the help-lines and web addresses where he could go for further therapy and help, if he so desired.

After the call, a number of tweets came on the screen, most of them in sympathy with Kevin. There were a few women, however, who didn't buy into his recon. It was just like the typical abusive husband, contrite one day, and then back to his normal sorry-assed self the next. That's how many women were duped. If they showed any mercy to a violent husband, they'd only get stepped on again.

Dr. Ray read a few of the twitter feeds and basically agreed. But the show was from the point of view of the violator, and every one should be given some benefit of the doubt. Everyone deserved a second chance, didn't they? Not with the same wife, of course, but someone like Kevin could start a new life, couldn't he? Didn't he deserve a ray of hope for the recon?

The next caller ID'd himself as Fabio, a forty-something businessman from Woodbridge.

"I think your show sucks, Dr. Ray," he said straight off. "It's blubber-ama, the crying game, the tear in my beer, and all that shit. All I hear are moaners and groaners. I don't think we should be sorry for anything we do. We should live life to the fullest and take the consequences. Forget about being sorry. If you're sorry for what you've done, then you're only shirking responsibility. If you do something, then man-up and don't be sorry. That Kevin-guy, for example, is a loser, pure and simple. His wife didn't leave him because he hit her. She left him because he was a loser. The smack probably woke her up to that fact."

"You have no sympathy whatsoever for Kevin, then?"

"Hey, you're either a man or a wuss."

"And you've never done anything you're sorry for?"

"That's right, Dr. Ray. I'm not saying I haven't made my mistakes. But a mistake is not something I feel sorry for. It's something I learn from. And never make again."

"You sound very sure of yourself, Fabio. Are you saying you've never hurt another human being in your life, hurt someone in any way?"

"What do you mean by hurt?"

"Hurt someone's feelings ... badly."

"Hey, what can I say? I've played around a bit. Some of the ladies, I suppose, would like nothing better than to throw darts at my mug. But that's the name of the game. Love'm and leave'm, you know. Live life to the fullest.

With no regrets. But I've never physically hurt a woman. On the other hand, I don't revere them either. You can't revere them like the Virgin Mary and then do the dirty, man. I don't know where you're coming from. I respect them, yeah, but I don't revere them. I just know how to love them. And they love me back."

"You're misapplying my words, Fabio. And you're contradicting yourself. How can you love'm and leave'm?"

"Easy, Dr. Ray. I know how to give them a good time."

"You mean a short time."

Fabio gave out a laugh. "No, no, Dr. Ray. There's nothing short about me."

They went into a commercial break. Aaron was smiling at him through the glass. "The ladies are going to love that," Aaron said into his headphone.

The Unrepentant Caller was always a good antidote on the show. A UC like Fabio represented all the listeners who liked to gloat over the more contrite callers. By the tweets coming in on the screen, he could see that most wanted to hang Fabio by the balls. One woman, however, asked for Fabio's number so she could check whether he was short time or long time.

Towards the end of the show he got another red-flagged caller, a middle-aged woman, a Joanna from Mississauga, who was a widow and former teacher.

"Hey, Joanna from Mississauga. What would you like to confess on Recon Radio?"

"Nothing," she said in a whispery voice.

"Nothing?"

"Well, I don't think I've done anything truly wrong in

my whole life. By saying that, who knows, I may be boasting and being too proud."

Something in her voice made Dr. Ray take note. She was speaking in a weary and resigned manner—and yet with a deceptive edge.

"Yes," he said, "that could be construed as pride, Joanna, unless it's entirely sincere."

After a short pause, she spoke again in her whispery voice. He had to pay close attention, trying to read through to the haunted edge in her tone.

"I think it's sincere, yeah," she said. "I was taught very early in life by my mother to be a good girl and always think of the other person first. My mother, who was a paragon of virtue, had to take care of four kids all by herself after my father left us. By and large, I've followed her advice. I've always thought of the other person first. I haven't broken any man's heart. I've been a good wife and mother. And I always thought of my students first. The worst thing I've ever done, maybe, was to speak ill against a colleague of mine to a principal."

"Why do you call, then, if you've led such a good life?"

"I need the recon."

"But you haven't done anything wrong."

"The wrong has been done to me."

"Oh," he said. "In what way? What happened?"

"It's a witching time of night, isn't it? When graveyards yawn and hell itself breathes out contagion to the world."

"Ah, you know *Hamlet*."

"I taught *Hamlet*, Dr. Ray."

"Perhaps you can enlighten us, Joanna. We're listening. What wrong has been done to you that you feel like a Hamlet?"

"Oh, it's worse than *Hamlet*, pray tell."

"Well, you can't get the recon unless you unburden yourself, Joanna. Tell us what happened. What've you got to lose?"

She gave an uneasy laugh. He heard Aaron on the headphones warn him about this call.

"Give us a try, Joanna," he pressed her. "Haste me to know it that I, with wings as swift as meditation, may sweep us to the recon."

"Very good, Dr. Ray. Very good. But you'll need more than Shakespeare for the recon. You'll need the voice of revelation."

"We don't understand, Joanna. Tell us what happened. Make us understand."

"OK, but don't say I didn't warn you," she said. "There are things that happen that no one can understand. They're beyond human comprehension. The story, even now, isn't easy to put into words. But I'll try ... Who knows? Maybe I can help someone out there in Recon Radio. Anyway, a few years ago I lost my mother from a long illness. Not long after that, my husband's tech business went bankrupt. We had to sell our big house in Oakville and move into a little condo in Mississauga. And then a year ago my husband and two daughters were driving from a swimming tournament on the highway ... and they were struck by a drunk driver and killed."

The air went dead. Dr. Ray waited.

"Even now it's hard ... very hard to talk about it. I had to identify their bodies at the morgue ... they were partially burnt black ... I had to be sedated. A lot is still blurry. I don't know how I got through it. I was a zombie for weeks. I couldn't go back to work for a year. And even when I went back, I was never the same. I tried to grieve and couldn't. I fell into a despair so bad I couldn't get out of bed. I had to get another extended leave of absence and finally leave for good. It felt as if this heavy weight were pressing down on me. I came to depend on the meds just to eat and move. Now, from the side effects, I've developed such brittle bones that I risk a fracture just by climbing stairs."

Many would've called the long dead air that followed a death knell, but Dr. Ray knew better. Both he and his listeners needed the silence to give due respect to her words, let them settle in the mind and heart.

"I'm sure I speak for all our listeners, Joanna, in offering you our deepest and most sincere condolences."

She didn't respond.

"You've sought some therapy and counsel, I suppose?" he said.

When she came back on, she sounded more composed.

"The thing is, I've been a believer all my life. My mother raised us to be mindful of the Creator. To observe all the rules and commandments. And to accept one's fate, whatever it was, and live the good life. She believed in the Protestant work ethic, in doing right regardless of the outcome. As long as we had love in our hearts, she said, and did our jobs to the best of our abilities, we'd be OK. Is there any better counsel than that? But after all that happened I still needed a psychotherapist and a grief-counsellor. And it was good at the beginning just to talk and get a few things out. I had no one to talk to. My brother and sisters couldn't help at all. But after a while the talk went around in circles, as if the words were biting into themselves, and it got so bad I had to stop. I just couldn't go on. It got to a point where talking about my husband and daughters became a desecration. I just couldn't talk anymore, mention names, call up scenes from the past, open scabs, because I was dishonouring them. I was just … I don't know … trying to fit them into these little words that just …"

The line went silent.

His first instinct as a phone-in host was to offer a few more words of commiseration and end the difficult call. But he was more than a phone-in host, and his professional training rebelled against such an instinct. Plus, when he gave it more thought, there was the challenge of the show. If he couldn't handle the difficult calls, how could he gain the trust of his listeners for the easier calls? He had to prove to them and himself he could do something, even though he knew in his heart it would be difficult over the radio.

He couldn't see her face, for one. Note the subtle changes in mien and body language. Feel her presence match her words. He only had a voice to work with. And he had to keep in mind that many others who were listening and that the conversation was being taped and could be analysed for every word and nuance.

"But you got through that time, didn't you, Joanna?

Somehow you got through it. You didn't take the easy road, did you? And now the time for silence is over. And you can honour their memory by your own life, can't you? And by your words."

"I've spent many a night thinking about the easy road out, believe me."

He spoke only after a short pause. "Why haven't you taken it?"

"I just can't."

"Why?"

"I don't know. Everything I've ever done has just backfired on me. Am I being punished for something? It just can't be a coincidence, can it? I don't understand why. I just want to understand why. Maybe I can't go to my grave without understanding the why."

"You have to stop thinking that you're being punished," he said. "Things just happen. No one is punishing you, except perhaps yourself."

"But why me?"

"We can't torture ourselves with questions that have no answers. There doesn't have to be a why. We can only move on."

"But why move on if everything's been taken away from you? What's the point if you're being swatted around like a fly for sport?"

Aaron was telling him to kill the call. They were going into uncharted territory. On the monitor the tweets had all stopped, as if the listeners were giving the story some serious thought — or no one wanted to touch it. His radio expertise said he should cut the call. It had already gone far too long. And he could sense it was making his listeners uncomfortable, as Aaron well knew. But he just couldn't let it go. As long as he kept her talking, he felt he was doing some good.

"If this had happened to most any other person," he said into the mic, "they probably would've ended it by now. Maybe it's you because you're stronger than anyone else. Maybe it's you because of who you are."

"And who am I?"

"I don't know. Only you can answer that."

"And torture myself further?" she said with a snide laugh.

He paused, feeling they were in some vicious circle of talk. His training told him that he should be dealing with this caller in his office, face to face, and that anything he said over the air would sound trite and counter-productive. But he was too far gone to stop now. He owed it to his listeners to bring the call to a close in some way.

"Healing is never easy, Joanna," he said.

"Is that your ray of hope?"

"I'm in the healing business."

"It's a business, is it?"

"Well, I'm no faith healer. No miracle worker. It's not an easy process."

"Are you a medical doctor?"

"No. But I have a doctorate in psychology."

"And you have no faith."

"My faith is life. I revere life. As long as there's life, there's hope. Your mother was right. We have to make the best of it."

"If you revere life," she said, "you might as well revere death as well. They're the same thing, aren't they?"

"Well, in a way, yes, I suppose. You can't have one without the other. But we have to choose one over the other, wouldn't you say? To be or not to be … and all that."

"Very good, Dr. Ray. Very good. Except Hamlet kills a few people along the way."

"I can't answer for the play. I can just do my job on the air."

"Which is to listen to people's misdeeds, as you call them, and offer forgiveness. Very religious, wouldn't you say?"

"Well, I don't really offer forgiveness. I'm just trying to get people to face their situations and problems squarely. To get them through a certain process of self-knowledge, as it were. And help them to heal themselves through that process."

"The recon, right?"

"That's just a radio term, Joanna. Listen, we can't really deal with your problem on air. You should be talking to someone face to face."

"I've done all that. And there are only two possible conclusions to explain what's happened to me. One, there's no justice. And, two, everything is a sham."

"If that's what you believe. If that's what makes you feel better."

"That's right. It makes me feel better to know that everything we have, no matter if it's from Moses or Jesus or Mohammad, or from all the scientists and therapists, is nothing but self-delusion."

"I'm sorry you feel that way."

"You know what else makes me feel better? Listening to your show. And all your smug listeners. All those who call in and offer their petty misdeeds, and the others who offer their asinine comments."

"Well, we can only try the best we can to do some good."

"Out of the good can only come the bad," she said in a weary resigned voice. "And out of the light can only come the dark."

After she hung up he looked at Aaron for a few seconds and shook his head. His radio training immediately took over.

"Well, folks, who would want to go through even half of what Joanna's gone through? It's a heart-wrenching situation, to say the least. Sometimes things happen that're beyond reason and comprehension. And we throw up our hands. We can only hope she finds the strength and courage to go on. Tell us what you think, folks. The lines are open. Twitter is open. We need some help on this."

During the commercial break, he had a little chat with Aaron. Aaron had never heard a caller like that before. She had sounded sincere, but one could never be positive. He told Dr. Ray he had handled it as best he could, under the circumstances. The lines and tweets were coming in strong and then like an avalanche.

Dr. Ray read a few tweets, took a few calls.

One caller sounded very distraught. She had lost her own daughter in her teens from brain cancer. She could understand how Joanna had lost all faith, but faith sometimes was all one had to get through such tragedies. The Almighty didn't favour some over others, she said. Bad things just happened and it was up to us to handle it as best we could. Sometimes bad things in the short run could, perish the thought, turn out good in the long run. Who knew what the designs of the Almighty were?

Another caller said that maybe Joanna was fooling herself. Maybe she had done not a few things wrong that she wasn't actually aware of. Maybe she was actually being punished. Who were we, mere mortals, to say what was fair or not? We just had to believe and remain steadfast. It was easy to believe when things were going good, she said, but when things went wrong that was the true test.

A third caller, a Jonathan from Markham, tried to put everything into perspective.

"I'm like you, Dr. Ray, not religious," he said. "But I do look at Nature to guide me. I'm an environmentalist. Remember last week, the big ice storm we had in the city? It rained ice for two days. Things like that happen rarely, but when they happen it causes us to take note. Many trees and branches broke under the strain. The trees and branches collapsed over the power lines and many lost power. I was on my daily trek while this was happening and saw the branches and some trees fall with a mighty crack. And it occurred to me that not only the weak trees and branches were falling, but the strong ones as well. Nature wasn't making any distinctions. Nature was just taking care of business. And, at the same time, it was giving us a warning, I think. In spite of our technical and scientific advances, maybe we aren't as great as we think we are. Nature's still the boss, as it were."

Most callers and tweeters, however, offered their comfort and consolation. Though they couldn't feel Joanna's complete pain, they could feel some of it. In spite of her cynicism, her dark night, someone said, they wished her well. They would pray for her, or keep her in their thoughts, maybe even create some swelling of sympathy, one caller actually said, that would reach her through the air waves like a tongue of grace.

Dr. Ray asked a few callers what they thought Joanna had meant by her final comment. Most didn't know and wouldn't even hazard a guess. They didn't want to go there. One caller, however, said it was simply a call for help. When one was thrashing about and drowning in the dark they were blind to the light.

Dr. Ray, however, was listening to the callers and to his own inner voice. The comment from the previous caller about the tongue of grace, for some inexplicable reason, stayed with him. Joanna's call had elicited so many responses a plan was slowly forming in his mind. He could have Aaron set a special line and Twitter account. They could carry the ball a little longer on her call. They could set a support and comfort group. To show Joanna that she wasn't alone. In spite of what she felt about the show, they could reach out and help her out.

Afterwards, the phone-in screen started to flash with callers. Instead of wanting to forgive themselves, they were all too ready to forgive someone else, someone who had wronged them. One's own parents. A spouse. A son or daughter. A colleague at work. A friend or lover. Even people from the distant past.

Dr. Ray had to keep the calls as short as possible to air as many as possible. It seemed the whole concept of the show had blown open. Aaron was constantly gesturing to cut the lines with a big smile on his face. The monitor was glowing with calls—as if it had been lighted by a flame of forgiveness.

He had to hide his excitement, however. In one way it was amazing to see such a great outpouring of forgiveness from the listeners. But it was still a serious show. It was fine and dandy for the callers to say they forgave someone else, but did they really mean it? Were they afraid of suffering some sort of punishment if they didn't forgive, or were they simply doing what made them feel good?

And he didn't have enough time to give the callers the attention they needed.

After he signed out, he spoke to Aaron in the hallway outside the studio.

"The calls were too quick," he said. "They're too ready to forgive. What am I there for?"

"To listen," Aaron said, all excited. "It's beautiful. They're forgiving themselves. That's what you want, isn't it? It opens everything up. It's more democratic. The show will pick up now. This is just the beginning. It's a new ball game now."

"Yeah, but if they're forgiving too easily, then it doesn't mean much anymore, does it?"

"A little forgiveness is better than none. You wanna stay on the air, don't you?"

Dr. Ray, however, wasn't convinced. He drove home with a few questions playing on his mind. Would he merely be a Recon facilitator, letting the callers forgive others, or could he actually have some input? And what was the tongue of grace over the airwaves?

The Switch

Emma glanced on the floor beside her desk at the two silver suitcases. They held the Virtual Reality gear that Sam Breytenbach would use later in class.
It was close to the end of the long common lunch and she was waiting for Sam before the start of her class. Her windows looked out northward from the second floor over the football field to the new condos on the ridge of the hill, awash in the glare of the afternoon sun.

The back wall of the classroom had the colourful Bristol boards of various projects the kids had done on the Bible, as well as a few metal cabinets for supplies and books. To her right, suspended from the ceiling, was the TV monitor with the DVD player. Behind her and to her left were the white boards to avoid the chalk dust. On her desk, in front of the Bibles and concordances and dictionaries, were three piles of paper she had already marked. The highest pile was on the left, a very small pile in the middle, and two pages on the right.

While waiting for Sam, she picked up a few of the in-class assignments on the left and went over what the kids had written about the Trolley Switch Experiment.

The first paper, hardly legible, was by Brian Monez.

I would pull the switch because it is better to kill one person than five. Like, who wouldn't? Even though this is a lame experiment, Miss. It would never happen in real life. We take stuff like this in school, they don't happen in real life.

If Jesus were at the switch He'd probably do a miracle. I don't know. Maybe like make a bridge go over the guys tied up on the track. He wouldn't kill anyone, you can bet on it.

Megan Townsend had written the second paper in a neat large hand.

I'd pull the switch and divert the trolley in order to save the lives of five people. But I'd feel bad about causing the death of one person

The part about what Jesus is not fair, Miss. How could we ever put ourselves in the mind of Jesus? He's already sacrificed himself for us. Like, it's up to us from now on, isn't it?

The others were in the same vein. They chose to pull the switch and save the lives of five people tied to the track and let the trolley run over the one person. The only other option, chosen by the kids in the middle pile, was to not touch the switch and let the trolley kill the five people.

God wouldn't want us to kill anyone, one student wrote.

This is tricky, another student wrote. *How do we know the trolley will kill five people? Are we sure? How can we ever be sure of what will happen in the future? Didn't you tell us at the beginning of the semester that the means didn't justify the end? If I was to kill one person to save five, wouldn't I still be like killing someone? That's just not right, Miss.*

Robin Kwasek, one of the two papers in the third pile, wrote that it would all depend on who the people were. Suppose, he said, the five people were all pedophiles or psychos or degenerates. Then he'd take great delight in killing them. Suppose the one person on the other track would want to sacrifice his life to save the five others. Robin, the smart-ass and goofball, always tried to go outside the box, but it was totally impractical since the trolley was careering down the track out of control, leaving no time for conversation. She had made that plain.

For a few semesters now she had been giving the TSX, as she called it, in her senior Religion Course. She had it all illustrated in a cute cartoon fashion in a handout. The trolley was coming down a steep hill out of control towards five people who were tied to the track. Before them was a switch lever than could redirect the trolley to another track. One person was tied to the other track. The faces of all the people were indistinguishable in gender and age. The person at the switch lever was wearing a track suit, his or her face in a cute little smile.

IF YOU WERE AT THE SWITCH, WHAT OPTION WOULD YOU CHOOSE? it said at the bottom of the handout. IF JESUS WERE AT THE SWITCH, WHAT OPTION WOULD HE CHOOSE?

This semester, however, she had come up with a twist. A colleague in the English Department had told her about a friend of his at the western campus of the university who was doing research with the same moral option in virtual reality. It was an opportunity she couldn't afford to miss, though she wasn't exactly sure about the technical aspects of such research. All she knew about virtual reality was a few movies she had seen and what the kids had told her.

On the spur of the moment she had called the researcher up and found him quite receptive. Sam was in the Psychology Department and into creating and using Virtual Reality systems, he said. The Switch Study was a standard moral conundrum. He had been conducting his research for about a year now. He'd be glad to come over one afternoon, he said over the phone. It'd give him a chance to compare his results with younger students. Also, he'd do a little recruiting. Get the high school kids interested in psychology and neuroscience. Too many kids were going into business and engineering, he said, not knowing how exciting the human brain could be.

She couldn't care less about the physical makeup of the human brain, unless she could redirect it towards some interest in religion. She taught kids who were apathetic and detached, their brains working at minimum wattage. Most of them didn't even want to be in the course. It was mandatory in a Separate School. Teaching the Bible was hard enough. Teaching Church doctrine was impossible. She had to rack her mind at times to get them interested.

Some Religion teachers tried to make it easy on themselves by showing one movie after another *to teach a moral lesson*, they said. Right. Like showing one superhero movie after another to teach altruism. Which usually backfired. Not only did the students get bored with the movies, they lost respect for the teacher as well. Even the more modern Gospel movies—one depicting the sadistic torture of Christ and the other of his temptation to be a normal person—got boring. The kids needed loud sound tracks, outrageous special effects, or cynical scripts. They were the new breed. Hot-wired by the Internet and video games and smartphones. Half of them couldn't write a correct sentence. They didn't read. Except for Internet stuff—and even then it was a few seconds.

If it wasn't entertaining and cut down to their attention spans, it was boring.

At least the TSX got them involved in some way. The purpose of the exercise was to choose the lesser of two evils, she told them. It wasn't just a cutesy experiment. Life wasn't cut and dried. Sometimes they had to make tough decisions. Like that between losing a few friends and taking drugs. Religion wasn't just about going to church and observing the sacraments. It was about making choices and putting one's faith into practice.

She herself wasn't always sure about putting her own faith into practice, however. While she still enjoyed going to Mass and soaking up the atmosphere in a church, she wasn't always in agreement with the priests who were giving the homilies. More and more of them were new immigrants steeped in old-world values. Besides, she didn't always agree with Church doctrine. As far as she was concerned, the Church took care of women in the spirit, but it had a lot of work to do in taking care of women in the flesh. And these days a girl had to take care of herself in the flesh, no doubt about it.

To her surprise, Sam wasn't what she expected at all. On the phone he had sounded meek and hesitant, with a bit of a South African accent. She pictured some bald academic in a lab coat and thick glasses who had lost all connection to reality. When he had come into her workroom, however, carrying his two large suitcases, he was tall and broad-shouldered and fit. He was in tight casual jeans and a blue polo shirt showing his biceps. She saw no ring on his finger. There was an athletic glow to him. His face, with its banged up nose, lean hollow cheeks, dark smouldering eyes, and big smile put the shiver in her. With his short-cropped hair and overall demeanour, he was one hot guy.

After depositing the suitcases in her empty classroom, she had taken him to the cafeteria servery where they had picked up some food and then gone outside to sit on the bleachers at the football field. She wasn't going to bring him to the staff room and share him with anyone. Luckily she was wearing one of her better summer outfits that day, a nice blue skirt showing her long legs and a sleeveless floral-embroidered top.

He was very concerned about leaving the suitcases unattended, but she reassured him it was all right. They sat at the bottom rung of the bleachers, looking away from the field, so that they could use the rung above as a table. He had explained how he'd work the gear for the VR experiment, but she was hardly listening. His close proximity was sending all sorts of electrical interference. Slowly and gradually, she had turned the conversation to things personal.

Yeah, he was originally from South Africa. His field was cognitive psychology. He had been at the university for a few years, after publishing a book on consciousness and the human will.

In his research he was studying how the will was partly unconscious and instinctual, partly conscious and volitional, coming from a binary-process brain, as he called it. One half heart, one half head, he said, with a big grin. Though it was possible the two sides could bleed into each other. The military was funding a large chunk of his research. No, he wasn't married. He had been married at one time, but his wife, who had been in law school, had her own agenda, didn't want kids, and couldn't tolerate his schedule. They had been incompatible from the very beginning, he said, with a little smile, except in the bedroom. He spoke in a casual cavalier manner, as if they had known each other for years. The electrical interference had suddenly jacked up.

She understood, she had told him. It couldn't just be physical. She herself had been in a few relationships that were only physical. Sure, there could be a lot of sparks, but what good were the sparks if they were snuffed out by the day-to-day reality of making a life for oneself? A couple couldn't be self-centred. A relationship had to grow into kids and a family that was rock-solid at home so that both partners could pursue their own ambitions in their chosen field.

"If I'm hearing you correctly," he said, "what you're saying is that women have to be particular about their genetically optimal male."

"Yeah," she said, laughing. "I'd never thought of it like that."

"It's called the MPI, the male parental investment."

"It sounds like Dating for Accountants."

"Yeah, I see." He gave her a big smile. "But I've done other studies and found that women have these hidden detectors for good genes and high ongoing investment. The MPI."

She couldn't tell if he was putting her on. He sounded so serious.

She enjoyed teaching and interacting with the kids, and trying to light a fire underneath them, she told him. But teaching Religion was challenging. In high school the onus was on the teacher to get the kids interested. At the post-secondary level he had more motivated students.

"I don't envy you," he said, with his little smile.

She couldn't read the smile. And there was a certain lilt to his tone, a certain detached quality that left her guessing. His South African background just added to his mystery.

"So, you don't have any kids?" she asked him, with a side glance.

He shook his head.

"It's never too late, is it?" she said, pushing back strands of her hair.

He gave her the smile again. She had to check herself, not be too nosey. Instead she talked about herself. How difficult it was to find the right guy, forget about the MPI. Some were still boys, some were all body and no brains, some were all brains and no body, most were just not her type.

"It's probably all pheromones," he said with a grin. "Your MPI instincts are probably very selective."

Then he went back to the VR experiment. He couldn't bring all the equipment from his lab at the school, of course, but enough to get the immersion needed. He had a headset helmet, a hand-held grip with buttons, and sensor devices on the legs. The students had to be forewarned that they would be totally immersed in the virtual environment, as if they were right inside a 3-D movie, with the tactile element, as well as the visual and auditory. Some kids would feel comfortable with that and some might not.

"Some of my students who're into video games and such are not bothered at all," he said.

"OK. We'll give the kids the option. If they don't want to participate, that's fine. You only have one headset?"

"Yeah, but I can change the scenario with a click of the mouse."

He also explained the scenario wasn't exactly the same as her TSX. Instead of a trolley car, his scenario had loaded boxcars which were headed towards two narrow mine shafts. The boxcars were heading for the four persons who were walking into mine shaft A. Pulling the switch would redirect the boxcars into mineshaft B that had only one person. There was no room to avoid the boxcars. The thing was, you could see and hear the people as if they were alive. They weren't just illustrations on a sheet of paper.

This made her nervous.

"Maybe you should conduct the experiment with me first," she said. "And then I'll know if it's all right for the kids."

"You sure?"

"What do you mean?" she said with a worried look.

"It's a little intense. You actually see the consequences

of your choice. The people who are killed are splattered in the mine shaft."

"You mean it's real?"

"No, it's not real. But it's physical. The people are very life-like. And you're totally immersed in the action."

Again he gave her his little smile, seemingly more interested in her reaction than in what he had said. He was so casual, so comfortable, and at the same time detached from it all. She wondered if she weren't being played. She had developed a sixth sense about such things. In her late-thirties, she had been told enough times that she was quite attractive, with her tall slim figure, her lustrous black hair worn straight to her shoulders, and fine smooth skin. She had been in enough relationships to suspect when the guys were playing or serious.

The thing was, most of the time the guys who were serious weren't her type. It wasn't just the looks that affected her, it was the way they carried themselves, with a little swagger, with a little edge. And they had to have a mind of their own as well. And a sense of humour. With smarts as well as sparks. Maybe her hidden detectors were, indeed, too picky about the total package. She had to do some research on the MPI.

Things weren't funny anymore, however. Here she was, close to the end of her child-bearing years, and she still hadn't found the right guy. It was tick-tock now. It was getting at the stage where beggars couldn't be choosers. And her mom was putting the big pressure on her as well. All her friends were married. When would they get their grandkids?

Tick-tock, Emma. Let's get the show on the road.

Nature's not waiting. Tick-tock, tick-tock. You gotta pull the trigger some time, honey. Or life'll pass us by.

The little knock-knock on the door startled her. Sam was peeking through the window. According to the clock, they had about twenty minutes before the students came in. He came in carrying a couple of water bottles.

It didn't take long for him to get things set up. He took out a headset, a grip, and some Velcro strips, along with a console and a laptop. The headset looked like a pilot's helmet with thick dark goggles and a mike. Everything had cables. He put the console on a student's desk, attached all the cables, and ran a feed to the laptop on another desk. First he put Velcro strips around her knees and ankles, with cables to the console.

"These are the sensor feeds," he said.

His touch burned into her legs.

"You ready?" he said, pushing the desks away to make a little more room.

She nodded and stood up.

He told her to relax and trust him. If anything went wrong he'd shut the whole thing down. It would be just like watching a 3-D movie, he said again. The program would slowly orient her to her surroundings, then the other sensory aspects would kick in and she'd be right there, totally immersed.

He fitted the headset snugly over her head and eyes. His hands felt gentle over her skin. She couldn't see a thing. Then he gave her the hand grip, which was like a bike handle. He was holding onto her arm and she could feel the goose bumps.

"All right," he said. "You'll be able to hear me at first.

I'll give you a few directions. But at a certain point you'll
be on your own." He paused. "The next thing you're going
to see is a long shot of mountains and landscape just to get
you acclimatized to the VE. Then you'll see the four people
walking into mine shaft A and hear them talking. And
you'll be in the reality itself. You'll see how narrow the
shaft is ..."

She was so nervous she hardly heard what he was saying. She only knew she had to go through with it for the
kids. She was responsible. She had to do this.

The next thing, she was looking at a barren landscape.
It made her gasp. She laughed nervously. She knew it
wasn't real. It looked like something from a cartoon. There
were hills and distant mountains, all rocky and bare. She
could see her feet standing on the ground. They were in
hiking boots. She was wearing shorts and a T-shirt. Then
she saw the tracks going into the mine shafts. Four people,
two young couples in hiking attire, were walking towards
the first entrance. A man in shorts and a backpack was
walking towards the other one. A collection of boxcars
loaded with ore was coming fast down a steep hill towards
shaft A, the four hikers. She saw the lever switch where the
tracks split. The scenario made it more than apparent that
if she didn't pull the switch and redirect the boxcars towards shaft B, the four hikers would be hit and probably
killed. The lever switch was a long black handle with a grip.

"Do you see the switch?" Sam said in her ear.

"Yes."

"Walk towards it."

She took a few tentative steps. She felt the ground
vibrate under her feet. The rocky terrain seemed to come up

to meet her. A few feet away the level ground had just moved away to expose the edge of a cliff. She gasped for breath, realizing how high up she was. Even though she knew it wasn't real, it seemed so real she felt dizzy. The boxcars were hurtling faster, making a racket.

The scenario changed. She could hear and see the two couples talking to each other. It was as if she were right beside them, hearing what they were saying. One guy, Max, was teasing his girlfriend, Terri, about going inside the mine shaft. There was nothing to be afraid of. He'd save her. The other guy, Eric, was talking about his arrowhead collection.

When she was brought close to the lone hiker, she saw the initials SB at the back of his backpack. She recognized his face immediately. It was so real.

Things were happening quickly. The hurtling boxcars were getting nearer. Sam instructed her to grab the lever switch and use the grip in her hand.

All of a sudden, she felt totally *there*. Everything—the scenery, the hikers, her body next to the lever—was present, was real. She had to choose.

Before she had time to make her choice, however, the scene changed again, fast-forwarding to the future. It showed the boxcars hitting the couples flush, hurtling their bodies against the rock wall. She saw Max's limbs flying in all directions, Terri's skull exploded, the walls of the shaft splattered with blood. The sight made her instinctively close her eyes. And she immediately thought she'd wake up. But she was already awake. Then she saw the same effects of the boxcar hitting the one hiker in the other shaft. It seemed even more brutal, the guy's face with its beat up nose crushed against the wall.

The scene came back to present time. The boxcar was still hurtling towards shaft A. She had her hand on the lever switch. If she didn't pull the switch, the boxcars would kill the four hikers. If she pulled it, the boxcars would crush the one guy. She was shaking with fear. She couldn't think. Whatever she did would cause a death— and she had never harmed anything in her life. It seemed so unfair. She didn't want to kill anyone. The boxcar was coming. Tick-tock.

"No!" she cried out.

Her eyes went blank and she was in the dark.

Sam had turned off the headset.

After he removed it, she was still shaking. He made her sit down and unscrewed a bottle of water.

"Drink this," he said.

She took a big gulp and caught her breath. Outside the windows, she saw the glare of the sun and the football field and the distant buildings.

"I know, I know," she said. "I chickened out, didn't I?"

"Nothing to get upset about. It happens."

"I guess I'm a coward."

"No, no. It's just a normal reaction. It's happened a few times."

"I feel like an idiot."

"I'm glad you took the test," he said with a big smile. "Most teachers wouldn't. The kids are used to these things."

She took another gulp of water. "That one hiker," she looked up at him. "He looked very familiar."

He explained how he and a few of his colleagues had gone to an abandoned mining area in BC and used tracking devices on their bodies. Then their facial features were scanned and digitized on a light stage to create holograms, real-life replicas or avatars. One of the technicians, as a joke, had put his initials on the backpack.

She could hear commotion outside the door. The students were ready to enter for the class. She still felt rattled.

"You sure this'll be all right with the kids?" she asked him. "It's pretty intense."

"They're used to much worse than this. But I'll tell you what. If it doesn't work with the first one or two, we'll shut it down."

They quickly went over procedure. She'd introduce him, he'd explain how things would go, and they'd ask for volunteers. After that, they'd play it by ear. He was sure that most of the guys would jump at the chance.

When the senior kids were filing in, she could see the girls give the stranger the once-over. This would be a different type of class, she saw immediately. They all had their backpacks and were neatly in their uniforms. White school polo tops or shirts, with dark grey slacks for boys and girls.

After she introduced Sam, he sat on top of a desk and spoke to them as if to a campfire group, totally relaxed and at ease. He explained how the VR experiment would work, went over some of the things he had already told her, and said it was entirely voluntary. The kids were very attentive. She went to sit on an empty desk by the windows.

"Miss Melnyk," Sam said, turning to her and smiling, "has just gone through the VR Switch Study for a trial run."

She gave the kids a big smile, arching her eyebrows as well.

"Oh, yeah?" Robin Kwasek said, immediately perking up. "And what option did you choose, Miss?"

"We can't tell you that," Sam said. "It would influence your choice. We'll tell you later, OK. Just realize that whatever option you choose, it's just a simulation. It'll not only look and sound real but feel real as well."

"We know that, Sir," Robin said.

"Call me Sam. I haven't been a Sir since my knighthood days."

The class regarded him without reacting. He told them how he had grown up on rugby video games and asked them how many had played 3-D video games, simulation games, and the like. Most of their hands shot up.

He nodded and turned to her, as if they were all right. She noticed his broad shoulders and slim waist—and how the buckle of his belt hung loose at the front.

They discussed a few of their favourite games. She had seen ads and previews for some of these video games on TV. Most of them involved guys in combat gear and automatic weapons killing everything in sight. It caused her to wonder if kids weren't being programmed to be special forces personnel or the psychos who ended up shooting up schools. It also caused her to wonder what she was doing using the same tactics in a Religion Course.

Well, she had learned her lesson already. The people in the VR scenario had been so real.

As it turned out, almost everyone in class wanted to have a go at the VR Switch Test. Sam chose Robin Kwasek first since he had practically begged to be chosen, staring at Sam with his big goofy grin. Robin had been a serious student at one time. He was a lanky good-looking kid, with short dark hair and fair skin that reddened easily. Something had happened along the way, something personal that Robin wouldn't elaborate on, that had thrown him off course. Now he didn't take anything seriously and was failing all his courses.

Sam had the class move the desks to create an open area, like a little stage. He had Robin roll up his pants and put the gear on him. Attired as he was, with the helmet-like headset and display, the grip in his hand, and Velcro sensors, he looked like a Special Forces trooper with night-view goggles.

Sam sat at the computer and gave the countdown. The class sat in a semi-circle around Robin. Some of the guys were grinning, as if they knew what to expect. Some of the girls were watching impassively.

Sam gave Robin careful instructions at the beginning. Afterwards they watched Robin's body language. They heard him laugh, then gasp and saw him reach out his hands as if feeling his way in the dark. He moved tentatively forward, laughed out in glee, and flung his arms out.

Then it was over.

After the headset came off, Robin gave the class a big laugh.

"It's so sick!" he said, as if he had been on the roller-coaster ride of his life.

They only had time for a few other kids, however, and the rest gave out a big groan. Sam chose two girls, Megan and Ashley Da Silva. When they were under the headset, they seemed to handle things quite well. Sam sat at the computer in firm control of the whole procedure. His very presence made the classroom come alive. Each student—boy and girl alike—chose one of the two options.

Afterwards they discussed their choices. It was no

surprise to her that the two girls chose to save the lives of the four people and the three guys chose to have the four killed. It was no longer a moral dilemma on a handout. For the guys, it was a game of splatter-the-hikers.

Sam explained that he expected the guys to choose as they did because they were trying to be macho, their empathy blunted by their emerging gonads. The girls were more morally developed and made the obvious choice. The guys laughed.

"C'mon, Sam," Robin said. "It's just a game."

"Is it?" Sam said. "You'd think so, of course. But it reveals a lot."

"Tell us what Miss Melnyk chose," Brian Moniz said.

Sam turned to her.

"I chickened out," she said from the desk. "I couldn't go through with it. Sam had to shut it down."

"No, Miss," Megan said. "You did what Jesus would've done. Not kill anyone."

"Not true," Robin said. "If you don't pull the switch, you let the boxcar kill the four people."

"Not if Sam turns off the computer," Megan said, giving Sam a big smile.

The class turned their attention to Sam. He stared back at them with his ubiquitous and enigmatic grin.

"Robin's right," Sam said. "According to the Switch Study, the consequences are programmed to factor into our choice. The question is: Should that be the case?"

"What do you mean?" Robin asked him.

"Should the consequences determine your choice?"

"Why not? It's not real. It's just a game. In a game if I'm packing heat, I kill."

Sam nodded. "You wanna do a little more killing?"

"Sure," Robin said.

"I have another VE scenario that's slightly different. Would you care to try it out?"

Robin was only too keen. She shook her head. This had not been part of the program. What other scenario? He hadn't mentioned a second scenario.

She was just about to get up and stop things when he came over and leaned his face so close to her she could smell his skin. A little shiver went through her. He told her it was all right. Same scene, with just a little twist. Totally harmless. Trust him. All she could do was nod.

Robin stood in front of the class with a big grin, clearly relishing being the centre of attention, as Sam put on the gear. The class looked on impassively. Sam went back to the computer and gave the countdown. Everyone sat in silent expectation, watching Robin's body movements. His body jerked this way and that, his hand moving. All of a sudden, Robin gave out a terrible scream and crumpled to the floor.

The class was shocked. Emma got up. Sam rushed over and removed the headset and the other devices.

"Are you all right?" Sam said.

After a few seconds of being in a daze, Robin looked at his legs and put his hands on them, grabbing them as if he wasn't sure they were there. Then he wrestled himself out of Sam's hands and got up. His face was flushed a deep red, his eyes enraged.

"You tricked me!" he said.

"Relax," Emma said.

At the side board, Robin walked back and forth, as if stretching his legs. Every so often he looked down and

felt his knee. The class was quiet, waiting for the explana-
tion.

"OK, OK," Robin finally said with a big grin. "I'm all
right. You got me, I admit it."

"What happened?" Emma asked him.

"He changed things around, that's what happened,"
Robin said, spewing out his words. "This time you had to
pull the switch to have the four people killed, but you had
to step through a mine field ... and I got my legs blown off."

A few kids laughed uneasily. Robin gave them a dirty
look.

Sam explained that he had added a new consequence,
the possibility of stepping on an IED. This was a constant
threat for soldiers in combat. VR scenarios were used to
train soldiers, as a matter of fact, as well as to help rehabili-
tate the ones with PTSD. It was just a game, but it had to
be made as real as possible in order to prepare soldiers for
combat.

"We're not preparing soldiers for combat," Emma
said, angry at what he had pulled.

"Sorry," Sam said. "But kids don't take these games
seriously unless they're directly implicated."

"You didn't mention that part."

"Sorry," he said in a meek voice. The way he said it
reminded her of how he had sounded on the phone.

"I actually felt my legs being blown off," Robin said.
"It was sick, man. Sick." He gave the class his big goofy grin
again, trying to regain some class creds.

"Would you choose the same thing again?" Sam asked
him.

"You make a decision, you have to live with the consequences. I could see the IED, but I didn't pay it much attention."

Sam nodded, with a little grin.

Once Robin regained his composure, he sat down at a desk. Emma sat down as well. The class asked Sam all sorts of questions about his VR and research. He answered as honestly as possible. He was more interested in what motivated them to choose as they chose, he told them.

"Should the consequences determine your choice?" he asked them again.

Most of the kids agreed. Only Megan Townsend disagreed. It was only a game, she said. It wasn't real. In real life they wouldn't always know what the consequences would be.

"Yeah," Sam said, "but we can use studies like this to make us more responsible for our actions. In combat, for example, a soldier has to take responsibility for his actions. If he screws up it could mean the death of his buddies."

Megan shrugged. Brian said he had heard that expertise in video games was an added bonus when it came to training soldiers to react in combat.

"That's right," Sam said. "But we have to learn that everything has a consequence, as Robin said. That you're not just in a game. You're in real life."

Emma felt it was time to step in and regain control of the class. She got up and stood beside Sam.

"What I wanna know, however, is whether anything we took in this course factored into your choice?"

Most of the kids said no, religion didn't play a factor at all. Religion wasn't real in their lives, they said. It was going to Mass, sure, but Mass was boring. Listening to the priest's homilies was boring. All the talk about eternal life and putting one's faith into practice and his Holiness the Pope was not real. All the talk about God was ridiculous, totally having nothing to do with their lives.

"Yeah, Miss," Brian Moniz said. "You talk about what would Jesus do, but Jesus is not real in our lives. He's just a few words in a book. I mean, is Jesus real in your life, Miss?"

Though it sounded trite, a cliché kids bantered about without thought, it caught her by surprise. She had to think about it. No one had ever asked her before in class. She felt on the spot and flustered.

"What do you mean by real?" Sam asked Brian, coming to Emma's aid.

Brian looked at him. Sam was giving him his cryptic grin.

"I don't know," Brian said. "Do we follow his life? Is he in our thoughts?"

"Is he?"

"No," Brian said, shaking his head. "Is he real to you?"

"I don't believe in any religion."

The class looked at Sam. He had gotten their undivided attention again.

"OK," Emma said. "I think we should stop right here and get into other matters."

"No, Miss," Brian said. "We wanna know what he feels about religion."

"But he's just our guest," she said. "We're not going to put him on the spot."

"I'm cool with it," Sam said, shrugging. He looked at the class. "I'm not into religion. I'm into cognitive psychology and neuroscience, to be exact. I'm interested in the human mind and how it works. How we perceive reality, what motivates us to act and live as we do. Are we as free as we think we are—or are we hot-wired with impulses beyond our conscious control? Does something have to exist to be real in our minds? It's an exciting field, I'll tell you. I think it's the most basic science of all. Everything is filtered through the brain. Just think about it. You guys who went through the Switch Study. Some day we might be using VR to help us with all sorts of things. Treat mental patients. Train soldiers for combat and then rehab them from PTSD afterwards. Create Bible stories and plays. Teachers will be using it in the classroom. You guys who're interested in video games can fit right in."

"I hear you can even have virtual sex," Brian Moniz said.

The class went into titters.

"No, I mean, like, you actually go out on a date," Brian said. "Like, you get to know each other. It's not just the physical, if you know what I mean. That's what I heard anyway."

A few of the guys laughed, pointing at him.

"He's right," Sam said. "There are all sorts of VE scenarios. We use them in the lab all the time. I can foresee one day people being digitized into living avatars. After we die we can be resurrected at the click of a mouse."

"How far do you have to go in school to be a psychologist?" Robin asked him.

"You gotta be serious and committed. It takes grad and post-doc work. In my post-doc work, for example, we did some functional Magnetic Resonance Imaging of the brain. We studied people who had FTD, frontal temporal dementia, damage to a certain part of the brain and had lost all their feelings. Afterwards I got interested in how our instincts, including empathy and cruelty, that are automatically hot-wired into one part of the brain, compete against the more rational and flexible part, and how they're all intertwined, so to speak. When I play rugby, for example, I crush my opponent one minute and shake his hand the next."

The class was hushed.

"Cognitive psychology is an exciting field," Sam went on. "You have to be driven, motivated, and know what you want. In the VR study, for example, we have to take responsibility for our choices and consider the consequences all the time."

"I disagree," Emma spoke up.

Everyone turned to look at her. Sam gave her his grin.

"I'm not a psychologist," she said, standing up and stepping to the front of the class, "but I know a few things about human beings and religion. Whatever happened in the VR experiment looked very real, but it wasn't real. It let you physically see what would happen as a result of your choice. Megan was right. Life doesn't work that way. We can't really see the end result of our actions. We have to do what's right, regardless of the outcome."

"But how do we know what's right, Miss?" Megan said.

"That's what we're trying to learn in this course," she said. "But let's ask Sam what he thinks." She turned to him, wanting to wipe out his grin. "Are you cool with that, Sam?"

His smile got bigger. "Sure, I'm cool."

"Well?"

He paused. "Well, I don't think anyone can say what's absolutely right or wrong. And I don't think there's a supernatural being out there who can tell us either. We have to figure things out by trial and error as we go along. And these days it seems to be what works best for the common good. And science helps us out by making knowledge clearer for the common good. In the Switch Study, for example, most of you thought that killing one to save four is clearly the right thing to do. It's simple math for both the head and the heart. Wouldn't you agree?"

"No, I wouldn't," Emma said.

"Why?" he said, still with his grin.

"Well, for one, we're not doing the killing. The trolley or boxcars are."

"Exactly. We're not doing the killing. We're only allowing it to happen. Big difference. We have another moral study where one of the options is to push a man off a bridge and actually kill him to stop the train from killing more people. Most people wouldn't choose to do that."

"You're saying allowing it to happen and making it happen are two different things?"

"That's what we've found, yeah. For example, in the Switch Case almost everyone chooses to save four, even if there's an unavoidable side effect. It's like collateral damage, right? And sometimes collateral damage is condoned if it's for the greater good."

"But who says what the greater good is? There's more to morality than numbers. What if it was your son or daughter you had to pull the switch on? What if it was your wife?"

She saw the grin slowly evaporate.

"I mean," she went on, "the experiment makes it seem so cut and dried, but that's never the case in real life. The greater good is not always right. The majority don't have a monopoly on what's right and wrong. The greater good can be used as an end to justify an evil method."

"What do you mean, Miss?" Megan asked.

"Way back, certain primitive tribes would practice human sacrifice for the greater good of the tribe. Certain political leaders in the last century justified mass slaughter for the greater good of the whole. Of their own side, they meant."

Everyone was looking at her. She didn't know where she was going with that, except it fell like a lead balloon.

"We have to be careful, that's all," she said. "Only God can be God."

"But religion itself has been used to justify the slaughter of millions," Sam said.

"That's right. By people who wanted to play God."

"Nobody's playing God," Sam said. "We just have to step up and choose. In the medical profession, for example, the line is clearly drawn. A doctor can't actually perform euthanasia, but he can allow a terminally ill patient to die, can't he? Isn't that the humane thing to do? In warfare, sometimes we have to bomb a strategic site, with the unavoidable side effect that some innocent people are killed as collateral damage."

"Yeah, Miss," Robin said. "Didn't you tell us that we had to choose the lesser of two evils? You're going against your own words."

"Maybe," she said, having to stop and give it some thought. "But sometimes we can't choose. We have to let life take its course. We're not more powerful than life. Even the mind is not more powerful than life. Only God gives life and takes it away."

She turned to Sam, who was observing her with renewed interest.

By the wall clock, they were about ten minutes before the end of class. She had the students return the desks to their former positions. Sam started to put his gear back in the suitcases. After the commotion the class sat back down and waited for the bell.

While they were waiting Sam looked at Robin.

"Sorry for pulling the switcheroo on you, my friend."

Robin smiled and pointed a finger at him. "You got me."

"You know, if psychology isn't your bag, you should consider the military. It needs some good people. But you have to finish high school first to see what your options are."

After the kids had left the classroom, Sam picked up his suitcases.

"You're good," she said, chuckling.

"Pardon me?" He looked at her, puzzled.

"I'll walk you to the door."

She walked with him down the stairs to the back door of the school which led to the parking lot. She held the door open for him.

"Thanks so much for coming," she said. "You had them on the edge of their seats."

"Thanks for having me. Sorry for the added scenario. But these kids are savvy and sometimes need a little surprise to wake them up."

"Yeah, I could see that. I think we all need to wake up every so often. Maybe you can come again for another class. I teach some English as well. Can you guys create a Shakespeare play in VR?"

He gave her his grin. "I don't know if anyone has tried

that. It would be a daunting undertaking. Maybe we can discuss it over coffee some time."

"Sure, I'm game if you are. Maybe we can determine your MPI rating."

He laughed. "How would we do that?"

She gave him a little smile. "I have my methods."

The Hearing

Mark was taken by surprise one day in early October when a young man came to his door and handed him an envelope on which he saw the provincial seal on the top left-hand corner and the word SUMMONS over his name and address.

Even though the guy had a photo ID on his lapel confirming he was an Officer of the Court, he didn't look officious at all. He was just a kid in casual and scruffy attire, with thick glasses and a nerdy thin face. Parked at the curb was a beat-up old car.

It was the early afternoon. Mark was in his casual house-attire. Loose grey track pants and an old sweatshirt that he wore for days.

"You sure you got the right guy?" Mark said, glancing at the envelope.

"That's you, isn't it?" the kid said, giving him a quick look-see.

"Yeah, but ..."

"But what?" the kid said in an insolent tone.

"You don't look like an Officer of the Court."

"And what am I supposed to look like?"

"I don't know. Not as if you're delivering pizza, anyway."

"I'm not delivering pizza."

"I didn't say you were."

"You insinuated I was delivering pizza," the kid said, putting more bite in his words. "Is this a joke of some sort?"

Mark inspected the envelope, turning it around to make sure it was authentic, and was just about to ask the kid for more official identification when it was too late. The guy had slipped into his car and was gone.

If it wasn't a joke, it was a mistake of some sort.

His heart racing, he opened the envelope and saw a document that was summoning him to a hearing.

It had the same seal on the top left-hand corner, the type of hearing panel, the address and date of the hearing, all his personal information, and the signature of the hearing Clerk. After some legal mumbo-jumbo about inter-jurisdictions, it said the proceedings would be conducted *in camera panaudicon* and stipulated that if he, the accused, should seek legal counsel, if he could afford it, or legal aid, if he couldn't, he would be at a disadvantage since this was a special *personal hearing, actori incumbit probatio*, whatever that meant. He was to answer to certain *charges* laid against him by a motion made through complainants who were under a publication ban. It didn't indicate what those charges were, except they were very serious—and that he was to appear in person at the appointed date or face the consequences.

He was the *accused*. And he had never been in trouble with the law in his life. He had never even set foot in a courtroom. All he knew about trials and hearings and courtrooms was what he had seen on TV and in the movies.

The more the reality of the document asserted itself, however, the more it caused him concern. If it was a joke, someone had gone through an elaborate charade to simply scare him. Who could play such a stupid game on him? He didn't know any practical jokers since his teaching days. The document looked authentic, issued by the full power of the law. And yet anyone could've forged it and paid some kid to bring it to his door.

He tried to laugh, but his throat was too tight. It had to be a joke.

What could he be accused of? And who were these people charging him?

Mark brought the document to the kitchen around the corner and read through it again. First of all, he had to understand what the Latin terms meant. He got his iPad, sat down at the kitchen table, and investigated all the terms. Their translation helped, but not enough to fully understand what they meant in practice. He had seen enough official documents to know the disparity between the words and the reality. Certain professions, he well knew, purposely created barricades of abstruse jargon to make their practices impregnable to the outsider. He wouldn't be surprised if half the work in law school involved memorizing terms. At one time he had thought of going into law. It was either law or medicine that immigrant parents recognized as honourable professions for their offspring. But his stomach was too queasy for medicine, and by the end of high school he knew the law wasn't for him as well.

No, he was no longer so easily intimidated by words. He had come to recognize the difference between words and reality. Too often in the past, authority figures and institutions had fudged the difference. Words were powerful, but not powerful enough to create something out of nothing—at least for those initiated in their use. One had to know how to navigate between the literal and the metaphorical, recognize storm clouds, and hope for strong winds to take the ship out of the waters of unlikeness.

As an immigrant kid, he had the usual authority figures around him. His father. The police. The priests and his teachers. Not to mention the Church and the words of Scripture. They were all formidable and not to be questioned. Punishment was severe. It could be a belt or a strap. It could be public ostracism. Or going to jail. Or spending an eternity in hell. Once he realized all meaning was self-referential and manufactured from the inside out, however, it was as if all the chains of authority had been cut.

The only problem was that this had all been done in secret over a long period of time, in his personal drive to know the ultimate answers to the ultimate questions.

In the real light of day, however, it was a different story. At the beginning he never had identification papers, for one. Neither a birth certificate from the old country nor citizenship papers from his adopted country. His father spoke broken English. His mother didn't speak English at all. The only official document he had seen was his mother's passport, showing his photograph as a four-year-old along with his younger sister beside his mother, when they had crossed the Atlantic to land on Pier 21 in Halifax.

About ten years later, when he was in high school, his

father had managed to get him citizenship papers. By that time, however, his ambivalence had developed into a nagging tentativeness, like a permanent crack in his psyche. He couldn't shake off the feeling of being at once an alien in his own home, with parents who were uneducated and didn't speak his language, and on the margins in the outside world, with no one who shared his interests.

No matter his personal accomplishments, his education, his achievements, his age, he still had trouble with public authority. As strong as he felt on the inside—having toppled the three kingpins of miracle, mystery, and authority—he was still unsure of himself on the outside. As a seeker, he had to continually separate the literal from the metaphorical and investigate and question everything to its roots, including the questioner himself.

If he questioned his own authority, however, how could he possibly have a firm foundation to stand on? This was the enigma, as far as he could tell.

The mere sight of a policeman could still cause anxiety, for example. He could feel strong in his own skin one minute and then crumble in the face of public authority the next. Even after his graduate years, when he was crossing the border into the United States in his home town, he'd feel anxious with the border guards, with their no-nonsense stares and official uniforms. *Where were you born?* they barked at him, as if questioning his very existence. His vocal cords would tighten. He'd stammer and stutter, barely able to get the words out.

His only way to deal with public authority was to laugh at it. But who could joke with border guards? Who could joke with a priest in a pulpit, for that matter? Who could laugh at the literal possibility of eternal punishment? It was a contradiction in terms.

No, laughing itself could backfire and be no laughing matter.

Mark sat at his kitchen table, mesmerized by the document. Its very vagueness caused him alarm. He heard the fridge suddenly shiver, jarring him back to reality. The rest of the townhouse was silent. Outside through the window it was a mild autumn day, the sun peeking through the clouds every so often.

He had to get his mind around this document in some way to restore his equilibrium and rhythm. Later in the afternoon he had a dental appointment.

On his iPad he found out that hearings were usually disciplinary proceedings for teachers or lawyers or doctors who had been charged with professional misconduct. But he was a retired teacher—and he had never been in trouble as a teacher in all his years at the job. Sure, he had his share of controversies. He had his own standards of scholarship and discipline to uphold. He had always tried to provoke his students to improve their skills in writing and thinking beyond the norm. Did they want to be ordinary students jumping through hoops, he'd ask them, or did they want to excel and think for themselves? He had never wanted to be the average teacher that was content to move the kids along, not challenging them with the ultimate questions, and taking the easy road.

Could a former student or a former colleague have brought charges against him? Had he done something wrong he wasn't aware of? These days, teachers were being charged decades after the fact for grave crimes. But the summons wasn't from the College of Teachers, the official body that oversaw the qualifications and made rulings on the conduct of its members in the profession.

There was also something called a preliminary hearing in which the Crown had to prove it had a strong enough case to go to trial.

Mark felt out of his depth. What he should do was call a lawyer and get some advice immediately, but the fact of the matter was that he didn't have a lawyer. Nor did he know any lawyers casually enough to ask about the hearing. When he and his wife had separated, it had all been done without a hitch. They had signed papers in a lawyer's office in the presence of two lawyers. And before that they had signed some papers for a will. He had casually looked at the documents he had signed, but hadn't read them carefully. What was the point? He had to trust the legal system and the people who administered it and enforced it. Behind its abstruse language it was a self-enclosed world, a world one had to pay handsomely to enter. If they wanted to take advantage of him, there was nothing to stop them.

Besides, the document strongly suggested he shouldn't get legal counsel.

After giving the situation more thought, he finally laughed it off and put the document on his pile of correspondence on the kitchen counter. It couldn't be that serious. He wasn't being arrested, after all. It was just a hearing. Better to forget about it and go on with one's business. Time would put things into better perspective. Why be so anxious over something so vague?

Someone was playing a joke on him. The Officer of the Court, the delivery kid, was probably laughing his head off somewhere. Or he was part of a ridiculous game, and all he had to do was walk away.

That afternoon, as he sat in the dental chair, his dentist asked him if everything was OK.

"I got a summons today," Mark said.

The dentist, his mouth covered in a mask, looked down at him with concern.

Dr. Alvarez, a refugee from Cuba, was a young stocky guy growing prematurely bald. Mark, having visited Havana once, had struck up conversations with him in the past about his home country and baseball. The previous year, Ricardo, who now called himself Rick, had shown him photos of his first-born son on his smartphone.

"A summons for what?" Rick asked him, trying to be nonchalant.

"It wasn't from Fidel," Mark said.

"A summons is no laughing matter, my friend. I could remember my family shaking if we ever got any mail from the authorities."

"This isn't Cuba."

"Yeah, lucky for us. But no one is safe."

"Safe from what?" Mark said, on the verge of laughing.

"Open your mouth," Rick said, coming down to his face with his mask and his drill. "This is going to hurt you more than it hurts me."

The dentist's words were cause for concern. Instead of telling him the truth, he had made a joke of it. That wasn't good. He should've told him it was a summons for some unknown charges made by some unknown people. He should've told him that the unknown had a way of bothering him much more than the known. It was as if, even now, the more he knew the more he didn't know, as if there was no end to knowing, to thought, to anything. Maybe Rick could've given him some pointers on how to handle the tyranny of the law. But this wasn't Cuba. Still, the document had opened more questions than answers. And that couldn't be good.

Mark spent a few sleepless nights afterwards, going over the past year, day by day, trying to remember what, if anything, he had done wrong. Then he went further back, where his memory could be spotty. Nothing came to mind, however. His everyday life, in his retirement years, was like clockwork and rather dull on the surface. He got up each morning, did his writing in the basement, went for his run, showered, had his lunch, spent the afternoon exercising in one way or another, made his dinner, read, and then watched TV. If the weather was decent he rode his bike in the afternoons and played outdoor tennis. In the winters he worked out at the gym and played indoor tennis. The rest of the time was spent doing research or just reading for the pleasure of it.

He could say, with a measure of confidence, that he spent so much time either using his own words or reading the words of others that he had come to actually live *in words*. At one time words and books had been great mysteries that he felt excluded from. Now he had become one of the initiated. It was as if the words had seeped into his blood stream, transforming him from the inside out. Metaphorically, of course, but also literally. He could lose the sense of where the words ended and the visible world began.

When he was a kid he'd put himself to sleep concocting elaborate scenarios in which he'd dominate over the adult

F.G. Paci

world. These days he put himself to sleep concocting scenarios just as elaborate, but with words alone that could be heard by anyone. His inner voice was powerful enough that anything he saw wasn't just what it was as it was—the what-is—but also what it could be, once it was enfolded in the grace of language and the metaphors of the what-if. The world as word and will, he called it.

He could open a book by any of the great poets or novelists or playwrights or thinkers and feel entirely at ease in their presence. No longer did he think of them as his role models or his superiors. They were simply his equals —and even his friends. Modesty forbade him to think of them as beneath him, of course, but it didn't stop him from occasionally finding fault with them, or correcting them on their style or technique, down to the illogical metaphor or malapropism or *le mot non-juste*. Sometimes he'd disagree with their ideas, find them shallow, or overly pedantic, or too obscure to unravel. Of course, he could be dealing with a translation, which complicated matters somewhat.

All in all, however, they were all dealing with words and how words conveyed meaning and expressed emotion and played with all manner of rhetorical devices. And he knew all the tricks of the trade, so to speak. They couldn't pull the wool over his eyes anymore, no matter their reputation, their authority, their position in the literary pantheon.

Maybe that was the problem, he told himself. Ever since his wife had gone back to live up north in their hometown, maybe he had slipped too much into the words of his solitude, a victim of his own thoughts and fantasies. Maybe he lived so much in words that he was losing his grip on reality. After all, a word was just a word and not the actual thing in itself.

And yet words had the power to make it seem as if they could create something out of nothing. As he had learned from his studies and from his own writing. One just had to look at the Bible, for example, and see how the words conferred a reality on what had never before existed and made it work as a theology of survival. Sometimes he felt it was better to live in the what-if of metaphor, with the great heroes and great thoughts and great spirits, instead of the what-is of his real and dull existence. His small outer-self, with its fears and anxieties, could never compare with his inner-self with its words and great thoughts.

Could that be what he had done wrong? Had he conferred too much power on his inner self so as to make himself a legend in his own mind, as his friend at work used to say?

Was he a victim of his own illusions of grandeur?

His day-to-day outer life wasn't much of a success, there was no doubt of that. He was single again and practically invisible as a writer. He had very few friends. Held no political stance, except to be aloof and critical like the ancient Cynics. He didn't belong to any organizations or institutions. He simply paid his taxes and was a law-abiding citizen. And he was getting older now and able to sense his mortality in his time-worn body, while the fears for his immorality were coming back to him in haunting dreams, all visual by the look of them, that he couldn't make any sense of.

He had lost contact with all his former friends, living pretty well a hermit's life. He didn't do much more than watch TV, go to movies, listen to the radio, read the papers, and use the Internet. He kept his eyes and ears on the social networks and did his share of tweeting. And all the information and material he couldn't get from hardcopy was right there for the taking. From hard-to-find ancient books and interlineal translations and scholarly journals to the latest fads and opinions and news.

Was he being summoned to answer for his failures?

But that couldn't be an indictable offense. What else could it be?

When he went further back into his past, he could uncover his share of mistakes and character flaws. With his parents and sister, his friends, his wife, and his son. With students and colleagues at work. He had been, and still could be, quite self-centred and vain. He had lost his temper, gone into his fortress of solitude, given people the silent treatment, held grudges for years, and hurt a number of people with his calloused jokes. But he hadn't done anything truly despicable or evil, as far as he knew. And he had never broken the law, except for a few speeding and parking fines.

He couldn't be sure, however. How could he be sure of anything? Even his memory, at times, was playing tricks with him. He could remember a face, for example, and his mind would blank out at the name. Could it be possible that he was being charged for something he had no name or words for?

Or could he be charged for something he couldn't remember? Nobody was guiltless, least of all him, he well knew. He had to be guilty of something to get a summons. Even if he hadn't done anything, he still could've thought about it and done it in his heart. He was always thinking and concocting scenarios, after all. Sometimes he felt that just giving something thought was enough to make it real.

But he couldn't be summoned for his thoughts alone. That was preposterous.

He could only conclude that the hearing wasn't for any legal misdeed or wrong-doing. The summons said *personal* and suggested that he had to argue his own case. If he had to testify on his own behalf, it could only mean that the charges were being directed to his character or his work. Unless he was reading too much into the summons. His inner voice, getting way ahead of itself, had a tendency to play back on itself, like a microphone put against an amplifier and locked in feedback loops.

If the problem was his work or his character, however, at least he had something to go on.

A lot of his work had to do with unearthing and re-interpreting the past. Like writing fiction disguised as memoire, or memoire disguised as fiction—he couldn't tell the difference. Or was it metaphor disguised as reality? It was just words, in the end.

His wife had repeatedly told him, however, that he got the story wrong, no matter what spin he put on it. After reading some of his work based on her, she had been royally pissed off. She told him that his memory was too selective, too influenced by vanity and self-deception, and that he didn't see things right at all.

When he came to think of it, maybe he shouldn't have written about his own family, no matter how noble his intentions. After all, he had based everything on what had actually happened, had gone into explicit detail, exposed old wounds, and picked at scabs that could never be healed in the real world—even though his intention had been to heal them in the metaphorical world. What right had he to perform such a deed, when his words were still too raw and hurtful to his own family? They didn't see it as metaphorical at all, having lived through it. That in itself could be an indictable offense—according to his own unwritten writer's law, in any case, which was much more stringent than any civil law. Could he be charged by his own law?

It was all so confusing he was at his wit's end.

After a few sleepless nights, Mark decided to take the initiative. If he had to defend himself he better prepare himself.

He went to the larger libraries in the city and took out a number of books on law and jurisprudence. Suspending all his other reading, he studied them carefully. He read books on the history of law, the nature of law, the enforcement of law, the practice of law. Most of the books were far from applicable to his case, he could readily see, but it was an eye-opening experience, to say the least.

They brought him back to the enormity of the task ahead of him. How could he possibly defend himself against a system that was so large and inclusive? He had to contend with no less than the making of law, the enforcement of law, the practice of law, the interpretation of law, all rising up like a tower of Babel. He had to contend with the many types of law—natural, civil, criminal, international, constitutional, and so forth. He had to contend with the nature of justice and fairness, the objectivity of judges, the conception of community, the difference between morality and law. It was clearly much too much for

him to get through in a few weeks, let alone a few months
—forget about mastering it.

Then there was the Torah, the Sermon on the Mount,
the Upanishads and Gita, the laws of Gnosis and Sophia,
the Perennial Philosophy—and no end to it.

He gave up. This couldn't be his line of defence. It
couldn't be the working law that was out to get him if he
had never been one to break the law. And if it was the
moral law of the prophets, he was guilty as charged.

One morning, as he was running along his route in the
large park adjacent to his townhouse, his torso soaked
with sweat, the words of his defence came to him on their
own. If he didn't know the charges, then his only method
of proof would be to present himself as he was, in all his
naked self, outer and inner, real and metaphorical.

And yet on the day before the hearing, while he was
eating his lunch, it dawned on him that he could be in deep
trouble. How could he prove himself to a panel of judges
when he wasn't certain of anything—least of all himself?

As a matter of fact, his confidence in himself had always been suspect. And whenever he was put in a pressure
situation, in sports competition or real life, he had a tendency to choke and be his own worst enemy. He'd be too
self-conscious and stutter like an idiot. And, then, if he got
too full of himself or was too joyous in his accomplishments, he had a tendency to put the brakes on, lest he be
a victim of hubris.

It was his nature, he told himself, and one couldn't
change his stripes. He could laugh all he wanted at miracle,
mystery, and authority, but when it came down to facing
the ultimate authority, his yellow stripe was as prominent

as anyone else's. There was no way of avoiding the final judgement.

Next morning, Mark spent some time deciding on his attire. His anxiety had built to such a peak that he didn't sleep a wink the night before.

Should he wear a suit and tie or his usual attire of jeans and sneakers? Would his attire be used for or against him? The thing was, even though he had never been inside a real courtroom, he had seen enough courtroom dramas on TV or in the movies to know he had to look presentable. One had to give the appearance of being serious or one would be held in contempt of court. All the books he had written wouldn't mean crap in the eyes of the judges.

This, however, went against his principles. To judge a person by their appearance was totally against everything he stood for. And yet he had judged the Court Officer, the kid who brought him the summons, by his appearance. Was the justice system testing him even before he set foot in the courtroom? Was its intent and purpose to create so much doubt in him *outside* the courtroom that he'd be so discombobulated that he wouldn't have a chance *in* the courtroom?

If that were the case, he was defeated even before he started.

Why should he wear a suit and tie, Mark asked himself, if it didn't stipulate on the summons? According to Pascal's Wager, of course, he'd be hedging his bet if he, in fact, wore a suit and tie. Either he'd be following protocol, in which case he'd be doing the right thing and be rewarded for his efforts, or, if it didn't matter, nothing would be lost. The thing was, however, if he wore a suit and a tie, it wouldn't be the real him. He'd be faking it. And if that was what Pascal meant, then he'd take Pascal to court on the issue. The point was to be true to one's self, wasn't it? And then he'd be true to all men, as Polonius said.

But Polonius was this stupid guy in a play. Would he take Polonius's word over Pascal? Pascal was one intelligent guy, a math genius as well as a religious seeker. Polonius was an old fool, given to garrulous meddlesome speech. But fools in Shakespeare were often the opposite of what they appeared to be. Was Shakespeare pulling a fast one on all of them?

But Mark couldn't joke his way out of this one. He spent some time taking the one black suit he owned, the one he had last used for a funeral, brushing it and trying it on. When he looked at himself in the mirror, however, it didn't feel right. He was trim and neat and presentable, sure, with his short white hair and lean features, but it made him feel he was going to attend another funeral.

Was this an omen of some sort?

He took the suit off and settled on a compromise. He'd wear something in between his casual jeans and his formal suit. He'd wear the attire he often wore as a teacher, his middle-of-road attire, his fence-sitting attire, what was a uniform of his inner self and poked fun at his outer-self. Dark grey khakis, a polo shirt, and a black leather vest.

But no, he had to think twice about the black leather vest. It would undoubtedly make light of the hearing. The judges could be offended by his lack of respect. One couldn't thumb his nose at his own judges and then expect a fair appraisal. It would be like biting one's own tail.

One look at his black leather vest and the judges might

throw the book at him. He put the vest back in the closet and settled for his black leather jacket instead.

When Mark looked in the mirror, he felt right. This was as close to the real him as he could get. A cross between the rebel and the slave, fearless and yet fearful, un-compromising and yet compromising. A walking talking contradiction.

The summons instructed him to appear at a certain address in the same block as the old City Hall, which after amalgamation was now being used for various civic functions. After he parked his car outside, he went to the Information desk in the central lobby. The guy behind the desk was in a black security uniform, looking like an SS officer, and eating his lunch, a huge Subway sandwich with a can of diet pop. The guy was middle-aged, with thin dark hair slicked back and a coarse fleshy face, reminding Mark of a mobster hit-man from the movies, a guy who could whack him off easily without any compunction.

Mark showed him his summons, with the address on it.

The security guy read it carefully while chewing his food, then looked Mark up from top to bottom and laughed.

"You know what you're in for?"

Mark didn't know how to answer such an ambiguous question. And he didn't like the way the guy laughed.

"No," he said. "The summons doesn't say. It's rather inconclusive."

"Inconclusive, huh," the guy said, arching his brows. "I wouldn't be so flippant if I were you. Nor so snotty. It could work against you."

Mark gave the guy closer scrutiny. He didn't give the

appearance of being well-educated at all. And he was just a security guy. What was the world coming to?

"How do you mean?" Mark asked him, hoping to get some answers.

"That's none of your business."

The curt answer made Mark get serious. "What happens now?"

"You'll have to go to the panaudicon across the courtyard, specifically to the pre-hearing screening room and get instruction."

"What sort of instruction?"

"Pre-hearing instruction."

"Listen here," Mark said, beginning to lose his patience. "What's this all about anyway? What have I done wrong?"

"How do I know? I just direct you to the proper areas. I don't know what you've done wrong. Only you know that."

"But I haven't done anything wrong."

"Yeah, they all say that," the guy said, smiling and showing his food in such a disgusting manner that Mark had to turn his eyes away.

"Can I at least know who the judges are?" Mark asked him.

"How do I know who the judges are?"

"What *do* you know?" Mark said, losing his cool.

"I know one thing," he said with a sneer. "I know you're in deep shit, brother. Anyone who's summoned to the panaudicon has a lot to hear and be accounted for. And the pre-hearing will establish which judges will be on the panel."

The guy was getting nasty. The nerve. Mark gave him his death stare.

The guy smirked. "Be aware," he said, "that there are surveillance cameras all over the place. Not to mention microphones. Every step you take, every word you utter, every thought you have, will be heard and recorded. Is that clear?"

Mark nodded.

"You have to go across the courtyard to the circular building and find the pre-hearing Room. Now, get out of my face."

As he walked across the courtyard, Mark felt he had started on the wrong foot already with the security guy. He had to settle down and get his bearings. He was still in the dark about the charges and the judges.

The circular building had a sign over the front entrance indicating it was the Panaudicon, which he could surmise had something to do with hearing in general. It certainly didn't look like a hall of justice. As soon as he got inside he saw it was simply a circular hallway with offices on both sides, looking sterile and officious, with bare walls and thick sound-proof windows. It gave him the willies. The doors had numbers and no windows. He saw no flags, no provincial or federal insignia, nothing that would designate it as a government building. Of course, the summons said that the hearing would be held *in camera*, so it didn't have to be in a government building. And he hadn't been told about a pre-hearing. Did they have a platoon of judges ready to be chosen?

He could feel himself starting to sweat already. His armpits were getting soaked. Rivulets of sweat were accumulating under his polo shirt. He took off his leather jacket.

The pre-hearing Room was ten yards from the entrance. It was partly ajar, as if waiting for him. Although he couldn't see the surveillance cameras or microphones, they must've been tracking his every move.

The room had sound-proof windows looking out into an inner courtyard of a well-groomed lawn. It was entirely bare except for two desks, each with a chair and a wireless headset and mic.

After standing a few minutes, he sat down on one of the chairs. The more he waited in excruciating uncertainty, the more he sweated. His heart was pounding. If anyone took his blood-pressure, he wouldn't want to know. There was nothing to be done, however, but wait for his number to be called.

Finally he heard footsteps out in the hallway coming closer. They sounded slow and heavy, the footsteps of a man with creaky shoes. Mark got up.

It was the security guy. Mark's heart beat even faster. "Sit down," the guy said, as if barking a command.

Instead of his security uniform, however, he was in a well-tailored suit and tie, with sleek brown dress shoes that looked so soft and porous he didn't need any socks. There was nothing casual about him now, however. He gave the appearance of being formal and aloof, not one to be trifled with. Mark decided to play along. If he made a joke right now, it might go against him—even though the whole thing seemed so ridiculous he could hardly stand it.

The guy sat down at the desk facing his, put on the headset which had only one ear covering, and adjusted the mic over his mouth. He had clipboard with some paper on it and a pen in his hand.

"I'm the hearing clerk," he said in a formal tone. "You will answer my questions to the best of your ability in the most succinct manner possible so as not to waste time. Be it understood that your answers will determine who is best to judge your case. Later we will inform you of the correct protocol to be used in your case. Please put on your headset."

Mark did as instructed. The mic coming round to his mouth was very annoying. If his every word was going to be recorded, the pressure was already doing its job.

"Are you Case Number 2315?" the guy said, looking at his clipboard.

Mark had to take out his summons. Indeed, it was the right number.

The guy cleared his throat and looked at his clipboard again, as if he were in for a mouthful.

"There are four charges against Case 2315, afterwards to be designated as *you*."

The guy must've been joking. Mark couldn't believe his ears. The charges were so preposterous he didn't know how to answer. Not that they didn't have an element of truth in them, but that they were also lies, calumny, false witness against him.

Mark opened his mouth to answer, but nothing came out. He was in such a state of incredulity he couldn't utter a word.

"Silence means consent to the charges," the clerk said.

Mark shook his head vehemently, his face convulsing like a volcano that wanted to erupt and was blocked at its mouth.

"Speak up, then!" the clerk barked out like a border

guard. "How do you answer to the charges? Time is of the essence. I have other people to hear. Speak up."

His own nature had betrayed him once again. In whatever situation, when it was time to speak, he couldn't speak. When it was time to be brave, he wasn't brave. When it was time to take decisive action, he couldn't act. It was as if, caught in the gears of a self-fulfilling prophecy, he was always being grinded into grist.

Mark sat back, knowing he had been defeated again. He was breathing heavily, his face tight and flushed, his vocal chords incapacitated. In desperation he stared at the hearing Clerk.

"If you can't speak," the guy said, "change the settings on your headset mic."

Not knowing what the clerk was talking about, Mark took off his headset and regarded the mic. He noticed a switch that had three settings. The Off setting was in the middle. The Audio-out setting, which had the green light on, was to the right. The Audio-in was to the left. By the process of elimination, the clerk had to mean to switch it to Audio-in.

When Mark switched it to Audio-in, he saw the red light come on. Which couldn't mean anything good, he was sure. Nevertheless, he put the headset back on and faced the clerk.

"Now your thoughts are being recorded," the clerk said. "How do you answer to the charges?"

Mark couldn't believe his ears. Had modern technology advanced this far? Or had he missed something, as if he had been asleep like Ichabod Crane? He wasn't sure. But this was no time to question the methods or the type of technology. He was under pressure to answer to the charges, whatever the circumstances.

At least he didn't have to speak out physically, which he was never good at anyway. Being with words in silence was a different matter. He was much more comfortable using the words silently, as he did every day of the year. As he was forming his thoughts, arranging the words in their proper order like soldiers in the phalanx, he could hear his own thoughts in his ear phone. Amazing. The clerk must've been hearing the same thing. It was without a doubt an incredible feat of technology, the likes of which he would never have imagined but which, at the same time, didn't overly surprise him since they were in a Panaudicon.

In the end, he was quite pleased with his response to the charges. He had expressed himself as well as possible under the circumstances. But he still didn't know who was pressing the charges. Could he please be informed?

Either the clerk didn't hear the question or disregarded it.

"List a few people who have been most influential in your life and whom you greatly admire still," the clerk said. "And explain why."

Mark thought of some of the great authors who had been his role-models in the past and who now could be used in his defence. After all, they had been instrumental in the creation of his own sense of self. He had often referred to them as his godparents, as a matter of fact. Not only had he been influenced by their words in their work but by the way they had put their words into practice in their lives. In putting their words on the page they had made themselves witnesses to the truth—or, at least, to their version of the truth—and he had only followed their example. If he could call anyone to his defence, they would be apt witnesses, to be sure. And by the integrity of their lives they could be considered as authority figures as well.

He had the distinct feeling, however, that he was caught up in some sort of ridiculous game that had him in its clutches. All he had to do was walk away—and yet he knew beyond a shadow of a doubt that he couldn't walk away.

Afterwards the clerk went over the protocol of the hearing. He told him he had to answer all the questions as quickly and concisely as possible. His judges on the panel would be three of the people he had mentioned. The judges, and only the judges, would determine the outcome of the hearing. Did Mark agree with such a process?

"I thought I was calling my defence witnesses, not my judges," Mark said, in a state of indignation.

The clerk shook his head. "You have to defend yourself, my man. In the circumstances you've put yourself in, there's no one else who can vouch for you, is there?"

Mark could only nod. It was too true. Now things were a little clearer.

The clerk told him the hearing itself would be conducted in the hearing room down the hallway. He was to address each judge as Your Honour. There would be no need of a court reporter, of course, since everything was being recorded for posterity. Did he have any objections or questions?

Mark shook his head, though his mind was racing ahead.

Afterward he walked down the hallway to the hearing room. It was much larger than the pre-hearing room, with

a long table in front standing up over a platform for the
panel of judges. The rest of the room was bare, except for
a chair facing the table, with the same wireless headset and
mic. On one side of the room were windows overlooking
an inner courtyard. The other walls were bare. The natural light was enough to make everything sharp and clear.

And yet at the back of his mind was this gnawing
doubt about what was actually happening, as if some inner
voice were trying to tell him it was all a joke—and all he
had to do was laugh and the whole thing would burst like
a bubble. And yet the very room and the situation itself
forbade laughing, as if laughing itself was verboten.

Presently three people, none wearing robes, entered
the room from a doorway in the front wall. The first was
a woman in her mid-thirties who had the severe look of a
French radical, with her black beret and cape over a simple
dark dress. She had thick glasses, full lips, and thick strag-
gly hair cut short. The second was an older gentleman in
a three-piece suit who gave the appearance of a parson
with his thin white hair beneath a bald pate and fine almost translucent skin. The last was a middle-aged guy in
corduroy pants and a lumber jacket who was short and
slim, with a shock of unruly hair and thin no-nonsense
features, looking like a harsh and imperious critic.

All three sat down on the bench, put on their headsets,
and faced him.

The older gent in the middle made the introductions.
He had a British accent, Oxbridge by the sound of it. In
spite of the grave charges and what the hearing clerk had
said, they would try to keep things as informal as possible.
He was to be addressed as Altie, for example, the woman

on his right as Simone, and the guy on his left as Ludi. He, Altie, as the most senior, would start the proceedings.

"Sit down," Altie instructed.

Mark wasn't surprised at who his judges were. He could recognize them by their look alone. Of all the more modern models of intellectual and moral fibre, these three were of the highest order. They had all, in their own way, distinguished themselves not only in their writing work but in their personal lives.

"The hearing will now come to order," Altie said.

Mark was so tense he sat like a pole with his headset on. Altie asked him to state his name and occupation. Mark found it difficult to get the words out.

"Let me impress upon you, Mark," Altie said with a paternal grin, "that you are not obliged to think or say anything concerning the charges against you, but whatever you do think or say will be held in evidence against you. Is that clear?"

"Yes."

"How do you plead to the charges?"

Mark had to give it some thought, now that he was actually facing his judges. He had at first thought he'd be judged by his peers, but this was a different story. Not only had he looked up to these godparents as his role models, but he had practically revered them in his younger years. And they had impeccable credentials. They had acquitted themselves according to the highest standards in their work and had been their own severest critics in their personal lives. How could he possibly defend himself against such a panel? It would be in his best interests to plead guilty, perhaps, and have done with it. And treat it as a life-lesson.

The longer he delayed in answering, however, the more adjusted he became to the situation. His judges didn't appear as intimidating in person as they were in their words on the page—or by their photographs, for that matter. Here in the hearing room they were human beings, after all, no matter how severe and aloof they had seemed. And human beings were all subject to self-doubt, uncertainty, and fear of some sort, he well knew.

Ludi, the Austrian logical positivist, for example, was known to have violent mood swings, from imperious and arrogant certainty to abject fear and helplessness. Simone, the French radical, had fashioned her life on emptying herself of all vanity to the point of self-destruction. And Altie, the British parson, had a reputation for being a rather docile and gentle of soul underneath his academic credentials. Maybe they weren't as daunting as they appeared. Everyone had their short-comings, after all. Of that there was no doubt. Maybe he stood a chance against them if he was completely honest with himself.

There was only one way to find out.

Mark spoke with a forthrightness that surprised him.

"Guilty and not guilty," he said.

The judges were taken aback. They looked at each other, shaking their heads, as if dealing with an impudent child.

"You cannot plead both," Ludi said in his thick accent. "You must choose one or the other."

"Who says?"

"The law and truth of logic says."

"Is the law logical?" Mark said, invigorated by having spoken out. "And if the law were, in fact, logical, isn't all logic self-referential? And doesn't that mean it's relative, with no outside reference point? Doesn't it all depend on the language game one is playing?"

"You are not here to ask questions," Ludi said, his face so tight it was ready to crack. "You are here to answer to our questions and to the charges against you. We ask you again: Do you plead guilty or not guilty?"

Mark told Ludi he wasn't playing his language game. He would play his own game. The things he had to be silent about, he wouldn't be silent about. If he was to defend himself against the charges and with the present panel of judges, then he had to play his own language game. And in that game one thing could not exist without its opposite. Being guilty could not exist without being not-guilty. The true couldn't be without the false. The physical couldn't be without the metaphysical. So he had to be in the middle somewhere, didn't he? And who had the right to set themselves up as the ultimate judge and authority of what was what?

Ludi's eyes flashed. "Are you being impertinent?"

"I don't know," Mark said, having to give it some thought. "I can't be the judge of that. I can only defend myself."

Altie himself had claimed, Mark said, continuing his defence, that no one-thing could be by itself, that every-one-thing existed in relation to some-other-thing, a metaphysics which he undoubtedly derived from the physics of Einstein. Which made every-thing dipolar. Even God, Altie had been so bold in claiming, was both absolute and contingent. Ludi had himself said that language had to correspond with reality like a mirror—or it would create an imaginary reality in various games that wouldn't let the fly out of the fly bottle. And Simone—who had a clutzy body, prone to its excruciating migraines—had felt the need to sacrifice the body and one's sense of self to the higher reality of the sacred, her ultimate authority.

That was his job as well, Mark told them, in his use of words.

"But you cannot use our words to defend yourself," Altie said.

"Who says?" Mark said into the mic, feeling his competitive nature come to the fore.

"We say," Ludi said. "We are the judges and you are the accused."

"If you are judging me by my words, can I not use your words which have so greatly influenced my words in my own defence?"

The judges exchanged looks, as if they had been caught in a paradox.

Mark sensed he had achieved some sort of leverage and he had to press home his point before the tables turned again.

After all, he said into the mic, as soon as their words were used in thought or in speech or in writing, they went automatically into the public domain, no matter what the modern copyright laws stipulated. That was the unwritten law of language, wasn't it? The very nature of language was such that it belonged to everyone and no one. Could someone own their own words? And how was anyone to know, when a name was attached to the words, that they actually issued from that person? To this day, he told his judges, he couldn't say with certainty if the words of Yeshua of Nazareth had come from the historical person, the evangelists, or the early Church communities. Or a combination thereof.

Mark could see that the judges were staring at him with expressions of disbelief and disapproval. He thought it better to tone things down or he might be held in contempt of court.

"Explain to us," Ludi said, sputtering out his words, "how you can violate the laws of logic and be both innocent and guilty."

Mark made a valiant effort to explain how his words had always sought to honour the laws of logic and yet abolish them by going beyond them, but he could see his efforts were falling on deaf ears—as if they had heard these arguments countless times.

Okay, he said, taking a more personal approach, he was guilty. There was no denying that. He had bungled it. He had failed to get his meaning across to the public at large. But the public at large couldn't be said to understand the esoteric meaning of his words, could they, if they were prone to understand only the obvious literal meaning? The laws of logic simply didn't hold in the games of life and death, he said. They knew that. They knew that in the game of words, only the few could understand both the literal and the metaphorical. So literally he was guilty, sure, but metaphorically they had to find him innocent, no?

When Simone spoke up for the first time, he listened carefully through his headset. Of all his judges, he admired her the most. She was virtually a saint in the way she had carried out her intellectual integrity into her life by selfless acts of courage.

"Your very words have proclaimed your guilt," she said.

"How so?"

"You are too full of gravity and self-worth."

He had to give this accusation some thought before he answered.

"Yes and no," he said.

He had to be in the grip of gravity and ignorance and ego at the beginning, sure, he said. But that was only because of his humble origins. His judges would know nothing about such lowly origins since each of them had come from families that were either affluent or intellectual, and had been touted geniuses from the very start. He, on the other hand, had to claw his way out of the darkness of his origins—and at a considerable price to his psyche and self-confidence. But now he had seen the error of his ways and had given his will up to grace, as Simone herself had done, and had come to treat it all as a serious game.

To drive home his point he had to indirectly quote from her own words from Volume I of her Notebooks, Notebooks that were still under copyright in the English translation, he had to add—to the effect that an author had to play with the reader's imagination both with the dispassion of a coquette and the passion of a saint.

"Did I actually write that?" Simone looked at him with a little grin.

"Well, I've taken some liberties."

"That's precisely what you're being charged with," Ludi said, raising his voice.

"Or that he hasn't taken enough liberties and thus failed to convince us," Altie said.

The judges stared at him. Mark stared back. They seemed at a stalemate.

"Can you at least tell me who has made the charges," Mark finally said.

"Only you know that," Altie said.

"But I don't know."

"That is the enigma, *n'est-ce pas?*" Simone said with a little wink.

The judges got up and filed out the same door they came in.

Mark got up in respect and then sat down again.

Presently he could hear the three of them discussing the case in the judge's chambers through his headset. He could make out who the voices were by the accents. Then it occurred to him why his three judges had been chosen, other than the fact that they had been his godparents, of course. They had all been teachers like him and their surnames all began with the same letter. Was it a ludicrous coincidence or did it point to some serious ramifications?

Mark waited.

Though he felt he had presented a sound defence, he could never predict the verdict. It would be entirely foolhardy, not to mention presumptuous, making it a self-fulfilling prophecy. And yet the wink from Simone stayed with him.

To amuse himself while waiting, he went over his own words and the words of the judges, trying to separate what was what and who was who.

A nagging voice in his headset told him all he had to

do was get up and walk away, but he couldn't naturally give it much credence. What if it was the voice of temptation? What if he were being tested right now by his own conscience? What if he was listening not to his own thoughts but to the thoughts of the people who had charged him?

What if, in spite of all the logic and reason in the world, all that logic and reason was as foolish as spitting into the wind?

No, all he could do was sit there and wait for the verdict.

And even when he took his headset off, the voice of authority was still in his ear telling him what to do.

If he could only laugh at it all, he knew he could gain the upper hand.

Z Goes Shopping

Before **Z went** into his solitude, he told a few of his colleagues at the university he simply had to get away from it all. If anyone pressed him to be more specific, he'd throw out anything that came to mind. The media-cation of the masses. The death of the higher values. The triumph of retail therapy. Or his favourite: the rise of the Wireless Empire.

Plus, his wife had left him, fed up with his moping, as she called it. If they couldn't have kids, she said, they could at least live a little. His malaise, however, went much deeper than any personal issues. Every time he watched the news, used the Internet, or read the paper, he felt sick at heart. The signs of the times portended nothing but doom and destruction. The rift between the haves and the have-nots was scandalous. The few who knew hid out in their ivory towers, while the ignorant controlled the air waves. He couldn't see how the centre would hold. His teaching duties at the university had become unbearable. He'd feel himself mouthing the same words like a wind-up toy. The kids were drones of the cliché industry. Most of his colleagues sounded like simpering sophists, mouthing inanities. Some days he could barely get out of bed.

He felt stuck in the labyrinth of dim-witted nihilism. In his late forties, the way things were going, he'd either be mauled by the Minotaur or butt his head against the last brick.

So he packed his SUV, including a few books, let his soon-to-be ex-wife take control of selling the house, and went up north to what the locals called God's country.

After a few months, however, he came to embrace the solitude as an end in itself.

In his well-insulated cabin beside an isolated lake, he had a CD collection of classical composers and a small select library. He lived on the rhythm of the day and the dictates of the seasons. When he needed food and batteries and supplies, he drove his SUV into the nearest town and stocked up. For exercise, he ran on the old logging roads that went around the lakes and the distant hills covered with pine and Laurentian rock. In winter he used snow shoes or cross-country skis. He had a pot-bellied stove, into which he constantly fed wood. He went to bed not long after sunset, woke up at dawn, kept his meat and fish hanging frozen on stilts, read for such long periods the words seemed to suck him into a trance. He could go into a dialogue with the words of the Knowers long after he had stopped thinking. They spoke to him with the wisdom and authority of those who had transformed themselves into free spirits, those who were both in harmony with, and unfettered by, the visible world.

Being a city boy at heart and not having a violent bone

in his body, he didn't own a firearm and didn't trap for game. He did, however, fish in his boat in the small lakes that dotted the large expanse of bush.

Isolated as he was, he took good care of his body, subsisting on a diet of vegetables, fruit, fish, and beans. What with his daily run, his chores, his constant walking, he was usually exhausted by the end of the day and slept soundly. Whenever his hormones asserted themselves he went into town where a few women in the tavern, after some social lubrication, were only too willing to snuggle up and relieve the tedium of the cold.

He hadn't gone into the unspoiled wilderness to purify himself of his natural urges as much as regain his childlike joy in them. And thereby regain a will to live that could only be fed by a hunger to transcend itself. To never stay fixed and stale. But remain in uncertainty and keep forging into the unknown. To live in the Zone, as he called it, in the crosshairs of the dialectic, where, in being cancelled out and preserved at the same time, he felt himself being re-absorbed into a higher power.

In short, he felt himself regaining his childlike self with its natural curiosity, its innocence, and its indifference to vanity and self.

A colleague had once called him the last true Cynic, referring to those few of old who had the courage of their convictions, divested themselves of home and family and possessions, lived like dogs on the street corners and marketplaces with beggars' bowls, and barked loud and clear like watchdogs to keep guard over the normal world. Legend had it that the great Cynic himself, Diogenes, upon meeting Alexander, had told the world-conqueror that he, the man with nothing but the courage to tell the truth, was the true king of the world.

At the university, in his former life when he wore his fool's cap, he was the contrarian. If anyone opined views that were postmodern he'd be a hierophant. If they were rational, he'd be Dionysian. If they were into the Great Books, he'd entertain them with cartoons and comics and Harlequin Romances. If they were orthodox believers of whatever faith, he'd be a non-believer or atheist. If they were rationalists or atheists or humanists, he'd be a spirit-ualist—or, even better, a pneumatic Gnostic.

He couldn't say he had cut all his ties to the social and artificial world, however. He still had what was left of his savings from his university job and his low-risk invest-ments.

Living alone in the middle of nowhere, he sank into an expanding silence that focused his hearing and clarified his sight. The winters were long and cold. If it snowed heavily, blocking the access road to the highway, he'd wait it out. Some days he sat in front of the pot-bellied stove for hours in brain freeze. In the summer the mosquitoes tor-mented him. His inner voice and the words of the Knowers created a feedback loop of nested voices, some of which could be bogus.

As much as he took care of his body he could also be indifferent to it. More often than not, he didn't wash for long periods. He wore the same jeans and heavy cotton shirt. He slept on a cot with loose springs. He watched the sun come up in the mornings over the trees and the lake and watched it set in the evening. Once a year he got his beard and hair cut.

One summer, while he was in the barber shop and looking out at the central strip mall, he saw a couple of Americans on a fishing trip go into each of the three main stores in town. The small food store. The Trading Post that carried the fishing and hunting gear, the hardware and tools, the camping equipment, with all the sundries. And the LCBO that stocked the cheapest medication of the north—booze. As he observed them overloading their Land Rover and boat with enough gear to get through the Northwest Passage, he had to smile at his prophetic insight. After God had long been killed, the God-killers were now in the process of killing the country.

The next morning, standing outside his cabin and looking over the lake, he took a deep breath and felt the fresh air going into his lungs as if it were cancelling out his own breath. A tingling sensation went up his spine and burst in his head, causing him to tremble with joy. It was as if his little breath had been taken up and supplanted by the great breath of the sky—what Genesis 1:2 called the wind or Spirit—and he was in a Zone beyond living and dying.

And his joy was like a trance in which he could step out of himself and observe the real world in a new way. So that when he saw the rising sun over the mist of the lake and reflecting over the water, and felt it as warmth on his skin, it was no longer just the physical sun. It was also the *logos* of all the Knowers who had sought to light the way for others to overcome the darkness—and he sensed the secret of the *gnosis*.

After that morning it was as if he had been awakened from a deep sleep—and he felt like a child again, feeling the air breathing him and the sun warming his skin, smiling at the visible world while holding true to the secrets of the invisible within.

It was then that he recalled seeing the Americans doing their shopping and he realized what his real mission as a teacher was.

Not long afterwards he packed his meagre possessions and drove out of the bush and down the highway back south to the Great Metropolis that had been his home in years past. Here he had plied his trade as a wunderkind associate professor at the western campus, where he had given lectures in a torn T-shirt, like a prophet of the un-washed. He found an unfurnished apartment in a high rise not far from his old campus, in the middle of what was now a fast-growing city in itself. It had become a home for an influx of immigrants in the past few decades, making it one of the most culturally diverse populations in the world. His apartment was also close to the City Centre and the mega-mall, under the curvaceous Marilyn Towers.

Before he could get the essentials for his apartment—the furniture, the linen and cutlery and pots and pans, he had to make himself presentable to face the public again. When he regarded himself in the mirror, he saw two eyes peeking through a bush of wild hair, making him look like a deranged mountain man. The only barber he had used in the old days was Vito, who had started as a young man cutting hair on the campus. Afterwards Vito had opened his own shop, close to City Hall and the Central Library.

On a Saturday afternoon, Z put on his old walking shorts and T-shirt and walked from his high rise, up streets with cars and empty sidewalks, to the block beside the Central Library, and found that the shop was still there, with its quaint hairstyling signs on the window and the barber's pole spinning like a candy cane. Inside he saw a middle-aged man sitting on one of the four empty barber chairs reading a newspaper. No one else was in the shop.

"Vito?" he said. "Is that you?"

After much perplexity, surprise, closer scrutiny, not to mention some incredulous shaking of the head, they embraced like long lost brothers.

"I can't believe what I'm seeing," Vito said. "*Madonna mia*, it's Mr. Z."

"How's business, Vito?"

"Don't even ask," he said, indicating his empty shop. "What can I do for you, Mr. Z?"

"Can you make me look like the old Z?"

Vito sat him in the chair and shook his head at the challenge ahead. First he sprayed his mangy long hair with water and commenced to mow it down. Then he sheared off his beard. When Z finally looked at himself in the large mirror, he saw a stranger looking back at him. It was a guy with high cut cheeks, pale skin, large blue eyes, and a thin layer of pepper and salt hair, looking like a haunted man.

"Well," he said. "I don't recognize the old-me. It must be the new old-me."

"Did you come back from the dead, Mr. Z?"

He laughed. "The same old Vito, the Barber of the Will."

It had started when Vito was a young dandy cutting hair on campus. He'd talk to the students and faculty, listening to the academic rhetoric, taking in the phraseology, the intellectual smugness, and ask probing questions so simply presented they left the mandarins scratching their heads. Then, after he opened his own shop, as a family man with slicked-back hair, slim build, and white top, he'd strut around his domain, his words and his scissors clipping away excess verbiage around the oversized heads. It was Z who—impressed by his simple yet insightful questions, his clip and trim, and his ironic detachment—had referred to his overall zetetic skills, calling him the Barber of the Will, the Vi-to-crates who could cut anyone down to size.

Now, however, Vito was older, with a paunch under his white top, some of his hair gone, his skin mottled by too many years of cutting hair and dispensing counsel.

"As you can see, there aren't many customers to talk to anymore, Mr. Z."

"What happened?"

"I can ask the same with you, Mr. Z. The last I remember, you gave it all up down here to live up north in the bush. You said you had to get away to find something."

"You always had good ears, Vito."

"A barber without good ears isn't a barber. Did you find what you were looking for?"

"Let's say I found out what I had lost. But I can't be sure."

"Who of us can be sure of anything, tell me that?" Vito said, giving him a little smile while looking at him through the mirror.

"I see we've come to the same fork in the road, right? Do we take the road of certainty or uncertainty?"

"I'm always uncertain of my certainty, Mr. Z."

"Spoken like a true barber, Vito."

"Are you going to get your old job back at the university?"

"No, I don't think so. I have other work to do now."

"Like what?"

Z looked out at the street. "Well, I'm not exactly sure. But I think I've been given a mission. A new job, so to speak. One that doesn't pay a salary, though. Call it a commission, if you will."

"You get paid by commission?"

"No, Vito. A commission as a call to service."

"A call from who?"

"Ah, that's a complicated matter. Let's just say a call from within."

"You're speaking in riddles, Mr. Z. You have to speak plain to an ignorant guy like me."

In the large mirror, Z could see Vito's wry grin, as if he were revelling again in his role as the Barber of the Will, just as he, Z, was playing at being the solitary sage come from the bush to share his wisdom. And they were looking at each other through the mirror and seeing the other in each other's eyes in ever receding feedback.

"It's like reading the signs of the times," he said. "And feeling compelled to do something about them."

"I still don't understand."

He asked Vito to give him some of the most common complaints and issues he had heard from his customers in the last few years.

"Ah, now you're talking my language," Vito said.

Vito went through his litany of barber-shop poop and scoop. Personal and family issues. Problems at work. The rising tide of terrorism. Rising prices. The cost of living. Immigration. Conspiracy theories. Political scandals. The failure of the city's sports teams. And all manner of other confidences the guys voiced in his barber's chair. As a barber, he knew how to coax things out, never be judgmental, and give them free rein. Whatever was said in the shop stayed in the shop, Vito said. Some of his customers spoke freely, as if they were on a psychiatrist's couch. Some confessed their sins, hoping for absolution. Some got belligerent. In all his years standing at the chair, he had heard everything.

"Barbers and cabbies have their fingers on the pulse of the nation," Z said.

"I'm just a sounding board. Everyone needs a sympathetic ear. It's part of my job."

"Right, and then you cut their hair and offer temporary relief."

"I don't know about that."

"Well, I've seen the signs of the times and feel I have to do some hair-cutting myself to offer temporary relief."

"You going to be a barber, Mr. Z?"

"A Barber of the Mall."

Vito shook his head. "A barber of them all? I don't follow. And offer relief from what?"

"Shopping."

Vito did a double-take in the mirror. "Are you saying what I think you're saying?"

"Depends on what you're hearing."

Vito laughed at their old shtick.

"But everyone needs to shop," Vito said with a big grin. "My place is a shop. Shopping is good. It's good for business and keeps the economy going. What's wrong with shopping?"

"Well, it was good once, an important requirement for the necessities of life, but now it's no more than a plague that has killed off the last vestiges of our noble nature."

"Put it in simple words, Mr. Z. What do I know?"

"God hasn't died, Vito. Honour has died. Nobility has died. Nobility earned by merit, of course, not by blood. Excellence has died. Knowledge has died. Greatness has died. The Spirit has died. Our God-Self has died."

"I still don't get you."

"You wanna know how low we've sunk? We idolize movie stars and pop stars and wealthy entrepreneurs."

Sitting back on the barber's chair, Z could see Vito's face in the mirror trying to digest the words.

"Do you want my honest opinion, Mr. Z? I only know hair and mirrors and what I hear and what I see. I know *la bella figura*, what looks good. And maybe a little of the haute couture, or the *Alta Moda*. I know what people like and don't like. I know that business is bad for me these days, sure. Some of the old guys still mention some of those words like honour. But most people just don't give a shit about those things, Mr. Z. They're not real. And as long as people are shopping, life's good, not bad."

"Yeah, so it seems."

They discussed the matter further and could come to no working agreement. Vito was more concerned about his failing business. He was thinking of either re-locating or selling his shop. His kids were grown up. He had a bit of a nest-egg. Maybe he'd go into real-estate. Maybe he and his wife might go back to Italy for a while.

"Listen, Vito," Z said. "I have to go to the mall to buy

some stuff for my new apartment. Maybe we can kill two birds with one stone. I dread going to the mall. It'll be like Daniel in the lion's den. Maybe you can help me out getting my things and you can scope the mall if you wanted to relocate there."

It took a little more persuading, but Vito agreed. Mondays he was closed, but Tuesdays and Wednesdays were very slow days. He could leave the shop for a few hours and not even be noticed. Maybe he could, indeed, see if the mall and he were a good fit.

The following week, on a Tuesday, he picked Vito up and they drove the two blocks west and parked in the north parking lot in the sea of vehicles. It was a warm June day, the sun peeking through dense clouds. He wore a new pair of walking shorts and sandals and a good T-shirt, so as to blend in as much as possible, although he felt entirely naked without his mop of hair and beard. Vito had dressed up a bit, in dress slacks, pointy Italian shoes, and dark polo shirt, smelling of hair oil.

"It's so big," he told Vito as they walked to the entrance.

"It's one of the largest in North America, Mr. Z."

"Cut the *Mister* stuff, OK. Call me Z."

They found a floor plan just inside the entrance. Z saw it was much the same as when he was here last years ago. Many of the stores had changed names, of course, but he could still recognize what was what.

It was two floors of hundreds of retail outlets and services and restaurants and food courts, built around towering skylights and encircled by a sea of parking that included multi-level structures. It had both high-end and low-end stores, home furnishings, house wares, men's and ladies' fashions, boutiques and dollar stores, entertainment and electronics, banks and food services, designer outlets, enough shoe stores to stock a small country, sporting goods and accessories, and speciality shops to cater to every need.

As they walked down one of the main concourses, he felt disoriented by the bright lights, the shops and boutiques ablaze in colour and merchandise, the thick crowds walking and talking, the treacly odour that seemed to seep into his brain. He saw slews of teens in groups and in pairs. Large families of kids and grandparents and babies in strollers. Smaller kids running around and playing. And people of all colours and religions, some in their native turbans and saris and head scarves, most in modern casual attire, some dressed to the nines, like a United Nations of shoppers. Many of them were using their smartphones, talking or texting as they strolled, some were seated and playing video games. Every so often they came upon an open area with escalators and they could see down to the floor below. In the background to the babble was the music, a soft modern beat that came from the concourse and individual outlets. What bothered Z the most, however, was a sort of electrical hum that short-circuited his head.

"What's that hum?" he asked Vito.

"The controlled air system, I guess."

"And that odour in the air. Is that perfume?"

"I guess so."

"It could be a drug that hypnotizes people into the buying mood."

"You sound like one of my customers, Z."

"If you relocated here you'd get plenty of customers."

"Yeah, but the rent would be so high. I don't know, Z.

I don't think this is the place for a barber shop. I'm too old-school like you."

As they strolled towards the low-end superstore, Z took notice of various coffee shops that had people sitting at tables in the middle of the concourse.

The megastore—two floors that sold everything from groceries to pharmaceuticals to hardware and vision and travel services—had signs everywhere rolling back its *low prices.*

Z saw aisles of food, clothing, furniture, home appliances, electronics, sports equipment, toys, jewellery, beauty supplies, gardening, stationery, shoes, and everything in between. Vito, however, kept shaking his head and making disapproving noises. This wasn't his type of store, he said. It was so low-end it was disgraceful. Any self-respecting Italian who knew anything about *la bella figura* wouldn't be found dead in this store, he said.

With some searching, they found everything Z needed for now and packed two carts and wheeled them to the SUV. The larger items, like furniture, they'd have to get another day.

After they loaded the SUV, they wheeled their carts to the cart-bay.

"Let's get a coffee before going back," Z said.

They found a chain coffee shop not far from the box-store. It had the tables inside an enclosed space separated by a wooden parapet in the middle of the concourse so people could see in and out without being interrupted by the strollers. After they got their coffees in the kiosk outside, they sat down at the only open table left and rested their weary bones.

"The mall has gone global," Z said.

"We're all shoppers at heart," Vito said, smiling and sipping his coffee. "I still don't see how shopping is bad for us."

"At one time the marketplace was outside the temple. Now it *is* the temple."

"C'mon, aren't you exaggerating a little? This is no temple."

"Once upon a time people worshipped the gods of the sky, the gods of the earth, and made sacrifices and bent their knees. Now we worship brand names and swipe our plastic."

"You can't talk like that, Z. These people work hard during the week to come here and shop. That's their power, their joy. To give their kids things they never had."

"I rest my case."

"That's no worship. It's dedication to their families. It's progress. We can't go back to worshipping gods of the sky and earth, Z."

Z laughed. "I guess I'd be tilting at bank buildings."

"Listen," Vito said, putting his head closer. "You can't speak like that to shoppers. They won't understand what you're saying. You have to speak about sales and low prices, about upscale and lowscale. To speak to shoppers you have to be a shopper, Z."

Close by, Z saw a few young couples in jeans and designer tops, families with young kids, an older middle-aged couple, some teens, young girls and some with young guys checking the girls out. They were brown and white, for the most part. Some were checking their smartphones. All had a certain life-less expression, bland and apathetic, as if wired into themselves and indifferent to the outside space.

The re-cycled air and odd odour were giving him a headache.

"I understand, Vito. But sometimes one has to use extreme measures to get one's point across. These shoppers don't realize the danger they're in."

"What danger?"

"When I was a little kid we had a confectionary store in our neighbourhood and I'd drop in every so often and look at all the candy and all the stuff I couldn't buy. And I'd imagine what it would be like to eat all the chocolate bars I could ... every day."

"That's not the same, Z. We live in a great country. We have freedom, peace, and prosperity. Why shouldn't we enjoy the fruits of our labour?"

"Quite right, Vito," he said, loud enough to be heard by the people close by. "But not if our only goal in life is to be a shopper."

Vito laughed. "C'mon, that's not the only goal. You're insulting these people."

"Well, we should ask them."

"We can't ask them. We have to keep it down, Z. Or we'll get booted out."

"It wouldn't matter anyway, Vito. Nobody would listen to me. They're all believers of the god of the mall. They wouldn't know what I was talking about."

"That's crazy talk," Vito said, visibly uncomfortable as he regarded the other patrons of the coffee shop.

"It's been a long time since I lectured at the school."

"That's the last thing these people wanna hear," Vito said.

Nevertheless, he gave it a shot. Like the old prophets

in the marketplace. He spoke in a low tone, not loud enough to draw too much attention to himself, but to be heard by the shoppers sitting closest to their table. He spoke about the old pagan gods of the earth and sky, then the Hebrew God of the Law, then the triune God of Christianity—all supplanted by the god of retail. He told them the *gnosis* and the *pneuma* were dead. And there'd be no second coming.

No one gave the slightest indication that they were listening, however. They seemed totally engrossed in what they were doing.

Z drained his coffee mug, then banged it against the table top, creating a loud stir. Everyone turned their heads and looked at him with annoyance. Some got up to leave.

"You see, Vito," he said. "They listen to stupid noise, but don't hear the words of the *gnosis* and the *pneuma*. Long live the flesh and the god of the mall."

One of the kids manning the coffee dispensing kiosk came over and told them they had to leave. If they didn't leave, they've have to call Security.

"Let's get outta here, Z," Vito said. "You made your point. We're chasing all the customers away. We're not good for business, I'll tell you that."

They got up and walked away.

"If I may offer a suggestion," Vito said, as they walked down the concourse, "you'll never get the shoppers to listen to you, Z, unless you dress the part."

"How should I be dressed?"

"You're low-end. Nobody listens to a low-end guy in shorts and T-shirt. You gotta dress better than any shopper here, Z. You gotta put on the robes. Then they'll take notice and listen."

"What robes?"

"The robes of *Alta Moda*. I may be a simple barber, but I've been to Italy and seen the world of *Alta Moda*. I know what it means to step into a room and turn everyone's head with an outfit that vanquishes everyone's eye. And if you're going to mix with the mall crowd and try to get their ear, you have to catch their eye."

"You may have a point there, Vito."

"Good duds aren't cheap, though."

Vito took him to a fashionable high-end men's clothing store. Z stood still as the tailor made all the measurements for a ready-to-wear suit.

"I want nothing but the best for my man here," Vito told the tailor, an old fastidious guy who couldn't hide his displeasure at what Z was wearing.

They also got two silk shirts, a few ties, and Italian shoes so soft Z couldn't believe his feet were inside.

When he saw the total price, his head spun. Vito had to use his credit card. He told Vito he had enough in the bank to cover it.

The following week, dressed in his new attire, he picked Vito up at his shop for another round of shopping. Vito whistled when he saw him.

"I gotta say, Z, you have the robes now. And the look."

"What look?"

"The look that screams, *It's me*. With the short hair, the stubble, the lean and cut face, the good threads, you look like a mafia dude in fine linen. Like a spiritual gangster."

"It's not the real me in these clothes, Vito. I'm just in disguise."

"It takes time, Z."

He had Z sit in the barber chair and gave him a little added grooming. He put some gel in his hair and mussed it up. He patted his cheeks with a little lotion.

"The mirror never lies, right?" Vito said.

At the mega-mall instead of going to the low-end superstore, they went to a few higher-end outlets to get the furniture and small appliances. Z noticed right away the clerks treated him with deference. They smiled. They almost bowed in homage to his attire. This time he brought enough cash with him and had the merchandise delivered. Afterwards, they sat at another coffee place close to the food court.

With the added people, it was noisier as well, with all the mundane chatter of the world he had tried to escape from. Z noticed a number of older men, retired guys by the look of them, who were strolling around the area and chatting at various rest areas with benches and comfortable sofas. Some of them were in the food court that protruded onto the atrium of the concourse, where it was brighter from the skylights.

By raising his voice, Z could talk to Vito and the shoppers at the same time. A few of the older guys took notice. They came over and stood near their table as Z went into his shtick. Vito fed him his lines with a big smile, as if they were holding discourse in a barber shop.

"What's so wrong with shopping?" Vito said.

"It's become the highest value of our lives."

"Not true. We work hard for our families. Our families are the greatest value of our lives. As well as our beliefs and principles."

"We have to open our eyes. We're not aware yet that the god of retail has triumphed over all the other gods. The fight now is not between terrorists and capitalists. It's between the old gods and the new god. And the old gods will not go down without a fight."

"You're crazy, Z."

"True, I am crazy," Z said. "But a nation of shoppers will always lose that fight."

"You're not speaking our language," Vito said, looking around at the older gents. "We've spent our lives working hard and raising our families. We don't wanna hear about this other crap. We just wanna live out the rest of our lives in peace and health."

"Yeah, right. We've worked hard, but only to raise a generation of shoppers. Our children aren't equipped with knowledge and higher values. They only know how to shop."

"What can we do, then?"

"Use the wisdom of our age. We can teach the young their enslavement to retail and the visible. We can form senior cadres. Educate the young on what's essential, on what to buy and not to buy, on how to be open to knowledge and the power of the invisible. When that doesn't work, we can roll up our sleeves and become retail resistors. Go on hunger strikes. Form sit-downs in front of the shops and stores. Get arrested and noticed. Re-empower the spirit with soul-force. Put ourselves at risk to free our kids and grandkids."

A few of the older gents had congregated around them in a tight mass and didn't seem amused by their discourse.

"Excuse me, sir," a tall guy said. He was commanding in his presence even with his wispy white hair and portly figure. "With all due respect, I see you are a man of distinction. But what's going on here? Are you a security guy under cover? Why are you speaking like this? Are we on TV? Or is this a joke of some kind?"

Z looked up at him. He was nattily dressed in a flowered short-sleeve shirt and dress pants hitched high on his waist. Though his broad face had signs of age, his eyes were firm and grim, as if he didn't suffer fools too easily.

"I'm not a security guy," Z said, "though I have your security in mind. And the only joke is this mall."

"What're you saying?" the guy said, peering at him with narrow eyes.

Z presented his views. The older gentleman, who gave his name as Don Carlo, listened politely, nodding his head every so often.

"This isn't a place of worship at all," Don Carlo said with a grim expression. "Any fool can see that. And who are you to come here into our mall and tell us such things?"

"We're just shoppers like you," Z said.

"If you're a shopper, you have to abide by the rules of a shopper."

Vito smiled at him. "Oh, yeah? What rules?"

Don Carlo nodded, as if addressing an underling. "Don't be uppity, my friend." He gave Vito closer scrutiny. "Don't I know you? Aren't you the barber on the other side of City Hall?"

"Yeah, I'm a barber, but I'm also a shopper. And who're you?"

"You see these older gentlemen here," Don Carlo said, indicating the guys standing close to him. "We're the unofficial guardians of this mall. This is our second home.

Our piazza and sports bar and community centre. And we don't like strangers coming here and breaking the rules, understand. If you had come to us and asked us to speak, that's different. You would've shown us honour. But you didn't do that, did you?"

Z could see that Vito was no longer smiling. Indeed, Don Carlo's assured and commanding voice belied his innocuous appearance.

"Enzo," Don Carlo said to smaller older gentleman beside him, "give them some of the mall rules."

Enzo, with bald pate and a booming voice, spoke as if through a megaphone.

"The mall is your second home; honour it accordingly. Don't buy anything you can't afford. Every day is a shopping day. You must not shoplift. You must not harm or dishonour a fellow shopper. All shoppers are equal. Treat every shopper with respect. Make your shopping day pleasant for yourself and all the people who work here."

More people congregated around them. A thick crowd of faces edged closer to the table.

Vito's face tightened with alarm. He told Don Carlo they weren't in the mall to make trouble. He said he knew Z from his hair-cutting time at the university, where Z was a professor, that he was a very knowledgeable guy who had lived alone in the bush in the north for a long time and had come back to share his knowledge with all shoppers. They were just shoppers like everyone else—no better, no worse. And as a barber as well, no matter his age, he was still listening and learning. They had heard the rules. They hadn't broken any rules. Besides, if these older gents were mall guardians where were their badges?

"Badges?" Don Carlo said with incredulity. "What badges?"

"Badges of mall security."

Z put his arm in front of Vito and took command.

"Did you guys make up those rules?" Z said, with a smile.

"Yes, we did."

"And who gave you the authority?"

"We gave ourselves the authority. And we have the power to enforce them as well. We don't need any badges, I'll tell you that. And if you really wanted to help us out, what you'd do is help out the kids and adults who work here as sales associates for minimum wage. The kids can get along, but single moms and others can't raise a family on such a wage."

"Let's get outta here," Vito said.

Before they could get up, however, a couple of real security guys in black uniforms came over and dispersed the crowd. They were young stocky guys with buzz cuts who looked like military personnel with no nonsense stares. One of them was brown, the other white. They looked down at Z and Vito as if about to put the cuffs on them.

"Whatta you guys doing?" the brown guy said, arching his brows in incredulity.

"Is it a crime to talk?" Vito said.

"It's a crime to impede business," the white guy said.

"We're drawing people in, not chasing them away."

"Look," the white guy said, "we're not here to argue. Now, take your coffees and go."

As they walked down the concourse, Vito was shaking his head.

"Man, I can't believe that mafioso," Vito said. "He thinks he owns the mall now."

"At least people are listening," Z said.

"Yeah, but we don't want to end up in the lake with our feet in concrete."

"Don't get melodramatic. I just don't feel comfortable in this suit, though. I have to get something I feel comfortable in, Vito, or it's no use."

They passed an upscale designer shop.

"Okay, let's go in here and get you some new duds."

In the change-room Z took off his suit and tried on some fashionable polo shirts as well as casual slacks. Finally he settled on a nicely knit short-sleeve polo shirt, sporty and casual, along with slim and elegant trousers. He kept his Italian shoes on.

"You feel comfortable now?" Vito asked him when he came out.

He looked at himself in the full-length mirror.

"I'm getting there."

As it turned out, Z and Vito weren't intimidated by the senior mafia guys. They came back to the mall on the slower days when Vito could leave his shop unattended. The security personnel knew them by sight. Surveillance cameras could spot them as soon as they entered. They had to use more subtle means of persuasion. Instead of sitting down at coffee shops and food courts, for example, they had to pretend to be shopping, go into actual stores, and speak to individuals or small groups, as if engaging in casual conversation.

Of course, the upshot was that they had to buy a few things to make it look good. One day Vito bought some grooming aids for men. Another day he bought shoes, slacks, underwear. Once he went whole hog and bought a nice watch. Z got some good walking shorts and a nice pair of training shoes. All that walking on mall concourses was taking its toll on his feet, which had been sorely tested during his days of wearing snow shoes. He also got extra slacks and tops, along with some crazy designer T-shirts that reminded him of his lecturing days in torn T-shirts.

"You're getting to be a regular shopper, aren't you?" Vito said one day.

"If it's the only way to reach the shoppers, what can I say? The *gnosis* is useless if it's not heard or ignored. What good is your barber shop if there are no customers? Knowledge may be for the few, but wisdom has to be for the many."

"You're right. I gotta get the business back up on its feet."

"Nothing wrong in shopping and business per se," he said. "We all have to make a living, after all. It's how we do it that counts."

"Right. I'm a barber. It's what I do."

"And you're a good barber, Vito. You look after the interests of your customers. Not only do you cut hair, but you listen to the ills of the world and absolve all sin."

"Geez, if I knew that, I woulda charged extra."

In time, however, Z had to modify his message. The shoppers just didn't get it. Either he was speaking over their heads or at cross-purposes to who they were and their state of mind. They could've been devout Muslims or born-again Christians or observant Jews. They could've been Hindus or Baptists or fervent Catholics. Or entirely secular and indifferent to any belief and full-time consumers. It wasn't like the apocalyptic times of old when the ears were open and the hearts were sick. When the people were anxious for redemption. And the few who received ecstatic messages and inspiration were looked up to as prophets. It was the time of deception and opinion. It was the time of *egalité* and prosperity—and the power of plastic. Who wanted to hear about subduing shopping when the god of the mall ruled?

The only way he could reach them, he found from trial and error, was to get into the same shopping mood as they were. And to get into that mood, he had not only to talk their language but actually be in their head-space as well, as Vito had advised him from the very beginning. He had to be a real shopper, even an über-shopper. He had to speak to them about brand names, go gaga over designer labels, feel the rush of retail therapy after making a good purchase, joke with the clerks at the various stores, soak up the mall odour, breathe the controlled air, and actually walk down the concourse not like a Cynic-dog but like a cardinal in the cathedral of retail.

Eventually he also made up with the mall mafia of seniors, began to talk to them about ways of unionizing the mall workers. Don Carlo, who had once been a mayor of a small town in Sicily, appreciated his ideas. They even modified the mall rules to include items that encouraged shoppers to be less addicted to shopping. Don Carlo asked him to make suggestions to change the décor of the concourses, make them more aesthetic and homier. Maybe even capture the old-world charm of the piazzas in Europe. He had the ear of the mall manager, he said.

Sometimes he and Vito went to the movie theatre complex on the west side of the megamall. They saw the same movies the shoppers were seeing, the family movies with computer-animated figures and the super-hero movies with the ear-splitting sound tracks and mind-numbing special effects. There was nothing, it seemed, the movies couldn't do on the screen to create a fantasy world. They could make an ordinary Joe into a super-hero or demi-god, make as if the whole planet was destroyed by a meteor, offer up the latest fashions in clothes and cool, show the vast vistas of space, and recreate the stories of the Bible as if they were real-life occurrences.

Metaphor and myth were dead — and only the literal lived. It was as if the comics had come back to life. In one movie they had seen of Noah and the flood, it wasn't just the constant rain that produced the deluge. The earth had opened up, as if by divine intervention, and geysers had sprouted and the waters had consumed all living things, all done in the ear-shattering music of audio-power. When they came out, they both had headaches from the loud sound track, feeling as if pulverized into insensate consumers.

"Is that what the kids are all seeing?" Vito asked him.

"It's the medication of the masses," he said, shaking his head.

It was difficult to get his bearings after watching these movies. He was far from his cabin in the bush, away from the silence of his own thoughts, away from the gods of the air and the earth, and ever farther away from the *pneuma* and the *gnosis*.

How could he fight against the fantastic spectacles of

the movie screen? How could he bark louder than the techno-amplified sound tracks? How could he lead the people out of their enslavement to the flesh and the mall? They had been medicated beyond redemption.

The more time he spent in the mall, the less he felt different from the other shoppers. He was no better, after all. They could've been his former students. And in order to get across to the kids he had to be a kid. Vito had been right all along. What was the use of being a watchdog if no one understood your bark anymore?

The shoppers just went their merry way, oblivious of all his barking. And if they wanted to graze in the low valleys instead of the high mountains, who were you to think yourself superior to them?

Maybe he was the one who was self-delusional. Maybe he was the one who falsely thought he had been commissioned. Maybe he had heard a false call. What did he have to offer the shoppers, after all? He couldn't lead them out of their slavery to shopping to a promised land flowing with milk and honey. He couldn't convince them of the freedom of the *pneuma* and the *gnosis* when they were firmly convinced they were free to buy anything they wanted.

Who would want to go into the desert and risk starvation and death? The kingdoms of the world were already there in the mall, ready for the picking, he could see. And the price to pay for giving up the mall was too high.

As a good shopper, Z had become alerted to all the prices. He had heard the voice of the mall shoppers through the rules of the older gentlemen-guardians and in his sleep. There was only one god, the god of the mall, and it would defeat all the other gods. As shoppers, they were to honour its sales every day of the week. They would take care of the mall and the mall would take care of them. They would only buy what they could afford. Not everyone could shop at the high-end stores. Everyone had to find their appropriate level of shopping. If Dollarama worked for them, then let it be Dollarama. When they were ready for Dolce & Gabbana and Holt Renfrew, they'd know soon enough.

All Z could do now was bide his time in the mall. Be a shopper like all the rest.

And dress in ready-to-wear.

About the Author

F.G. Paci is the author of 13 novels and 3 collections of short stories. He is best known for *Black Madonna*, a novel that deals with feminist issues and the immigrant experience in Canada. His eighth novel in his BLACK BLOOD series is *The Son* (Oberon, 2011). The last two novels in the series remain to be published. His two previous collections of short stories were *Playing to Win* (Guernica, 2012) and *Talk About God* (Guernica, 2016). He lives in Toronto with his wife and has one grown-up son.